HARD GOLD

NUGGETS FROM THE MOTHER LODE

Jim Reiley

Turnpike Press of Northfield
Northfield, MN

Turnpike Press of Northfield

P.O. Box 491
Northfield, MN 55057
jimtpike@charter.net

This is a work of fiction.
Names, places, characters, and incidents are products of the
author's imagination and are used fictionally.
Exceptions include historical figures Manuel Armijo,
Gertrudes Barcelo, William Becknell,
Charles and William Bent, and Ceran St. Vrain.

ISBN 0-9740382-2-9

Manufactured in the United States of America

This book is dedicated to the women in my life:

Betty, Melissa, Mary, Jill, Jodi, Jaclyn, and Anne
(my late wife, two daughters, and four granddaughters).

ACKNOWLEDGEMENTS

Cover: "El Embudo," by Betty Reiley
Editor: Marie Gery
Design/Production: Nancy Ashmore, Ashmore Ink

My thanks, too, to the staffs of the Northfield Public
Library and the Carleton College Library, to Richard
Maus for his technical assistance, and to Daniel
Reiley, for opening doors in New Mexico.

As a long-time student and teacher of history, I have been fascinated by the interlocking of events and people. At the same time I have admired the determination of many individuals to maintain a sense of independence. In recognition of the need for some degree of separation, I have written *Hard Gold: Nuggets from the Mother Lode* in three distinct yet related stories that I have chosen to call: Book I – Exodus, Book II – Transit, and Book III – Terminus.

The saga revolves about the lives of some of the people you may have already met in my first book, *Soft Gold: A Tale of the Fur Trade*. It is not necessary that you have read the first book – though I admit it would be nice to know that you have read it. I tried to develop the characters and their adventures in such a way that *Hard Gold* stands on its own.

Since the publication of *Soft Gold* my creations – the Ross family, the Gallagher family plus a few others – have struggled to free themselves from the pages where they had to do what I told them to do, say what I had them say, and react in the ways I thought they should. They have demanded that I continue their lives, but in a manner they determined. They weren't about to let me do it my way; *Hard Gold* is really their narrative.

In Book I my people wrestle with growing tensions and nastiness of the slavery issue in Missouri. The resolution to their dilemma is forced upon them, and their response is the West – the largely unexplored and unknown regions of the fledgling United Sates west of the Mississippi River. The completion of the Louisiana Purchase in 1803 only whetted the interest and sparked the imagination of many Americans. The Ross and Gallagher families were among those touched with this bit of fire.

In Book II finds my people on the Santa Fe Trail in the late 1820s on their way to the foreign country of Mexico and its northern province of

New Mexico. Their trek to the West takes them over oceans of grass and brings about "sea changes" in their lives. Those who plod beside their Conestoga wagons into Santa Fe are not the same who departed the East only two months before. Packed with their merchandise to be sold for what they hoped would be fabulous profits in Santa Fe are determination, resourcefulness, and adaptability. Which of these commodities will find a market in Santa Fe?

In Book III my people search for answers in the Land of Enchantment – New Mexico. The roots of people from the Highlands of Scotland, the hills of Carolina, and villages of the Mandan Indians barely had a chance to grow in the soil of an unhappy Missouri. Can these roots be replanted in the strange and challenging soil of a foreign country that both welcomes and keeps them at arm's length? It is in Santa Fe, a village of mud houses and dusty streets, that push comes to shove and iron wills are tested to the breaking point.

Read on – I think you will be intrigued with their decisions and their solutions to a new life in a vastly different environment.

Northfield, MN,
November 2005

A crash. A shattered window. The simultaneous thud as a large object hit the floor of the commons room of the schoolhouse. Everyone leaped out of bed.

Peggy screamed, "What was that?"

"Lie on the floor away from the windows and keep quiet."

Duncan Ross crawled across the room and slowly eased the door open an inch at a time. Naomi, his wife, avoiding the window, slid to the corner of the bedroom where Duncan kept a loaded gun. Not a sound could be heard within the schoolhouse. Down the lane at the foot of the hill, the horses were stomping and whinnying in the barnyard. The sound of footsteps and the soft calling of Thomas' familiar voice calmed and quieted them.

"Give me the gun. You and Peggy go back to bed. I'll slip over to the woodshed and keep watch there. When Thomas comes back from the barn I'll post him in the wash house."

"Dunc, no one is going to sleep. Let's all meet at the wash house and figure out what we are going to do."

"Fine, but don't walk around. In the morning we may learn something from footprints."

The Ross family met, talked quietly, and planned what they would do at the first light of day. When there was sufficient light, plans became action.

"Thomas, do you remember your track to the barn? Work your way back there keeping to the same trace. Look for footprints other than yours. Make a circle around the barn and barnyard. Naomi, you and Peggy spread out and make a slow circle of the schoolhouse. I'll go back inside to see if I can find anything to give us a clue."

Two hours of searching turned up very little. Thomas reported no footprints other than his own going to or from the barn, nor did he find any in the ground surrounding the barn. Duncan carefully measured the point at which the large, black rock that had smashed the window lay on the floor. He estimated the angle from which it had been thrown, and he went outside to see what he might find at the spot where it was hurled through the window. The footprints he found matched those Peggy spotted as she and her mother scoured all sides of the schoolhouse.

Peggy reported to her father, "It looks to me that there was one person, and he used the road from Uncle Jack's place."

"You don't think one of his children did this, do you?"

"I didn't say that. I said he used the same trail. It could have been anybody."

"Speaking of the Gallaghers, look who's here. Good morning, Jack. What can we do for you?"

"Seems to me y'all needin help. It's the middle of the mornin and I ain't smellin no coffee, no bacon. Somebody sick here?"

"Sit down, Jack. I'm about to fix something, and you can join us. We might have something to tell you."

"Mighty nice of you, Naomi. Now, what's on your minds?"

Duncan, Naomi, Peggy, and Thomas began at once to tell four versions of what happened during the night.

"That's quite a story if'n I could tell what's going on. One at a time, please."

The four began again.

"Maybe I should come back another day when y'all calm down. Now, Peggy, supposin you lead off."

"Somebody threw a heavy rock through that window last night. We spent the night in the wash house waiting for daylight."

"Guess I'd be scar't, too. Looks to be about a three or four pound goonie."

"Nobody's touched anything," Duncan said, "so after we eat, why don't you have a look."

The group demolished the breakfast set out by Naomi. Jack examined the commons room, then looked at the footprints, tracing them along the building until they disappeared in the woods.

"Well, my friend, what do you think?"

"Beats the hell out of me. Know anybody what's holding a grudge agin y'all?"

"Can't say that I do."

"I'll send Billy to town to pick up some glass. 'Tween the two of us, we can fix this here window sash and have her back in place by sundown. Then y'all come over and have supper with us. Eleanor said just the other day she don't see much of you people since you got to runnin your school."

"That's very kind. I'll fix something to add to Eleanor's supper." As she spoke Naomi knew exactly what she would prepare – everyone loved her corn fritters.

📖　📖　📖

Duncan's hours of planning along with hours of tramping about the countryside for sites along with his investments in land and buildings brought this school into reality. Duncan, Naomi, and Thomas Archer, a young man recruited to teach art and music, formed the teaching staff. Academic subjects complemented "hands on" teaching. Both Duncan and Naomi believed in and practiced that type of instruction. Students worked inside the classroom on academics and outside where they had farm, barn, and vegetable bed chores.

Fields of wheat, corn, oats, and hay were cultivated from the outset. The small orchard produced apples, pears, and cherries to add to the table.

In the barn were a riding horse and a team of work horses, two milk cows, five or six hogs, a small flock of sheep, and a clutch of chickens. Though they were not completely self-sufficient, the farm furnished the majority of the school's food and fiber.

The schoolhouse was built of logs cut locally, dragged to the site, and fashioned by hand. It had begun as one large building housing three classrooms, two small bedrooms, and a kitchen in one corner of a commons room. Another small bedroom and a large general purpose room were added the second year. Now, in the fourth year, the students, teachers, and several handymen were hard at work on an addition that would house a larger kitchen and two "collections" rooms. As the school grew so did the woodshed and storage buildings. Yet another building served as washhouse as well as an auxiliary kitchen for busy summer and fall seasons when foods had to be prepared and put up for the winter.

Sorting out the chatter from serious talk took time and patience as everyone gathered around Eleanor Gallagher's table filled with good food and equally good fellowship. A few threads from last night's incident at the schoolhouse were identified.

"That rock that smashed the window was smoked recently."

"How'd you know that, Duncan?"

"When I was cleaning up the broken glass and seeing what could be salvaged from the sash, my hands were covered with soot."

"Why would anyone go to the trouble of blackening a rock only to throw it through a window?" asked Naomi.

"Seems to me," Jack said, "somebody's wantin to send a message."

"Message? Why not come knocking on my door?"

"Well, you got a Negro family that sends their kids to your school."

"What of it?"

"Ain't every one in these parts cottons to nigger kids goin to school."

"That's just plain crazy, Uncle Jack," Peggy broke in. "They had only to come to the school and tell Papa Dunc what they thought."

Jack looked at his longtime friend. Not everyone would be comfortable talking to Duncan Ross about his school. He was all of six feet in height, a little over two hundred pounds in weight, trim and fit, and he could be blunt and unvarnished. To his wife, Duncan was "Dunc." Her voice was low and soft and at times slipped over words. It reflected her mixed-blood heritage of a Spanish father and a Mandan Indian mother. Their daughter, Peggy, followed the same speech pattern as her mother – Duncan came out as "Papa Dunc."

"What's been done is done. What are you going to do now?" asked Eleanor, Jack's Mandan Indian wife. Usually the quiet one in the group, when she spoke all listened.

Thomas Archer, who lived at the school four days each week to work with his charges on music and art, spoke up. "Well, Eleanor, I guess we'll just go on with school as if nothing happened. If we don't, it will only encourage that set of footprints to try something else."

Thomas kept his room and studio in St. Louis for the three days remaining in the week. He insisted on this arrangement though Duncan and Naomi had on several occasions pleaded with him to make his home at the school for the full week. Thomas was about five feet four inches in height and might have felt lost in this group of six footers – Duncan and Jack, Naomi a tad less, and Peggy soon to be as tall as her mother – but he knew how to hold his own. He pleaded, and won, his case for the split week and his own time in the town of St. Louis.

The night was quickly falling, and the Ross family and Thomas left Jack's place and headed back to theirs. "Shall we divide the night into two watches?"

"I appreciate your thinking of that, Thomas, but no. We could wear ourselves out in a week and learn nothing."

The shattered window was repaired. Work on the addition to the main building proceeded. Life continued at its usual pace. When it was Naomi's turn with the students she spent time nearly every day outside of the school. In nearby woods, meadows, and stream banks she discovered many of the items needed for her winter's supply of medicines. Various leaves, roots, fruits and nuts, bark and moss formed her pharmacy. She matched her homemade medications with her skills in knowing which item alone or in combination with others gave relief from pain or put an end to infection. Her calm manner added a sense of security to all in neighborhood.

The students loved this special time with Naomi. The woods were her home; there she moved easily and quietly, and managed to transfer her sense of the beauty and mystery of the forests and fields to her charges. All eleven students were from the school itself or nearby farms. It might have seemed that there was little that Naomi could teach children who had grown up in the environment that was her laboratory. But it was her perspective of the interlocking of all systems of nature that made her classes so special. She was patient and respectful of each student's desire to help, but was also quick to discipline when needed.

Everyone in the little community centered on the school knew of Naomi's background. Her father was a Spanish fur trader sent to the Mandan country from New Orleans by his *bourgeois* (owner or boss) about 1777. He met and married a native woman and had a child by her – Naomi. Some of her father's people came to the Mandan villages and forced him to go back in captivity with them to Mexico to face the charge that he was "living in sin." It did not matter to these strangers from Mexico that there were no officials of any rank to perform a ceremony acceptable to the Church. He was in defiance of the law and custom of an Old World set of practices that was difficult to adhere to in the New. Naomi never saw her father again.

A few years after that tragedy yet another cruel blow fell on Naomi and her mother. They were taken prisoners by Crees who sought to avenge the death of one of their warriors at the hands of the Mandans. Her mother was claimed by one of the Cree men. She made a home for herself and her daughter, but never forgot her Mandan roots. Her mother died when

Naomi was nine years old. She never saw her child mature into the remarkably handsome young woman she became.

Naomi lived among the Crees, but was never made a part of them. When she and Duncan met for the first time, at a trading post in the North Country of Canada, the attraction was mutual. This young, red-headed Scotsman she felt was the one her spirits had sent into her life to make it possible for her to live as a free woman, not as a captive. Duncan married Naomi *a la facon du Nord*. Peggy, their lively child, was rapidly becoming her own person and more and more an image of her mother, tall and attractive – and a bit feisty.

Jack Gallagher, a long-time friend of Duncan from their days as clerks for the North West Company [the leading fur trading company in North America in the late 1700s – early 1800s] had several successful businesses in St. Louis that provided a comfortable life for his wife Eleanor and their three children. Two livery stables plus a cartage business in the town and two large farms on river bottom lands worked by men on a share basis comprised his little empire. Tall and lanky, Jack compensated for his lack of physical strength and education – he'd never gone beyond the fourth year in the small Carolina hill country school he attended – with innate shrewdness, a large measure of common sense, and an uncanny ability to observe, identify, and remember the countless events of each day.

Frequent visits by Jack to the school were welcome, and the two old friends could immediately fall into conversation without preliminaries.

"Anything new at the school?"

"No, we're just puttering along. Got the addition all but finished."

"Good! There's just me and you, so listen. I got some leavins to chew over with you."

"Go ahead, my friend. I'm all ears."

"I hear talk when I'm tendin to business at the livery stables or over at the freight yard. More and more men are arguin this touchy slavery thing and gittin mighty hot under the collar whilst they're havin their say."

"Just what are they saying? What gets them so riled?"

"Some of them say if'n a man can't agree with slave owners he should get his ass out of Missouri. They aim to keep this a slave state."

"That sounds political. It can be settled by the men in Jefferson City."

"Ain't gonna be settled there. Takes too much time to get them people in Jeff to agree on anything. Talkin ain't gonna do it. They're callin for action."

"What sort of action?"

"They want burnin and beatin. That's the only thing people will understand; only way to teach a lesson to them that won't open their eyes and ears."

Duncan appreciated things of this nature from Jack. He had an ability to judge what he heard and separate reality from the boasting of loud-mouth types. If Jack was concerned, then Duncan felt he should listen and learn from a man who was close to the source of happenings in town.

📖　📖　📖

A few days after the window-smashing incident Jack came back from town with a letter for Duncan. Recognizing the writing, he tore it open at once and began reading. It was from his older sister in Scotland. She and Duncan had traded letters over the years, starting with his first days in Montreal as an apprentice in the North West Company.

Dear Duncan and Peggy,

Your letter was such a relief to us, and yet such a worry. What ever has happened in your life that you and Peggy are in St. Louis, but not with Naomi? I can only sit here and make up all kinds of stories to fit your situation. What happened? I am left to assume that you two are healthy and active, but you must give us details.

Jennifer has but one more year in school then must

decide what she wants to do in life. Her father says he needs her in his work at the iron foundry. She has fine penmanship and is quick and accurate with her numbers, just like you. Jennifer has not shown much enthusiasm for that option, but she hasn't come up with a plan of her own. She keeps talking about the life Peggy had growing up in a fur trading post and doing all that travel on the Missouri River.

The iron foundry has grown and prospered as Rory and his partners have poured their lives into it. There are many, many days we hardly see him, and he has aged considerably since your visit with us about five years ago. I worry about his health, but he brushes that aside and says he will soon ease his workload. But soon never seems to come.

I have read and reread your letter many times since it arrived – it took nearly four months to get to us. You talked about starting a school, and if I know you, you have made it happen. Are you serious about wanting me to come over and manage it for you? I am beginning to feel useless just running this big house, and Jennifer marches more to her own drummer, but only she can hear the beat.

Please find time to write to us, there are so many things we want to know. Jennifer suggested that now that Peggy is getting some schooling she and Peggy should begin to exchange letters. It could only enrich both their lives, and I am sure that we would learn more about you and the life you now live in this strange place you call Missouri. All our love,

Louise, Rory, and Jennifer

Duncan devoured the letter from Louise. He realized that a prompt reply had to be written.

Dear Louise, Rory, and Jennifer,

We received your letter yesterday, and the questions you asked of me demand a prompt reply.

My last letter was sent at a time we were separated from Naomi, but now she is back with us and our family is again as one. Her flight from the fur trade post that was our home and her attempt to return to being a Mandan woman became a disaster for her, but she made it possible for Peggy to be freed from a difficult situation. The details of her misadventure are slowly coming to light, but are not as important as having her with us once more.

Am I serious about you and your family coming to the States and starting anew here? Of course I am. Everywhere I look I see opportunities for Rory. I would be comfortable with you, a naturally born manager, running our school. Jennifer and Peggy could spend hours finding interesting things for both girls to do. Serious? Absolutely!

One aspect of our St. Louis experience is the chance meeting with a friend from my N.W.C. days as clerk, Jack Gallagher. He and his family have supported me every step of the way as the school has taken shape. His farm is but a mile from the school, and two of his children are students.

Jack's wife is also a Mandan. She is full-blood whereas Naomi is mixed blood. Our two families are much like one on many occasions, but I sense a difference between these two women. I can't put my finger on one reason, it's just a feeling that they think differently and arrive at their conclusions by different paths.

I promise to write more often. With the passing of Mr. MacQuay and Uncle Simon, you are my sole connection to the Highlands and to our old home.

Our love to all,
Duncan, Naomi, and Peggy

Summer faded into Indian summer, which gave way to serious cold and cloudy weather. One blustery day Duncan was working in the wash house with Mrs. Crawford to make it ready for a hog butchering. Florence Crawford and her husband, Amos, traded help with the farm and school chores for their two children's schooling.

A passing shadow drew his attention to the school building. A well dressed man riding a high-stepping horse with top quality gear – saddle, reins, and stirrups – slowly circled the building.

"A good day to you, sir, is there someone you're looking for?"

"Be you Duncan Ross?"

"I am. Tie your mount to the hitching post, and we can go in for a cup of tea and a place by the fire."

"That's mighty neighborly of you, Mr. Ross."

The stranger followed Duncan into the main building. They went to the kitchen where, Duncan knew, the makings for tea were always at hand.

As they sipped tea, each man sized up the other. Duncan saw a man in expensive clothing draped over a powerful figure and a manner that did not set well with Duncan. He sensed that this man's apparent wealth and his airs of a gentleman of the old school were but a veneer. But at the same time the visitor exuded an expectation of instant compliance that was definitely was in character with his commanding manner.

"Well, now, Mr. Ross, your school has made quite a reputation for itself. I have heard nothing but good recommendations in St. Louis. I have a son of twelve years who has outgrown his tutor and needs a school such as yours. I might add, sir, I am prepared to pay a handsome sum to have my boy placed here."

"You are very kind to tell me these things, Mr. … ? I'm sorry. I have yet to learn your name."

"Forgive me. I am Winfield LeBaron. My home is about twenty miles down river from St. Louis. So you see, Mr. Ross, in traveling this distance I am serious in the request I make of you to accept my boy. Are you in a position to show me the complete facility here? If it's not convenient, I will return at a time more to your liking."

"Why don't we step outside and begin a tour of our little community? It will be my pleasure to give you a full picture of what we try to do here with our students. But I must warn you, Mr. LeBaron, we are somewhat unorthodox in our methods."

"That's one of the reasons why I am here, Mr. Ross."

"The students are with my wife this morning. Much of her teaching is outside the classroom. For instance, she has the group in the woods learning the way some trees grow better in the company of certain trees rather than those of similar specie."

"Can your students comprehend such complexity?"

"I have no doubt. Mrs. Ross is an unusually fine teacher. Look, she is bringing them back here. Notice all the branches and twigs the students have for her 'collections' room. Every one of her classes becomes a laboratory."

"Yes, yes. I see that. I am taken with that style of teaching. But tell me, do I not see several Negro children in the group?"

"You see correctly. We practice open enrollment in our school. All students from whatever family are welcome here."

The fashionably dressed Winfield LeBaron turned abruptly away, stepped to his horse, mounted, and swung around to face Duncan.

"You, sir, are nothing but trash to permit a mixing of color in your school. I pray to God, Mr. Ross, you see the error of your ways and cleanse this school of the blot you have placed upon it. I bid you good day."

Several days of intense activity at the school prevented Duncan and

Naomi from mulling over the unsettling visit of Winfield LeBaron. As was their custom, the comfort and security of their bed was the place where problems were thrashed out. Problems were not always resolved, but they were usually talked over thoroughly,

"When that man got on his horse to leave, he took a minute to tell you something. Something that made his face turn red as he dug his spurs into the horse in anger. What did he tell you?"

"He called me trash and said I should get rid of the Crawford children."

"Did he threaten you?"

"Yes, but not directly, more by implication."

"Am I wrong to think a pattern is emerging?"

"Well, let's add up what we know. First was the stone through the schoolhouse window. Jack several times has told me what he hears in town at the stables and freight yard about growing tension between free-soilers and slavers. Then this Mr. LeBaron shows up. What do you think?"

"Thomas told me just the other day he is hearing heated talk in St. Louis about slaves. He said some people want to shut down the slave market. I didn't like the looks of that LeBaron. I didn't talk with him, but something about the way he carries himself hints of danger."

"I should ask Jack if knows anything about him. He said he had a farm about twenty miles south along the big river. There's something here that does not sound right to me."

Although not forgotten, that conversation was laid aside as the school made the transfer from fall to winter with an emphasis on inside pursuits and a subtle switch to academics. At great expense in terms of time and effort, Duncan had made contact with his friend and former business partner in Montreal, Samuel Rawlinson. They had severed their business relationship in Montreal when Duncan decided to go to Mandan country to search for Naomi and Peggy. The parting was more in anger than the friendship they had nurtured over many years as fellow clerks in the North West Company and banking partners for a number of years in Montreal. Time and the vast distance between Montreal and St. Louis had mellowed old grievances, and Samuel's response to Duncan's request was swift and complete.

Duncan asked his friend to buy a collection of maps and books about the lands of Canada and the expanding United States. Not only to make such purchases, but to have them shipped to the school. The maps especially added valuable resources Duncan could share with his students. Geography had always been his favorite subject in the little one-room school in the Scottish Highlands.

📖 📖 📖

"Duncan, take a minute to look at these."

He and Thomas Archer, the art and music instructor, were in an empty classroom where Thomas had spread some of the work of one of his students on a table.

"What do we have here? Is this some of your work? These drawings look quite professional."

"You have a discerning eye, but this is not my work. It's your daughter's."

"Really? It is good work, isn't it? I know Peggy has always liked your classes and works frequently on her sketching."

"I'm pleased you can see quality in what she has put on paper. I find more than a sense of perspective and proportion, there is some of Peggy herself in each one of these drawings. I would call it art, very good art."

"I'm pleased to hear you say nice things about our daughter's work, but I think you have something else on your mind."

"Right you are. I would like your permission to send these to Pierre Galvan for his judgment. He is a friend and a former art teacher of mine now living in New Orleans."

"I see no problem with that, Thomas, but what can he do for Peggy by just looking at her work and giving criticism of it?"

"He is an artist who sells his work in New Orleans."

"But why would he promote another's work in opposition to his own? Aren't you being the dreamer, the wishful thinker?"

"I am acquainted with his work. He works in oils, and much of his success and his income come from doing portraits of prominent people in his area."

"What has that to do with sending Peggy's work to him?"

"Her work is in pen and ink. A newspaper that can feature sharp and recognizable sketches to add depth to its news and articles is a step ahead of its competition. Book publishers, too, are always in need of such work."

"Go ahead with your plan, but have you asked Peggy's permission?"

He turned a bit red in the face and said that he and Peggy had been not only talking but preparing to send some of her work out for critique. As he stammered this admission, he pointed to the name Peggy had signed at the bottom of each piece: M. L. Ross, not Margaret Louise Ross.

"The general public does not seem ready to accept women as being equal to men in certain fields. That's why I advised Peggy to always sign her work, but use initials, not her given names."

"You are a devil, Thomas, clever and a bit conniving."

"I didn't intend to be disrespectful. I have only Peggy's advancement in mind."

"Relax. No offense taken. And I admire your foresight in seeing her work prepared in an acceptable manner. Well done, my friend, well done."

Naturally Naomi and Duncan talked over this surprising development that night. He made no attempt to hide his excitement over the prospect of recognition for Peggy's art. Naomi's response was quite different. There was no reaction.

"Can I ask you a question?"

"Of course. Ask it."

"What is the one thing you like to do more than anything else?"

"What an odd question. I thought we were talking about Peggy."

"Answer my question and you will know why I asked you."

"I would have to say it is how I have learned to make medications from all the things we gather from nature."

"That gives you more satisfaction, more pleasure?"

"Yes, that is my favorite thing to do."

"Peggy's sketches, what Thomas calls her art, give her satisfaction. Would you agree?"

"Of course I would agree. She seems happiest when she is drawing."

"Why do you seem to resent the possibility of Peggy finding an outlet for her talents, her ambitions, and her dreams?"

That last question ended the discussion. In fact, it deepened the gulf that every day in little ways appeared between Naomi and Peggy and between Naomi and Duncan.

The reunion of Duncan and Peggy with Naomi had been such a joyous occasion. It restored the family circle that Naomi had broken more than six years earlier when she took Peggy, seven years old at the time, and fled to the Mandan villages. But something was lacking. The Ross family was together again, a complete family, but tensions emerged from time to time. It should have been a picture of serenity and contentment.

"I have no idea of what may come out of Thomas sending some of Peggy's work to his friend. Whatever, I think Peggy should know both her parents support her efforts, not just her father."

"Peggy knows I support her. I don't have to tell her."

"I'm not sure that is so."

"No? And just why do you say that?"

"You came back to us at the time Peggy was becoming a woman but not knowing why certain changes were happening to her body. She asked, but you gave no answers. You turned your back on your own daughter."

"Well, she didn't need me."

"She needed you more than at any time in her life, but she had to turn to Eleanor and Florence Crawford for answers and advice."

"You see, she didn't need me. She had all the help she could ever want."

"You have always been the core of her life, the one person she could turn to for comfort and assurance. You were here physically, but not with your spirit, your love, your caring for a bewildered little bird, for your own child."

"Now she has answers to the strange things that happen to a woman's body in keeping with the cycles of the moon. What more does she need?"

"She needs you, Naomi, all of you, not just the part you choose to give her when it suits your mood."

Neither of them slept much that night. In the morning there was no effort made to continue the question of Peggy's art. Thomas carefully packed six of Peggy's pen and ink sketches and sent them to his friend in New Orleans. Everyone knew the long time involved in sending and receiving mail, but none could guess at the time the artist in New Orleans would need to make a judgment regarding the worth of her efforts.

📖 📖 📖

The proximity of the schoolhouse to Jack Gallagher's place was duplicated in the closeness of the two families. For Peggy, Jack and Eleanor Gallagher were a second set of parents. And for the three Gallagher children, Billy, Grace, and Charley, Duncan and Naomi Ross were the same. Add Thomas Archer's friendly and pleasant nature to the mix and anyone could quickly sense the bonds of love and respect flowing back and forth among the people who formed a friendly community centered on the school.

Billy Gallagher was much like his father. He was a natural jokester, a touch excitable, and a protector of all younger than he. Physically, he was more like his mother – short, compact, and wiry. He sat a horse well. What he could do with a horse made him special. If ever a boy was meant to be on the back of a horse it was Billy Gallagher. He had grown up with horses. He even boasted to Peggy that he could talk to them.

"Billy Gallagher, you are impossible! Nobody can talk with a horse."

"Want me to prove it?"

They had been sitting on the top board of the fence that surrounded the livery stable in town nearest to the river. Jack and Billy had driven Duncan and Peggy into St. Louis that morning. The men had some business to tend to. Then Duncan had shopping to do. The two young people were told to stay at the stable where Billy was to do some chores. Billy had other things on his mind. He never let a chance go by to impress a friend, and he reckoned Peggy Ross was his best friend.

"See that roan standing over at the gate?"

"She's a pretty one. What are you going to do with her?"

"Just watch and listen."

Billy spoke softly as he slipped off the fence, took a few steps and stood still, not moving a finger. The roan turned, tossed her head and slowly began to step toward him. Only two paces from him, she stopped, then with delicate side steps placed herself at Billy's left shoulder. He didn't make a move for a few minutes. She lowered her head and gave him a nudge. He still didn't move, so she gave him another nudge, a little harder this time. No movement. When she lowered her head the third time, Billy spoke to her. She flicked her mane and with her head erect, she walked to the gate and stood there with her tail pointed to Billy. He spoke again, and she walked into the barn.

"Now, what do you think, Miss Ross? Do I talk to horses? Didn't I tell her what to do? And didn't she do what I said?"

"I think you trained her to do those things."

"Don't you understand? I talked to her, that's all I did."

"Billy, you're just funning me. I know you. You think this is a joke!"

"Well, I can tell you something I know you don't know."

"How do you know I don't know?"

"You're a girl, and girls don't know anything."

"All right, Mr. Smarty, tell me what you know."

"Some men were here at the stable asking my daddy if he knew where they might buy mules. Not horses, but mules. Said they'd pay top dollar."

"Why would anyone want a dumb old mule instead of a horse?"

"The men said they're going on a long trail to a far off place called Santa Fe. The men told my daddy mules are tougher than horses on a long trip and can pull heavier loads given their size, and a mule doesn't eat as much as a horse."

"Would you like to go on a long trip like that?"

"Golly gee, sure I would! Wouldn't you?"

"I don't think so. It's nice at my daddy's school. Did you forget the remote fur trade posts where I lived? I know my time in a Mandan lodge was an unhappy time, but the long trip down the Missouri River on a keel boat to St. Louis was enough adventure for me. Why would I want to go any place so far away as Santa Fe?"

"Girls! Don't you want to know what's over the next hill or around the next bend in the road? You'd best stay home and draw pictures with old Mr. Archer."

"He's not old, and I like to draw. So there, Billy Gallagher!"

Duncan and Jack returned and other matters had to be taken care of. On the drive back to Jack's home the men sat and talked in the front of the wagon. Billy and Peggy rode in the back with the bags, sacks, and packages of things purchased for both households and the school. Billy wanted to talk, but Peggy gave him the keep quiet sign. She wanted to listen to the men as they talked. She'd heard what Billy had to say about a trail to Santa Fe. Now she heard Jack telling about gold mines near Santa Fe that were producing not just gold dust, but real gold, hard gold. Gold that was found in something called nuggets, chunks that were bigger than a hen's egg.

Peggy knew Billy liked to make things sound bigger than they really were. Now she knew where he got that – his daddy. Gold nuggets as big as a hen's egg? Nonsense! These Gallagher men knew how to string the long bow.

□ □ □

One of Jack's farmers, Daniel Forsyth, worked shares on some fine river bottom land west of the school. He had a boy he thought belonged in Duncan's school. The distance from farm to school was prohibitive for daily travel, but the boy himself was the greater problem.

"My boy ain't said more than a hundred words in the past four years. I never knew of any time I couldn't speak, and my wife, damn it, Mr. Ross, there's many a day I can't shut her up. But the boy's a good one, ain't nothing wrong with his mind, he just can't talk." Forsyth looked down at the silent boy by his side. "Maybe it's because he don't want to talk."

"To tell you the truth, Mr. Forsyth, I'm no kind of a medical man. I don't think I can do anything for your boy. You want him to have an education. That's the right thing to do, but our school may not be the best place for him."

Naomi was standing to the side of the men watching John Forsyth as his father laid out the problem. After deep thought she spoke up. "Wait. Maybe we should try to see what we can do. Can't we fix up a room for the boy and give six months to see if we are helping him?"

"I'm always ready to give a man a chance, or in this case a boy. But what do you think we can do?"

"I'm not sure. But I think we should try."

"Mr. Forsyth, you and John go back home. Give us a few days to get ready for your boy to stay with us for six months. Come here the first of next week. Bring John's clothes and things he might want to have with him."

"Much obliged to you. We'll be back come Monday."

Duncan and Naomi stood and watched Daniel Forsyth and his son climb back in the farm cart and disappear down the road and into the woods.

"Whatever made you speak up? I don't have the slightest idea of where to start or what to do. What is your plan?" As much as Duncan admired his wife, she remained a mystery, a stubborn, lovely mystery.

"I don't have a plan. I just have a feeling that we can help."

"So where do we begin?"

"I think we should have him as near to us as possible. I don't want him to think he is alone and that he is here just because he doesn't speak. He's going to need a lot of attention, but we can do this in a way he will not notice."

Young John Forsyth became a member of the Duncan Ross family and, in a short time, of the Jack Gallagher family as well. Billy led the rest of the students to include John in whatever they planned. The children in the school soon picked up on Naomi's way: She spoke to John as if he had no problem. He never said a word to her, but she acted as though he had. Even though this was difficult and tried the patience of all, Naomi's determination and Billy's tenacity became the model.

The first month was devoid of any sign of change, of anything that could be called progress. In that month, John learned to adapt and adjust to this lively, active, noisy, and sharing community. Peggy gave him a lot of her attention, and he began to regard her as a special friend. He was bright, attentive, and a good listener. He gave indications that he understood everything that was said to him or around him. He just didn't speak, no sounds, not even a whisper.

On a beautiful spring day in April, Thomas Archer took his class to the far side of the meadow behind the barn. Each student had a piece of paper, a stick of charcoal, and the assignment to sketch anything they saw, anything that took their fancy. But it had to be alive and moving. He told them to work alone and at some distance from each other, no talking and no calling back and forth.

After nearly two hours of intense bending over drawing boards and suppressed giggles, Thomas lead his class back to the main building. After trips to the outhouse and turns at the water bucket, the class settled down. Thomas had each student show what he or she sketched and tell why that particular living thing was chosen. Crows, squirrels, and a bewildered raccoon had wandered across the meadow and found themselves on the paper of several students. And the same for a doe that poked her head out of the woods. Students were commenting and at times sharply criticizing each other's work. When it came John's turn he eagerly displayed a neatly sketched field of meadow grass.

"But it isn't moving, is it, John?"

John nodded his head as if in agreement with Thomas. Then to everyone's surprise he blurted out, "Grass moves! Grass grows. It moves!"

Thomas quickly moved to other sketches. He thought it best not to make a big event over John saying something everyone heard. On their next outing to do sketching, John sensed he had done something wrong. His steps lagged and he was soon at the back of the pack. Thomas directed the class to a clearing in the woods where trees were to be the focus of their work. As they returned to the main building, John again lagged. Thomas saw this and casually matched his pace to that of John and could hear him muttering, "Grass moves. I know it moves."

"Yes, John, grass does move because we know it grows. But it moves so slowly we can't see it. Can you see grass move?"

"Sometimes. When I hide from my mom. I see all sorts of things move because I have to be quiet. I make any noise, she'll find me."

"And if she finds you, what happens?"

"She marches me into the house and makes me sit in a corner while she reads the Bible out loud. Then she screams at me in tongues. I don't know what she says."

Thomas was dumbstruck. In two minutes this troubled boy had spoken more than he had in months. Why? What in this exercise in sketching had released John from his verbal prison? Thomas decided on the spot. Tell no one, make no fuss, and work with John as though nothing happened. Without being obvious, he would observe John as often as possible. He would create activities for the class where John was expected to participate, but was not signaled out as being different.

📖 📖 📖

Jack Gallagher continued to soak up local gossip, noting who was hiring horses or mules, moving goods, bragging and boasting, taking on too much rot-gut in the local taverns and talking too much. Jack shared this store of information, usually in evenings over coffee and cake at either the schoolhouse kitchen with Eleanor, Naomi, and Duncan or at the Gallaghers.'

"I think Naomi has it right," Duncan said one night. "A pattern is emerging. Slavery is the big problem of the day."

"But what is being done?" Eleanor asked. "Talk is one thing, but action is another. Which is it?"

"It's both from what I gather. The talk gets louder, seems to be on everyone's mind, and I'm sure plans are hatchin."

Naomi had been quiet at this evening's get-together, but now she spoke. "I have a feeling something is going to happen. Do we have to wait? Can't we do something? Make our own plans?"

"What can we do? Who'll be with us, who'll be against us?" Jack continued with his thoughts. "Them that want slavery are the loud ones, but them that want to get rid of it ain't so loud. So who can you count on? The deer that breaks from cover is the one gonna get his ass shot."

The friends chewed on this topic a little longer, but Jack's news about mule buyers and drovers talking about the riches to be found in Santa Fe sparked a growing interest.

"The last I heard, some fella by the name of Becker, or Buckner or somethin like that [William Becknell] made a trail followed by a bunch of others and they all ended up in Santa Fe with pockets full of money. Does that get anybody's interest?"

"Not mine," said Duncan. "We've got our hands full running the school. And I told you all right from the start, it wouldn't be a money-making scheme. It was to be an adventure. Hasn't it been an adventure?"

"Can't argue with you, but an adventure to where? Where does it end?"

"Why does it have to end, Naomi? I know of schools back in Europe that have lasted for hundreds of years. Why? Because they made the effort to train others to take over when the time came. Couldn't we do the same?"

"Let's start training tomorrow. Tonight I have some medications that should be filtered and put in jars before they spoil."

📖 📖 📖

Two months later Peggy was overcome with surprise and pleasure. Her cousin in the Highlands, Jennifer McBride, had sent her a letter, her very first one! A letter addressed to Peggy Ross, her name written in neat script on the envelope. She opened it and read the letter through, then she read it aloud to her parents.

Dear Peggy

It is so exciting to write to you. I have never written to anyone before. My mother thought it would be a nice thing for us to do, exchange letters. I hope you think the same.

I have just finished all the schooling I can get in Glasgow where we live. I liked school and miss going to the classes and being with my friends. I go to my father's place of business and help in some of the office work he has to do. I like helping my father, but I really don't want to do that the rest of my life.

Some day I would like to travel like you have. My father came home with a map of North America and we all sat down and figured out how far you had to travel to get from the North Country to that place on the big river where you now live. Was it exciting? You must write and tell me all about it.

We send our love to you and your parents. Please write.

Cousin Jennifer

Duncan shared Peggy's delight at receiving her first letter. "You must keep in touch with your cousin. Who knows? Some day you and Jennifer may get the chance to meet and really get to know one another."

📖 📖 📖

Days turned into weeks and became months. The triumphs and struggles of the school community trickled by. Naomi's collections of samples from nature delighted her and perplexed her. As she taught, she realized she would always be a student. There was so much to learn.

Naomi quietly began to do something else that came to her slowly. She determined she would learn how to read. For this she turned, not to Duncan, but to Peggy. Her daughter became her teacher, and a fine teacher she was. It was not difficult to conceal their secret from Duncan, for he was so busy with all aspects of running a school that he took little note of the growing hours Naomi and Peggy spent together.

Jack's ever-inquisitive nature absorbed more of the angry talk and threats from those debating the slavery issue. He also absorbed the growing awareness of increasing travel to the West, to the fabulous wealth supposedly pouring into Santa Fe from trade and from gold mines.

Thomas had mixed feelings about the progress he saw in John Forsyth's return to the world, speaking openly and freely. Some of his art projects bore fruit. John talked normally, but only when he sensed he and Thomas were far from the hearing of others, especially from females.

Duncan's work keeping his school together and operating smoothly still left time to ponder other matters. He, too, worried and was deeply concerned about the issues passionately discussed: the politics, the morality, and the impacts of slavery on his world.

He was pleased that Samuel Rawlinson responded so quickly to his request for maps and books vital to the school's insatiable appetite for the tools of solid learning. Duncan wondered how he might induce Samuel to come to St. Louis and enter into business there.

Peggy was becoming the young woman. Her winning smile and natural grace and ease of movement plus her constant attempts at styling her long, black hair gave her an air of confidence. Still Billy's best friend, she was outgrowing him at the rate of about an inch every year. And Billy gave up trying to figure out why his voice sounded so strange at times and why his face had blotches and red spots even though he made a daily practice of using soap and water.

Eleanor was the one who did something about the changes in Billy. She could bring her world into focus and share it with sharp questions and useful observations.

"I think it is time for you to have a talk with Billy, Jack."

"And just what am I to tell our oldest boy?"

"About what it means to become a man and the changes in him that are happening."

"He's around animals every day. What do I need to tell him?"

"Billy's a young man, not an animal. Tell him what men think about."

"I can't tell him that!"

"You can, and you must, Jack. I caught him washing out his underwear, and it wasn't because he didn't get to the outhouse in time."

"That just shows he knows how to care for himself. Why do I have to tell him anythin?"

"I think his problem comes at night when he is in bed."

"Holy Hannah, Eleanor, he ain't old enough for them wet dreams!"

"He is, and it is better for you to talk to him than have him learn about it from the stable hands you hire at the liveries in town."

"I'll have Duncan or Thomas take him aside and explain these things."

"No, Jack Gallagher, you do it, and do it soon."

📖   📖   📖

It was one of those evenings in early fall when the sharper nip to the air was a welcome change after summer heat. In January this day would be like manna from heaven. Jack came home after a round of his businesses, the two livery stables plus the cartage trade in from St.Louis, with the news that the town was to have a large celebration. He thought it had to do with getting another hook and ladder company of the fire department equipped and trained. But that was not as important to Jack as the opportunity for a celebration. Parties, hoedowns, anything that promised good fun were always high on his list, not only for himself, but also for his family.

An invitation to join with the Gallaghers was extended to the Rosses. Duncan had already accepted an invitation to talk to a group in the village of Saint Charles about the realities of starting a private school. Because of Naomi's deep involvement in their school, he insisted that she go with him. She was reluctant to attend and even more reluctant to explain her views of what impact a school could have in the lives of its students.

"You are the one who pushed me into making the chores of our students in farm, field, kitchen, and woodshed a part of our teaching. Who can better explain this?"

"You know I have never shied away from telling you what is on my mind. But to do it in front of strangers might ruin what you want this group of people to know."

"I am not the least bit worried about what you might say. Maybe I should worry about how to get you stopped."

"Dunc, no more of that! I will go but only if Peggy and Thomas go with us."

"Fair enough. I will talk to Thomas when he has finished his project. He's having students learn ways to mix different clays and crushed rocks to make a variety of colors."

Peggy agreed at once. Thomas provided a different answer.

"Duncan, I would like nothing better than to go with your family. But I can't. I promised John I would stay with him in the classroom. He wants to work on a big drawing. He said he thinks he can put on paper with color what he feels about why he doesn't want to talk."

"He talks to you? You never said he was coming along well enough to tell you personal events in his life. Why do we not know this?"

"I decided to keep this to myself until John felt secure, ready to talk on his own terms in his own way."

"Sounds reasonable, but did you ever consider that we might help?"

"I don't think so. One thing about John I noticed right off was the look of fear that fills his eyes whenever a female is nearby. I'm sure Naomi,

Eleanor, or Florence did nothing to frighten him. As for Grace and Peggy, those two young women are the leaders in looking after John and making certain he is always a part of the group."

"Thomas, careful what you say here. None of those women would knowingly add to the burden he already bears."

"It's just that they are women. His mother is a woman. And I am led to believe his mother might be the root of his problem."

"What brings you to that conclusion? Does she abuse him in any way that you are aware of?"

"I don't think it is physical punishment. I think we would call it mental abuse."

"You will keep me informed if you learn more of the role his mother might play in his unwillingness to speak. We shall miss you, Thomas. And I think at the meeting you would add ideas about a school that we might not consider."

"I have my doubts. Art and music are my ways of talking to people."

"If you think John can work out some of his anger and fear by painting, then stay with him. Jack hired a guide for us to and from Saint Charles. This man knows some roads that will save a lot of time. We should be back by dark."

As the Ross family rode to the meeting in Saint Charles, John Forsyth was the topic of constant comment and discussion. Duncan related the story Thomas gave him about the amount and content of John's private conversations. The attention of Peggy and Naomi was matched with the questions building up in each of them.

"I give Thomas full credit for the unlocking of John's tongue, but I do admit that I am upset about his keeping all this to himself."

"Papa Dunc, why be upset? I think what Thomas did was the right way to handle John's problem."

Naomi added, "Of course Thomas was correct in the way he gained the confidence of John. What would you have had him do?"

"I don't know. I just feel that all of us might have been able to add to what Thomas was able to do with him. Remember when we get back tonight, we will all take our cue from Thomas. There is the possibility that he got no response from John. Maybe the boy crawled back into his shell."

The afternoon meeting with the folks in Saint Charles who asked Duncan to talk with them about starting a school went along rather smoothly. Smooth until the leader of the group opened the meeting to questions. Questions came thick and fast from a great variety of viewpoints. But when someone asked Duncan to explain what he meant by "open enrollment" the meeting took on another tone.

Civility was replaced by anger, and name calling flew about the room voiced in blunt terms and raw language. It was apparent to all that the leader was no longer in charge of a meeting called to set in motion actions that could bring a school into this community. Instead he was now a willing partner in the destruction of community spirit over the slavery issue.

"I think we should get back in the carriage and head for home. We can't add anything to this free-for-all."

Naomi stood and began to move toward the door.

"Come, Peggy. I don't see anything that will quiet this bunch."

The Ross family was relieved to see their guide loitering nearby and as ready to get away from the scene as they were. Nobody questioned their leaving. No one came out to thank them for coming; there were no words of appreciation. Duncan brought his team in behind their guide, who knew the way. After a fast ten minutes on the road he signaled to Duncan to slow the pace and relax.

"For the first time in many years I was afraid. I had no idea people could get so angry over slavery. Don't they know it's wrong? Why do they get so ugly and mean?"

"For many, slavery is way of life they want to preserve. The slave owner's way, of course. It is a separate culture we know little about."

"I saw that Winfield person. Did you see him, Dunc?"

"No. He was at the meeting? I must have missed him."

"He was slipping around at the back of the hall. He wasn't dressed in fine clothes. He looked like a working man."

"I guess he has the right to be at a public meeting."

"He was there to get people stirred up. He's a trouble maker."

"I'm glad I don't know much about slavery. I don't want to think it can involve us."

"But, my dear Peggy, you are involved. Did you forget about the Crawfords?"

"I thought you said Mr. Crawford is a free man, not a slave."

"Yes, Mr. Crawford is free. Except he isn't really free in this part of the country."

"I don't understand. How can a man be free and not be free?"

Both Naomi and Peggy listened as Duncan tried his best to explain what he knew about the attitude many people held of Negro people. Conversation flew back and forth among the three of them as they made their way back to the schoolhouse. None of them paid much attention to where they were, nor was anyone aware of the passage of time.

All four realized that it was almost dark. Norman Shirey, their guide, reined in his horse and said, "I'm leaving you folks. I gotta get back to St. Louis. Jack's place is just a mile ahead. Nice to meet you, Mr. Ross. If ever you need a guide you know how to get in touch with me. Ain't many places around this countryside I don't know about."

All the students at Duncan's school – save John Forsyth and Peggy – were day-students at Duncan's school. At the end of the day they either walked or rode a mule or pony to their homes on nearby farms. There was no sign of the Gallagher family at their place so Duncan continued on the familiar trace to the schoolhouse. As he guided the carriage onto the road that passed through a heavily forested stretch, he stopped abruptly. A large tree had been felled across the road.

"I'll tie the horses to this tree. You and Peggy stay here. I'll go get John and Thomas and a couple of axes to get this tree out of the way."

Before anyone could say a word, several rounds of gunfire broke the stillness of the evening. These were followed by another volley of small arms fire. Then a flash of searing red and yellow and orange filtered through the woods. Fire! Fire at the schoolhouse! Another brilliant flash. Duncan knew from its location it had to be the barn. Yet another flash and there went the woodshed. Last to be torched was the wash house. Complete and total destruction, for even though the Ross family was at least a half a mile from the fire, the heat and noise, intense light and acrid smell of burning wood said it all.

They stood in a trance. Peggy screamed, "Thomas, John, we must get to them.

"Follow me; I can see enough of the road to find our way."

Peggy took the lead. She and the Gallagher children had traveled this road countless times as they grew up more as one large family than as two separate ones. Peggy was the first to see the crumpled figure of John Forsyth; he was lying about twenty-five feet from the schoolhouse. She bent over the figure of her friend, her silent friend. His body was riddled with holes oozing blood. No one could survive such a blast of lead. Naomi dropped to her knees beside Peggy and took her daughter in her arms as her eyes confirmed what her senses told her. There was no hope.

Duncan ran to several places where doors or windows might have furnished a way out for Thomas. He knew if John managed to escape, perhaps Thomas somehow got out of the building. He stumbled and fell heavily. A flare of flames gave light enough to see he had fallen over Thomas' body. He picked up the limp form and carried it to where Naomi and Peggy were dragging the body of John Forsyth back from the searing heat of the fire.

"He's been shot. This little boy who never harmed a soul has been shot like a hunted animal. He's only a boy, Dunc. They killed a boy!"

"I know. Here's Thomas, shot just like John."

It was the end of two lives. The end of the school. The end of Duncan's dream. The end of Naomi's haven, and the end of Peggy's future.

Nothing could escape a fire so cleverly carried out, so thoroughly prepared for the arsonists' torches, and so completely successful. Neither John nor Thomas had a chance against the diabolical schemes of angry men bent on destruction – mindless destruction without purpose and lacking any moral justification.

The day's outing in St. Louis for the Gallagher family ended as it began, with laughter, good-natured banter, and plans to go to the school house to share their pleasant adventure with the Ross family. Jack began to help Billy unhook the span of carriage horses, lead them to water, brush them down, give them a bait of hay, but stopped in his tracks. The unmistakable odor of burning wood was nearby. Only one building, the schoolhouse, was that close to his place.

"Billy, I'm gettin a powerful smell of smoke. Do it reach you?"

"I smelled it as soon as we stopped."

"Fetch one of them torches we made. We ought to get over there to the school right smart. I don't like this feeling I got in my gut."

He went to Eleanor to tell her their plans. She met him at the barn and told him the same, "Jack, that smell of smoke is too strong and it's coming from the schoolhouse way. Oh, Jack, look at those flames. They're everywhere!"

"Me and Billy got us a torch we're gonna light off and get over there."

The horses Duncan had tied to a tree were tangled in the carriage traces and near death from fright.

"Billy, help me cut these critters loose. Careful, watch them hooves. Good, now let em go, they'll run back to our place."

Neither Jack nor Billy was prepared for what lay ahead. The first sight was the shell of the big building. Fires flared up from time to time as puffs of wind gave new life to old embers. The light from these many fires gave a clue where the Ross family could be found. Seated on the ground Naomi held a sobbing Peggy in her arms as she gently stroked her hair and softly sang a native song of death. Stretched out on the ground beside them were two bodies, one small, one large. Jack and Billy knew instantly they were looking at the bodies of John Forsyth and Thomas Archer.

In a voice filled with fear of more dreadful news Jack asked Naomi, "Where'll I find your man?"

"He went to see what he might be able to do at the barn."

"Billy, you stay. I'm goin down there. Duncan'll need a hand with the stock. They'll be mighty skittish, if'n there's any left."

He made it about half way down the lane to the barn when the shape of Duncan loomed out of the smoke and flaring light.

"No use to go down there. The barn's a total loss and the bastards ran off all the stock. Nothing remains. Did you see Naomi and Peggy? They are the ones needing comfort."

The suggestion from Jack that all of them go to his place for the night was heard and brought an immediate refusal. "We can't leave John and Thomas. We'll stay here till morning comes."

Jack told his son to stay, but that he was going back and help Eleanor get things organized. The Ross family had lost everything they owned. Only the clothes on their backs survived. As he made his way home Jack began to piece together some sense of what had happened. To level that large building quickly and thoroughly meant a lot of men were involved. A lot of guns were used to pump out so much lead making sure no witnesses got out alive. Hours of planning had gone into this night of total destruction. It was not an accident.

Other thoughts came to mind. The Forsyth family had to be told of John's death. People in St. Louis needed to know of Thomas Archer's fate. Lawmen in town had to be informed that there were killings as well as a devastating fire. Even as Jack mulled over this item, he guessed some among the lawmen didn't have to be told anything.

Eleanor met him at the kitchen door. "How bad is it? I know something bad took place over there."

"Ah, woman. I don't know that I can tell you. It's total. Little John and Thomas kilt, all the buildings burnt to the ground, their stock run off. Billy's stayin with Naomi an Peggy an Duncan."

"Eleanor, we're all they got. We gotta make some sort of home for them. I know they'd do the same for us."

"We will do everything we can. The first thing in the morning you ride over to the Forsyth farm and tell them about John."

"And after that I'll ride to town and tell the sheriff there's been a shootin out at the school. I think I know where Thomas had his room and studio. Best nose around there and see if'n I kin find somebody."

Jack and Eleanor sat down at the kitchen table and began to figure out how to fit three more people into their home. Eleanor moved her children to make a room for Duncan and Naomi; she put Grace and Peggy together, but she had to move Charley in with herself and Jack. Billy came back at daybreak and said a place in the barn would do for him.

Jack's morning ride to the Forsyth farm gave him time to review his thoughts. The speed of the fire through all the buildings and the intense heat told him that something had been thrown on the school building from all sides to accelerate the blaze. This dastardly act had been carefully thought out in every detail. "But what am I to tell the Forsyths?" Jack mused out loud. "Dan'l will understand, but what of his wife?"

"Mornin, Dan'l, mornin, Mrs. Forsyth. Got some news. Sit down, cause you ain't goin like what I'm sayin."

"It's 'bout John, I just know'd it. It's him, ain't it?"

"Yes, mam. I'm afraid tis."

"What happent him?"

"There was a fire at the school last night. Little John and the art teacher, Thomas Archer, they was shot and kilt afore the bastards torched the school and all the buildings. Everything's gone, burnt up."

"Who done such a thing?"

"Don't know, Dan'l, but I'm aimin to find out."

Mrs. Forsyth began to sway and mumble. She threw herself on the ground.

"She's fixin to go plumb crazy. She gets like this when she's upset."

The men watched as she fled to the woods, screaming in her strange tongue, tearing at her clothes and shrieking obscenities.

"Let her go, Jack. Ain't nothin we kin do. I'll fetch her back when she's done screamed herself to the point she's worn out. She'll be all right."

"There's one more thing we gotta talk over. We gotta bury your son. Do you want him brung here? You gotta another place you'd like for him?"

"Lemme think on that."

"You do that, and if'n there's anything you need, you let me 'n Eleanor know. We want to help you and your woman through this here dark patch."

"Best get on with other things you gotta do. We'll get along here somehow."

With that sad encounter behind him, Jack turned his horse toward St. Louis. He thought of what he might have done if Billy had been gunned down in last night's tragedy. Heavy thoughts weighed on his mind as he directed his horse to the sheriff's office.

"Well, Jack. What brings you in here wearing such a long face? Some one run off with one of those broken down nags you rent out to unsuspecting people? Well, out with it."

"Sit down and listen. I ain't wantin your shit!"

"Christ, man, take it easy!"

"You're the one takin it easy, too easy. Some of those damn slavers burnt out the little school that's just a mile from my place. Burnt it to the ground and kilt two people at the same time. Now, what are you gonna do? Tell me, Sheriff, what you gonna do."

"How in the hell am I gonna do anything til I know the details?"

"This here's serious business, Sheriff, and we're gonna get to the bottom of it. When we do, you damn well better be at my side!"

Jack laid out the whole story for the lawman, sparing no details, but refrained from passing judgments until the sheriff had his say.

"Now, we gotta look at this from all angles, one of which you ain't give me one name or one bit of hard evidence for me to go after anybody. That's the way the law works, give me evidence."

"The people expect a good lawman to go lookin for what he needs to string up the guilty sons a bitches. Not sit on his fat ass and wait for a citizen to bring it to him."

"That's pretty tough talk. What can you back up in this long tale of burnin and killin? That's where we gotta begin."

"To start with, them buildings went up in a matter of minutes. It was a fire that had somethin damn powerful to make her go so fast."

"And what else can you tell me?"

Calming down, Jack recounted the episode of the rock through the window of the school building; the visit of Winfield LeBaron with Duncan; the meeting at Saint Charles where LeBaron was present and stirring up trouble; how the meeting got out of hand when Duncan Ross tried to explain his school's policy of open enrollment. The sheriff listened to Jack without any comment. He got to his feet, put his arm around Jack's shoulder, and eased him out the door.

"Was I you, Jack, I'd be careful where I try to dig up evidence. I'd be damn careful."

"I'll be careful, count on it. But you had best show me action or we may have to dig around in your backyard!"

Fuming over this unsatisfactory conversation, Jack began to drift into a part of town that had mostly small private houses and cottages. He had some idea of where Thomas Archer had his studio and room. A few knocks on doors turned up nothing useful, but Jack was determined and kept knocking. At the sixth place he was met at the door by an attractive woman, who asked him into her modest, well-kept house.

"I think I know who you are, Mr. Gallagher. Thomas often described you and all the people at the school. My name is Myrna Wilson. What can I do for you?"

"It's more like what I can do for you, Miss Wilson. I bring sad news of Thomas. He was kilt last night in a fire that burnt up the school."

The woman fainted and fell to the floor before Jack could react. Revived with a glass of water, she let Jack help her into a chair. She sat for five minutes without saying a word.

"Thomas was my friend, my very best friend. He has lived with me for the past four years. We're not married, but we're close, very close. Can you accept that, Mr. Gallagher?"

"We all knew there was good reason why Thomas kept three days of each week for comin back to St. Louis."

"We were living outside the law, if you chose to take that view of our relationship. I loved that man, and he loved me."

"I think I know how hard it is for you to tell me this and I 'preciate your openness. I'm not here to pass judgment. I'm here to help."

"I am stunned. I cannot think clearly."

"If there is anything you want or need, why you just get word to me at one of my livery stables in town."

"Yes, Mr. Gallagher. I'm glad you told me. It would have crushed me had I learned of Thomas through town gossip."

"I want you to know me and my woman and all the people out at the school share this tragedy. Our hearts go out to you."

"You will get word to me about burying Thomas? I must be there."

Nothing more could be accomplished in town. Jack directed his weary horse and his own weary body toward home. As he rode he thought of all the things to be done. When he got home he was surprised to find decisions already had been made on a variety of problems. Duncan and Naomi were two capable people, and Eleanor had demonstrated time and again that she was equal to anything that confronted her.

"Jack Gallagher, you come in this house, pull off your boots, stretch out on the floor on that buffalo robe, and don't move until I tell you to."

Even as she was giving her husband these directions in such stern, no-nonsense terms, Eleanor had her arms about Jack and held him close. He did as ordered, but when he relaxed and realized his wife was busy elsewhere, he let the tears roll. Tears for the two dead men, one young, one not yet old, who had established a bond now forever severed. Tears for the dreams and aspirations of Duncan and Naomi, who labored to build a school designed to be a rock, a safe harbor, a spring of wisdom, not for themselves, but for young people. Tears for Peggy whose talents had been discovered and developed by an unselfish young man. And tears for his own family. The sheriff's parting remark was a warning that they, too, might be the target of the fury and blind hatred of those angry and determined types who seemed to be in control of the countryside in and around St. Louis.

At the supper table that evening the fatigue and shock of the past twenty-four hours gave way to a slow but detailed accounting of what had been done and what remained to be done. Daniel Forsyth had sent word to Jack that he wanted John to be buried with the young man who had tried to help him. Duncan's decision, supported by Eleanor, Naomi, and Peggy, was that their friends should be buried on the school grounds.

Peggy picked a place halfway between the school building and the barn on a rise of ground with a copse of young trees and a view over their little valley. Duncan marked out the grave sites, and he and Billy began to dig. Peggy insisted that this was hallowed ground and that she had to help with the digging. Eleanor came that morning with cloths and a bucket, sheets and cord. She and Naomi knew what must be done to prepare bodies for their journey to the next world. They did it in silence, with hands that were gentle, caring, and so touched with their love for these two men.

Sorting through the still smoldering wreckage of the main building, Duncan found some boards that had not been totally consumed and were still useful. All agreed the finished caskets need not be fine cabinetry, but made with wood from this special place. He set himself to this task with renewed vigor and determination. It gave purpose to the final memorial for John and Thomas.

At dusk that same evening they gathered at the burial site. Naomi and Eleanor, Duncan and Jack reverently laid the bodies in their respective coffins. All family members touched one then the other, and with Jack's help, Duncan nailed the lids on the caskets, sealed now with the thoughts and prayers of a little community not yet fully at grips with the tragedy of the moment. The men set the caskets on the ground beside the open graves with a carefully arranged mound of ground and rocks to cover them and protect them from animals drawn to the place.

The next morning Billy and Jack rode to pass the word of a graveside service that afternoon at the school. Other men uncovered the caskets and prepared the ground for the final service. Though Jack and Billy had specific destinations to inform friends and neighbors, news of the destruction of the school and the senseless killing of two innocent people spread as fast as the wildfire that had consumed the school.

People came to the school on foot, on horseback, in farm wagons, and in fine carriages. Many came with expressions of sympathy, of genuine sorrow, and offers of assistance. Some with expressions of sorrow that had a ring of insincerity, for they saw justification in what had been done here. They believed a lesson had to be taught to those who could not, or would not, see the true light of the cause.

As Duncan began to gather thoughts about a memorial service his mind drifted back to the North Country of Canada. To a little trading post in the vast wilderness more than a decade ago that was home for him and Naomi and Peggy. *Lac de Truches* was also the home of their *bourgeois*, Jonathan Graham, the owner and manager of the trading post. He had died of a heart attack as his brigade of canoes was returning to its home post from the annual *Rendezvous* of the North West Company at Grand Portage on the shore of Lake Superior. It had fallen to Duncan to see to his burial and to hold a service in honor of that remarkable man.

Once again, the burden of such a service was on his shoulders.

As the time for the service neared, a natural separation of the people gathered for the memorial began to take place. Those directly connected to the school, close friends of the Ross and Gallagher families, Daniel Forsyth, the Crawfords, and Myrna Wilson circled the graves while others pressed in behind them. Jack had thoughtfully sent one of his men and a carriage to bring Myrna to the service.

Duncan read a selection of verses from various parts of the Bible.

They were selected without any determination on his part, but by the spirit of Jonathan Graham, his friend and mentor from their days in the fur trade. Some were the same verses read at that service many years ago in the remoteness of the North Country. Duncan also asked any who felt the desire to express their thoughts about John and Thomas.

He began with a short, but deeply felt expression of the impact these two brought into the lives of all in this close-knit community. Jack followed with his own thoughts expressed from the heart without rehearsal or prior planning. Eleanor and Naomi trilled a death song of the Mandan people. Peggy tried to add her bit to the service, but broke down in a flood of tears. Billy, too, tried but could not get the words to come. Florence Crawford sang "Swing Low Sweet Chariot." Daniel Forsyth managed to mumble a good-bye to his son. Last to speak was the stranger, Myrna Wilson. She stood apart from the group, but in a voice filled with love, said her farewell to the man who had enriched her life for such a short time.

Earlier Naomi had slipped into the woods where she knew there was a growth of wild roses. She gathered an armful and now gave everyone standing at the graves two roses. After those who wished to speak said their words of parting, the caskets were lowered in the ground. Naomi stepped forward and, kneeling, ever so gently let a rose slip to one casket and then the other. All the friends did the same until the caskets were covered with a blanket of color. Jack took a shovel and used it to add a gift of earth to each grave, then passed it to the person standing next to him. And so it went around the gathering of friends until all who so desired had added their final tribute of earth to the two men who were now part of it.

At Eleanor's invitation, the little community turned their steps, their horses, their wagons and carriages toward the Gallagher place. More than the proverbial wine and bread awaited. Eleanor's home was an invitation to relax, to share the burdens of the past two days through talk with friends and to permit thoughts of celebration to enter the gathering.

Each in his own way John and Thomas had accomplished much in the briefness of their days. Their lives merited celebration. Naomi and Peggy were the last to leave the site of the graves. They thought they were the last, but silently Myrna Wilson fell in step with them.

"I hardly know where to begin but, Peggy, I have things to tell you."

"Peggy, you walk with Miss Wilson. I must go and help Eleanor."

"I want you to know as well. Please stay with us for a minute. Peggy, I helped Thomas prepare your art work for shipment to his friend in New Orleans. As he picked up each piece he commented about it and pointed out why it was truly art and not just another sketch. You must continue with your art. You have a true talent."

"I don't know, Miss Wilson. I don't think I am really very good."

"I would like it if you and your mother call me Myrna. I feel that through Thomas we are all very close. I should like to keep that feeling of closeness."

"But what is Peggy to do? Who will give her the kind of support that Thomas did?"

"At this moment I can't answer that. But I know when the artist in New Orleans sends his judgments to Thomas, I will know of it, for his reply will be addressed to my home in town."

As the three women slowly made their way to the rest of the group they discovered a little more about each other and resolved to visit back and forth.

"I have one more thought I would like to share. I cannot think of a more fitting tribute you could give Thomas than to continue with your art. I know he more than taught you, Peggy, he inspired you. Keep his inspiration alive in your art."

It was a long, sad day, but a day in the closeness of friendship and sharing of grief. At times it was possible to find the right words to express the feelings and the emptiness this tragedy brought into the lives of so many. At other times it was an embrace, a hand on the arm, a firm hand-shake that conveyed the message. But through it all Duncan found himself wishing he could find a moment of solitude, a time to let inner feelings replace the surface expressions, to just stop all senses, all earthly contacts. He needed time to set his soul free to find a resting place of its own choosing.

As evening took over from the bright light of an eventful day, Duncan stepped outside the house and walked toward the woods to find the peace he sought. A familiar voice softly spoke his name. He turned to find Amos Crawford standing in the fading light at the edge of the woods.

"Mr. Ross, I needs to tell you sumpin."

"Yes, Amos."

"Me 'n my woman 'n two little ones, we's leavin. We has to, Mr. Ross."

"No, Amos, you don't have to leave. We'll find something for you to do. I don't want you to leave; I need you now more than ever."

"No, we has to move on. Them what did all this evil to you got their eyes on us. Last night they cum to our cabin, ride around on their horses, shoutin and makin threats."

"We'll get a bunch of men together and watch your place. I won't let another tragedy like his break up our community."

"It ain't gonna work that a way."

"We can make it work. I know we can."

"Brother's comin tonight, late. He bring a wagon 'n mule. We's headin north."

"But where will you go? What will you do?"

"Don't know, we jus gotta move on, maybe to Chicago. Hear a black man kin git work there."

"I wish you'd give this more time. We'll figure out something."

"I knows you would. But we knows the signs, we knows what comes next if'n we stays around here. Ain't no use, Mr. Ross, we's leavin."

"Let me give you a little money, you'll need it along the way."

"Jus a little. Ain't nothin but trouble if dem slavers find a nigger whats got money."

"I think this is so unfair."

"Jus the way things is. We brung more than 'nough troubles when you took our two in your school. I stays round here, and you'll git more trouble. Goodbye, Mr. Ross. You tells your woman she's a good lady, and your girl, Peggy, she's a fine un."

Amos Crawford was gone as silently as he appeared. He left behind a saddened and angered Duncan Ross. A bewildered man thinking that all he touched seemed to meet tragedy of some sort — little John Forsyth, Thomas Archer, now Amos and his family. Years ago he had left the Scottish Highlands thinking of the great things he would accomplish in this New World. Now, look at this mess of porridge he had stirred up!

Two days after the burials at the schoolhouse site, Duncan learned that when Daniel Forsyth returned to his home after the funeral he had found his wife's body hanging from a tree in the woods.

📖 📖 📖

On the fourth day after the destruction of the school Duncan rode into town with Jack, who said he must get back to tend to business. He hadn't told any of his family or even Duncan about his talk with the sheriff. All this time gone by and not one deputy had come out to investigate either the fire or the killings.

"Duncan, you wanted to ride about town to see if'n there's a place you might rent. Was I you, I'd start lookin to the southwest. Anything long the river is gonna be a bit large, a bit pricy."

"That's what I had in mind, Jack. What time you figure on riding back home?"

"Bout an hour afore sundown, I reckon."

He didn't want to tell Duncan he was going to pay a call on the sheriff. He watched as Duncan rode off. Jack thought he should drop by the freight yard to tend to some business before he went to do battle with a lawman who dragged his feet on such an important case.

"Mornin, Sheriff. Me and you gotta talk."

"Can't you see I'm a busy man?"

"Maybe I gotta get busier and ride over to Jeff and have a session with the boys there about a sheriff who ain't made a move to investigate a suspicious fire and two killins. Want to ride along?"

"Jack Gallagher, don't you try to threaten me, hear?"

"I ain't makin no threats, I do what I say I'm a gonna do, and you know it."

"Now just take it easy. These things take time."

"Are you gonna do somethin? Tell me, Sheriff. Or am I the one to take action?"

"I'll ride out tomorrow or the next day and have a look. That satisfy you?"

It didn't satisfy Jack, but what was he to do? It was clear to him this sheriff had no intention to investigate either the fire or the murders. Jack knew a stacked deck when he saw one. He rode back to the riverfront where he could lose himself in the work at the livery stable.

Meanwhile Duncan was busy riding and looking for a furnished house to rent. On the way home that evening he told Jack what prospects he had found and where they were located and asked what steps were next.

"We'll ride around tomorrow and see what you turned up. I know some of the men in this here town who own places to rent, but I don't know em all. We'll do some door knockin and askin."

"There's just the three of us. We don't need a mansion, just a place that doesn't need a lot of fixing in a safe part of town."

"Safe? My friend, me and you, we're marked men! This slavery thing is damn near out a hand. Don't volunteer too much. Don't be askin too many questions."

That night after supper Duncan sat down to write a letter to his former partner in Montreal.

Dear Samuel:

This is far more than a thank you note for sending the maps and books I requested. Your selections were exceptionally useful and everything arrived in fine condition. It made my teaching of Geography much more complete and believable for the students. What I must write from this point on will be most difficult.

In Montreal you may not be hearing of the deep division growing in the States over the question of Free Soil or Slavery. A division deep and passionate that has struck us right where we live. I organized our school around the principle of open enrollment. In this part of the country you can take that to mean enrolling all children, even Negro children.

The school and all its outbuildings were put to the torch a week ago. They were total losses, but most hurtful and crushing to all of us were the deaths of one of our students and of our art teacher.

Devastation seems so inadequate a word to describe our situation. We lost everything, Samuel. As for my family? We are getting along but have only the clothes on our backs. I have much to ask of you.

The requests I make are based on the assumption that my personal wealth has grown with the investments you recommended a few years ago and that my assets can be made liquid and available to me within a reasonable time. I wish you to convert 25% of those assets into cash or cash equivalents. I will leave it to your judgments which paper in my portfolio you will select for liquidation. I am enclosing the name of the banking house in St. Louis with which I have had satisfactory relations.

We find ourselves in the position of having to start all over again – everything, and I mean everything. We are searching for a house in the town of St. Louis adequate to our modest means that can be rented furnished.

At this point I cannot tell you what I shall be doing. I have no stomach for starting another school. Opportunities for business ventures are beckoning, and some are tempting and must be considered. In fact, Samuel, many times I find myself thinking that St. Louis would be a profitable pasture for you to graze. Ever think of leaving Montreal? We here have word that since the demise of the North West Company your city has been severely jolted.

The address you used to get the books and maps to me should be the one to use as we continue to reestablish my financial roots in St. Louis. Advise as soon as you have the transfers underway.

My best to you and to Jeanette.

Duncan

"Look over there. See that big wagon what just pulled into the yard?" Duncan and Jack were standing at the side of Jack's freight yard. "Know what it is?"

"No. Looks like a boat on wheels under full sail. What is it?"

"Called a Conestoga. They don't stay round here very long. Most of 'em is sent on to Franklin or to Independence."

"Why there?"

"Them towns are the jumpin off places for the Santa Fe Trail."

"You can't get going West out of your mind, can you?"

"Ain't tryin to, and you should be thinkin on the same thing. Big chance for both of us to get a fresh start and not be hurtin our wallets whilst we're doin it."

"How would we ever start? Would Eleanor want to move? You two have a nice home in the country. Why change?"

"Hell, Eleanor would be the first to get in the wagon and the kids would be right behind her. I don't see Naomi holdin back. We know she's unhappy livin in St. Louis."

"Yes, she's not at ease living with neighbors so close, and she misses going to the woods to find the things she needs for her lotions and teas and medications."

"You miss it, too. But you're too stubborn to say it."

"Now don't go giving me one of your lectures about my being stubborn. You know I'm not stubborn."

"The hell you ain't! But no mind. All I'm askin is for you to think on movin West."

   📖   📖   📖

As days drifted into weeks, Duncan thought about moving on to the West. Instead of coming up with reasons for staying in Missouri, he found it much easier and more exciting to speculate about the Santa Fe Trail and new opportunities. But what were those opportunities? He heard about gold mining near the village, but that was a risky business. How about becoming a merchant there?

"Didn't you have enough of clerking with the old North West outfit?" he muttered to himself. "Face up to it, Duncan Ross, you liked being a partner in the NWC and the manager of five trading posts." He continued in the same vein, "You want to be the boss, no matter what you get into. You like being the head man."

Speculation about the future was fueled by the actions of his friend in Montreal, Samuel Rawlinson, and the figures he sent along about the growing wealth of his investments. He now had money in the bank in St. Louis and a substantial backup sitting in Montreal. What was holding him back?

Naomi.

He had not said much to her about what was churning in his mind. What was on her mind? And Peggy? She had had a cruel blow laid on her young back with the deaths of two very dear friends. Would change be the best thing for her to face right now?

Naomi and Duncan reserved the night for hashing out problems as they had done in years past. Lately, discussions that became quite heated were the only hints of passion. Duncan resolved to raise the question of moving to the West.

"Naomi, are you sleeping?"

"You know I'm not."

"I have been thinking about moving West. Get on the Santa Fe Trail and see what we might find out there to build our new lives around. What do you think?"

"It's about time you asked me. You've been walking about in a fog for months."

"I asked you a question."

"We might as well go. We're not really doing anything of importance in this hateful town. And Peggy is becoming impossible."

"Am I to take that as agreement?

"Yes. Now, I wish to sleep."

That night's brief conversation with Naomi was the basis for Duncan going to Jack to begin a series of questions and to develop firm plans of action. Jack learned that William Becknell was expected back in St. Louis following a successful return trip over the Trail from Santa Fe. "Soon's I hear of him bein in town, me and you is gonna meet up with him and sign on for the first out bound trek come spring."

"Now that is what I want to hear, but do we have to wait for him? Aren't there some things we might do right now?"

"Well, seems to me we might buy us two wagons, you know, them Conestogas that people are usin over the Trail."

"You have been in the freight hauling business for several years. What kind of wagons do you use?"

"I like Missouri wagons, been usin em without any problems. I been told the man what makes the best wagons in St. Louis learnt his trade in Pennsy with the Dutchmen."

"Which should we buy?"

"Them Conestogas are a tad bigger and have larger wheels, and the freight box can be made watertight. Ain't that much difference in cost."

"Sounds like you want to get the Conestogas. Fine with me! But why two? Won't one hold all the stuff two families will need?"

"One time you was a man of business. Why not fill one with stuff we kin sell when we get to Santa Fe? And think about mules or oxes. Horses ain't gonna be what we want pullin wagons for an eight hunnert mile slog. I'm selling all the mules I kin get my hands on to them that are headin out. For myself, I lean to oxes."

And so it went. Plans were made and buying of family needs as well as a stock of goods that would be the most profitable to resell continued. Duncan took over amassing their merchandise; Eleanor managed the purchases of family items. Naomi seemed not to care at all what plans were taking shape and seldom indicated a preference or a dissent. Peggy brightened at the prospect of the journey and spent much of her time and effort with Eleanor and with Grace and Billy. Charley ran from person to person trying to help.

Days when Duncan was not able to drive Peggy out to the Gallagher home, she turned to her art and roamed the water front with her pens, inks, and sketch pads. She was recognized by most of the men who worked there, and having those men know she was the daughter of that big red-headed Scotsman and the same as a daughter to Jack-the-livery-stable-man was like having two silent guardians at her shoulder.

Another guardian, anything but silent, was Billy. On the days he came into town with his father it was to do chores, but as soon as they were done he rushed to the riverfront, where he was sure to find Peggy. He quickly learned that there were times to put a leash on his teasing chatter and fade into the background. When she was ready to speak he would be there, eager to be her errand boy, her beast of burden, her sounding board for news and ideas.

"Do you ever think about missing all this scenery and activity when we go West?"

"Miss it? What's there to miss? I know this old town from one end to the next. I want to see something new and different."

"I heard your daddy say we will never see a river as big as this when we get on the Trail. Think of all the things we have seen going up and down this river."

"Think of all the land we're going to see. I heard we'll see mountains so big they always have snow on their tops, and animals so big that to kill one and cut out all the good meat one family can live off it for a month."

"Billy, you make me laugh. Mountains that always have snow on them? Oh, you are impossible! Why don't you write stories and I will draw pictures for them."

"Great! That makes me the boss. You will have to draw what I tell you. Yes indeed. I like that idea."

"Oh no, Mister Gallagher! Nobody will read your stories unless they have my pictures to make them seem real. So there!"

"Well, if you don't put down your old pens and start learning how to ride a horse you won't last two days in the West."

"Oh, poo! Anybody can ride a horse. There's nothing to it."

A new school began for Peggy Ross. It was harder than she ever imagined. She had to unlearn thinking she could do anything she wanted. She was forced to learn, to watch and listen to Billy, and to be ready for bumps and bruises. Perhaps she didn't realize it, but she could be as stubborn as her daddy. She learned to ride a horse, do it well, and to care for a horse.

Sketching, chores at home or at the Gallaghers, reading lessons with her mother, and riding lessons with Billy filled her days. Still, she managed a letter to her cousin in Scotland.

Dear Jennifer,

I want to write to you. It will be my first letter. I have so much to tell you. I will have to tell you that our school was burned. It was all burned down, nothing is left.

One of our students and one of our teachers were killed. We are all safe, but we have nothing. We now live in the town of St. Louis. I go to the river to do my sketches.

My friend Billy comes with me some times. Do you have a good friend? Billy is like my brother. I can tell him things I won't tell to others.

We will be moving to a far away place called Santa Fe. We will have to go many, many miles. We will have two wagons to carry our clothing and food and things to sell in Santa Fe. My father said we will have to walk most of the way.

Don't stop writing to me. Somehow I will get your letters. We send our love to all of you in Scotland.

Your Cousin, Peggy

Since their move into town, Naomi and Peggy made several casual visits to Myrna Wilson. One day the roles reversed. Myrna came to see them at their new quarters in town. "Peggy, I have such good news for you. Do you and your mother have a few minutes?"

"Of course, Myrna. Come in, please. I'll call Mother. She's mixing some of her medications in the kitchen."

"Myrna, how good to see you. I suspect it is Peggy you will be wanting to see. I'll go fix some tea, and I promise not to get tea confused with the other things I am doing."

"Thank you. But this will take only a minute. As you know I am a tutor to two children here in town, and I must get back for a class with them. Here, read this."

Peggy read the letter Myrna handed to her and read it a second time, her eyes growing wider at each word.

My Dear Thomas:

It was good of you to send me the samples of your student's work. My congratulations to both, for I am duly impressed and take pride in seeing the talents of one my students transferred to the work of one of his.

I showed the samples to a Lester Browning of New Orleans. He is a publisher and has been scouting the area for someone to illustrate a book he will shortly place on the market. What a happy chance that what he searches for is exactly the kind of work you submitted. At present the book has a tentative title of "Life in the Territory of Missouri."

I have taken it upon myself to act as agent for Miss Ross and have sold her complete portfolio to Browning. It gives me great pleasure to enclose a draft in the amount of $32.40 U.S. currency. It represents the full purchase price for six sketches at $6.00 each less a 10% commission which I have reserved for myself. I trust these arrangements meet with Miss Ross's approval.

And, Thomas, I hope you see fit to encourage Miss Ross, and I would be pleased to act as her agent in New Orleans. The subject of her art is her choice. As you well know, artists do not take kindly to having others dictate the direction of their endeavors.

My best to you and your student, Thomas. I commend your teaching and your discernment that your student is indeed an artist worthy of Mr. Browning's investment. May I hear from you shortly with word that your student wishes to continue this relationship?

I am your servant, sir, and share the pleasure in your discovery of a new talent.

Pierre Galvan

"Oh, Peggy, I am happy for you, and sad that Thomas is not with us to share our joy. I do hope you will act on Mr. Galvan's suggestion that you continue with your sketches."

"I don't know what to say. I thank you for bringing this letter as soon as you received it. It was very kind of you. It must have caused you pain to have to open mail addressed to Thomas. We miss him so, all of us."

"It would be less than honest, Peggy, to say there was no pain. But I think this is a wonderful thing to happen. Just seeing your happiness offsets the sadness of not having your teacher here to share the moment."

Myrna Wilson seemed to forget the pressure of her students' class and continued with another cup of Naomi's tea while the three women caught up the news and rumors of the coming trip on the Santa Fe Trail. Just saying that the Ross and Gallagher families would leave in mid-April with their two wagons for Independence and a rendezvous with the larger group heading West brought an end to the sense of joy and accomplishment. The three women had grown close, more so than any one of them realized. When a definite date for the departure was mentioned they knew separation was an irreversible reality.

📖 📖 📖

One morning Peggy persuaded her father to hire a rig at Jack's stable and drive her to the ruins of the school. At the last minute Naomi said she wanted to go with them. "I feel a change in the weather is coming and there are many items I need for my medications, especially those that seem to work when you come down with what you call a cold. I don't know why you insist on calling breathing illness a cold, but you do."

"Mother, you know I will be working with Eleanor the whole day."

"I will need a lot of leaves, and I was hoping you would help me."

Duncan spoke up. "May I substitute for Peggy? I have a few things to do, then I am your slave. I promise only to gather what you tell me to."

The Ross family piled into a light, four-wheeled carriage, called a Dearborn, and drove to the site of their school. This little trip had been made many times since the disaster that totally consumed the school. Always it cast a blanket of gloom over the family. The trip was never made without a gathering at the graves of Thomas Archer and John Forsyth. Reliving the night of the fire was inescapable.

Peggy's efforts were directed to the gathering, sorting, and packing of the personal items to be taken on the trek to Santa Fe. She liked working with Eleanor and with Grace, the second oldest of the three Gallagher children. Their work was serious for they both realized only they could make decisions about what to take and what to discard. The two young people still managed time for themselves and the trading of dark secrets that only sixteen-year-old girls can discover, invent, or imagine.

Duncan and Naomi lingered at the ruins, not saying anything but aware of the huge gap left in their lives when the schoolhouse went up in flames and Thomas and John perished. It was more than a building, it was their home, the focus of their lives, and the center of their dreams. John's progress and Thomas' coaching of the young man had generated a feeling of success, now dashed and ended in a pile of ashes.

"Come, Duncan, I have much to do."

Duncan went to the carriage and retrieved the canvas bags Naomi had stitched together for collecting such things as starwort, snake root, valley cottonwood leaves, and the flowers of chamomile, items which she knew could be converted to useful medications. He followed her and became the gatherer and packer. It saved much time for Naomi not to have to do these things herself, and she found herself many steps ahead of Duncan.

"I'm going to take these back to the wagon. If I try to jam anything more into them I may ruin what we have already gathered."

"Poke around for something else to use. I want to keep working. If we get a sharp wind with rain some of the leaves I want will be made useless."

As he shouldered the heavy bags Naomi watched him walk away. He was still the rugged, well-set-up man she had fallen in love with over seventeen years ago. A handsome man with a ready smile, she also knew him a man not to be taken for granted. His mind was like a mountain stream of pure, cold water; it ran swiftly and ran deeply.

When he returned, it was with a large wash tub that had escaped destruction in the fire. "Think you can use this? It'll hold a lot of your leaves and roots."

"Well, I suppose so. Drag it along."

"I think we should take a rest and munch on this."

Duncan extracted a small parcel wrapped in a napkin from his jacket pocket and offered it to Naomi.

"What's this? I'm not sure I want anything that's been in that pocket."

"You don't recognize your own baking? What am I to do? Toss it away?"

"Give me a little piece first."

"Not so fast, my lady. A little piece will cost you a kiss."

"Dunc! None of your games. Either I share or you can throw it away."

"The price has to be paid, and I can tell you this corn bread tastes mighty good. And I'm not throwing it for the squirrels or raccoons to eat. Last chance."

Naomi turned and walked away quickly and didn't stop until she had reached the Dearborn. "I'm ready to go home now. Drive us over to Eleanor's place to get Peggy."

The day had not provided the opportunity Duncan sought to have with Naomi. They worked together, but their conversation was mostly bits and pieces spread over a wide variety of topics. He wanted to talk about the strain in their relationship, but she evaded all such talk. Later that evening when he and Naomi were in bed, he tried again.

"My friend with the long legs, what have I done or said that makes you turn away when we have important things to talk about?"

"I never walk away from you, never!"

"This morning as we gathered your nature samples you did just that. You walked on into the woods and never answered my questions. Why?"

There was no response. She turned her back to him and made like she was sleeping.

"I know you are awake. If you choose not to talk to me, fine. But at least listen to what I want to tell you. Ever since you came to St. Louis after living in Mandan country with Armand you have built a wall between us and between yourself and Peggy.

"If you were happier living with Armand then I think you should go back to him. If that's what you want I will help you go to him."

Naomi stirred restlessly and turned to say something to Duncan. Changing her mind, she continued to pretend she was sleeping.

"I always felt that you lived in fear of the man and that your reason for allowing Peggy to go with Jack and me on our return to St. Louis was to get her away from Armand and his strange and fearful lodge."

Still there was no response from Naomi.

"Eleanor is working hard to collect and carefully pack all that we will need for our coming trek to Santa Fe. Can't you see the hurt you are causing with your standing aside and not plunging in to help your sister Mandan? Why? Tell me, Naomi, why?"

Silence.

The next morning Duncan arose at first light, made a breakfast for himself, and walked over to Jack's stable. Some of the hostlers were already at work and paid no attention to him. That was not upsetting to Duncan, for he wanted more time to think through what was on his mind. Suddenly Jack was standing in front of him.

"You spend the night here? Where's your blanket roll? Come up with two bits or get ready to work out what you owe me. I ask for and get two bits for a night in my stables. I ain't got time to fool with strangers."

"Go stick your head in a bucket of cold water, you old horse thief. Let me take you over to the hotel and get some coffee in you, for we have serious things to hash over."

"Now you're a talkin. Gimme me a minute to lay out what I want my men to do this morning."

Coffee turned out to be a full breakfast for both men as they got into the heavy end of all the things Duncan had on his mind.

"I've been thinking about what you said about favoring oxen over mules for our wagons. You know and I know oxen have to lay down for as much as two maybe three hours and chew their cud at some time. And they need a fair amount of water to keep them going. Right?"

"Right you are, but I ain't gettin your drift."

"Well, I'm thinking that a line of mules will be better than trying to manage a string of oxen plus some mules plus some horses. We could end up in Santa Fe with oxen that are so beat up from working the Trail they won't be worth much on resale. And if our luck turned on us and we had to kill a few to survive they wouldn't produce much eating meat."

"Damn me eyes! You have been doin some thinkin. It goes against my better nature to say you might be right. But you might be."

"It's not important that I'm right, Jack. It's important that you share your thinking. Do you still favor oxen?"

"Can't say I do, can't say I don't. But you old beaver skinner, I know you figered out that we'll need a heap more a mules than them oxes."

"Yes, I figured on that. But how many more? That's your department. You know a sight more about mules and horses than I'll ever know."

"It rests my mind to know you're a thinkin that a way. But I'll have to sit down and scratch at some numbers a fore I kin answer all your questions. Much obliged for the meal. I gotta get my butt back to the stables. But keep worryin this over in your mind, my friend. Once we're on that damn Trail it'll be too late to make changes."

In the end Jack's decision was to go with mules for the wagons. He felt he knew a lot more about managing mules than oxen, and always with an eye to the future, he felt strongly about selling mules in Santa Fe. Have something to sell where there's a market, he often said to anybody who listened to his homespun advice.

It was Peggy who brought about a change in Naomi's self-imposed distance from the day-to-day preparations for the trek over the Santa Fe Trail. The change was also noticed by both Jack and Eleanor Gallagher, but wise to the ways of the tall and attractive woman, they kept their opinions to themselves. It was Duncan who ventured to comment to Naomi about her willingness to join the families in their work.

"It's a tough job. You know, trying to make sure we have everything we will need on the Trail, yet not taking a stitch more than necessary."

"Yes, but what I see tells me Peggy has done a good job. What I don't see, Dunc, is space for all the medications I've made. You know as well as I do that things happen and we'll need them."

"Not going to argue that point, but where do you want these things? In the family wagon or the merchandise wagon?"

"What's the difference?"

"The one wagon will be like a little store for the two families. That wagon will also be the storage place for our food. When we get to Santa Fe we will be selling our merchandise out of the other wagon."

"My medications might be needed in a hurry. Which wagon will be the best one to carry them?"

"Good question. What do you think of this? We will store all of your medicines in one place and on top of everything in the Santa Fe wagon."

"Very well. Let me load that wagon after you get everything you plan to sell loaded on the bottom. I will know where each item is placed and I won't have to dig through bolts of material or piles of clothing, blankets, or cooking pots to find what I need."

And that was how the two wagons were set up for the nearly eight hundred miles to be covered on the Trail. Jack and Eleanor were in agreement with that plan and were pleased to finally have Naomi become a working part of the group. Duncan was also pleased, but more than a little puzzled. What had Peggy said to her mother that brought about the change in Naomi's attitude?

What Peggy said remained a secret between the two women. But slips of the tongue do occur. Peggy had set some books alongside the art materials she wanted to go with her to Santa Fe. When she learned that her mother's medications were to have top space in the merchandise wagon, she assumed her art materials would be given the same consideration.

"What ever will you do with these books on the Trail? I can understand you want sketching materials, but books?"

"They're not just my books. Some of them are for Mother."

"Your mother wants to take books? Peggy, this isn't a time for jokes!"

"It's no joke. Mother needs them for her reading lessons."

"And just who is giving your mother reading lessons?"

"I am. Oh dear, I think I spoke out of turn."

"Perhaps you did. But why is this a big secret?"

"That's the way Mother wants it. She was going to surprise you when she felt confident enough to show you what she can do."

"Is she doing well? Foolish question, isn't it? If you are her teacher, I am sure she will do well with her reading. We'll keep this as our secret."

"That's good. She might quit if she knew her secret was out."

Duncan was both pleased and a bit upset about this bit of family development. He wanted to rush to Naomi and take her in his arms and tell her how happy he was about her decision to learn to read. From years of living off and on with the Tall One, he knew that a silent tongue was often the best tongue. Taking that desirable woman in his arms at this point in their touchy relationship was not going to happen.

There was another secret Peggy had. This one she managed to keep to herself. On the fourth or fifth day after the schoolhouse fire she had walked over from the Gallagher place and poked around in the ruins. As she looked at the remains of what had been her bedroom she saw under the charred rafters of the collapsed roof the little tin box Duncan had bought for her the day they reached St. Louis after the long trek down the Missouri River from Mandan country. It had a tight fitting lid and when Peggy managed to pry it open she was overcome with joy in what she found – the piece of tartan her mother gave her when she was leaving Armand's lodge in Mandan country. It was the same swatch of tartan that Duncan's mother had given to him when he left his Highlands home to begin his voyage to Montreal. Naomi had always made an effort to care for and protect this bit of Scotland, for she knew its importance to Duncan. Now Peggy had the precious keepsake in her hands. She resolved that she, too, would protect and care for it. Somehow it had escaped serious damage from the fire, and even the tin box could again be useful. She thought to herself, "If I hide this among my art supplies nobody will find it."

📖　📖　📖

On another of the morning trips made to the Gallagher farm both Peggy and Naomi accompanied Duncan. Jack and Duncan were to go over the two Conestoga wagons they had purchased. One had recently arrived in St. Louis on a barge from the manufacturer in Pittsburgh. The other had come from Pittsburgh overland, and while new when it left the wagon shop, it had to be gone over carefully before they set out for Santa Fe.

"Peggy and I are going to walk to the ruins. And then I am taking her with me to show her how to gather the bark of scrub oak. I want to make a lotion to ease the pain of sunburned skin. Drive over to the school when you are ready to go back to town. We won't be far from there."

Duncan and Jack went to work on the wagons. They took on the new wagon first. As they went over each part to familiarize themselves with it, they also grew in their admiration of the well-crafted piece of work.

"Them Dutchmen back in Pennsy sure knows how to build a good wagon. This here tub will haul a heap o goods and never crack a board. If'n we load her proper it won't strain no part of her nor cause the iron tires she has to jump of'n her wheels."

"What'll we do if this fine wagon should bust an axle?"

"I heard talk we make a stop at a place they's callin Council Grove and cut ourselfs some pieces of hard wood to sling under the wagons. If'n we have the time there, I reckon we'll shape an extra wagon tongue, an axle or two, some double trees, maybe even some spokes and hubs. Lord knows what we'll need. Can't leave it all to the Man up there."

"How about this used wagon? See anything needing replacement?"

"Well, let's have a look. I don't like the fit of them end boards and I don't like the set of this here rear bolster. Get ready to sweat your jacket, my friend. We gotta heap of work to do afore this here'll be fit for the Trail."

Several hours of hard work solved a few of the problems the men found to fix on the second wagon. Time for a break, for some minutes of rest and reflection.

"Know what I was thinkin while we was poundin on that bolster?"

"Can't say that I do, Jack, and can't say I want to know."

"Well, I'm a gonna tell you anyhow. I was thinkin 'bout up in the fur country we had to get our canoes ready for the dash to Runnyvoo every summer at the Portage."

"You're right. We had to do it and do it right! Once on the rivers and lakes on our way to Grand Portage for the annual *Rendezvous* there was no time to make repairs. Do you miss those days?"

"Sometimes I do. We was good at what we done for that damn old North West Company. But them high 'n mighty partners paid us no mind. They took us dumb and they took us cheap."

A sharp reply died on Duncan's lips. He wanted to remind his friend that for a few years he was a partner in the NWC, but he had to admit to himself that Jack had it right. The "little people" in the big company – the clerks and the *voyageurs* – were seldom treated fairly. Yet the powerful NWC had lasted for over thirty years in a fiercely competitive business.

Each day both families, the Rosses and the Gallaghers, made progress in their preparations for the many days and nights they would spend on the trail to Santa Fe. All knew that surprise after surprise awaited them; perhaps there would be setbacks and problems beyond their ability to solve them. But no one talked about quitting, about finding something else they might do in the St. Louis area.

📖 📖 📖

Winter's grip seemed to be easing. Hints of spring appeared briefly but with determination. All signs seemed favorable and familiar. Then came an interruption, an unexpected happening that would have great impact on the group.

Jack raced to the Ross house in St. Louis, out of breath, and so excited that he could barely blurt out the message given him by a stranger who just stepped off a riverboat from New Orleans.

"Duncan, get your ass down to my riverside livery. There be a man who's askin for a Duncan Ross. He described you so's I know he knowd you."

"What's his name?"

"Samuel. Samuel something, last name's high fa luttin. Says he's from Montreal."

"My God! It's Samuel Rawlinson. He's at your stable? Let's go!"

There was no mistake. It was Duncan's old friend from the NWC, his former banking partner from Montreal. Why? What was wrong?

The two men looked at each other absolutely speechless, so pleased to see and be with each other after years of separation that words were inadequate. Emotions found release in bear hugs and repeated slaps on the back.

"Samuel, what in the hell would ever bring you to St. Louis?"

"You, my friend. You brought me here with your honeyed words about the great opportunities awaiting me in this shabby town on the banks of this muddy stream."

"Well, yes. But I never thought you would pay attention to anything I wrote. Meet my friend and partner, Jack Gallagher. Jack, allow me to name Samuel Rawlinson."

"Pleased, Mr. Rawlinson. I reckon anyone who calls this redhead a friend be welcome in St. Louis. So I say welcome to you, and if'n there's somethin you be needin, why you just ask me."

"That's mighty nice of you, Mr. Gallagher. I appreciate your welcome."

"Let's get off on the right foot, I'm Jack. Mister ain't a word I know much about. I expect I'll be callin you Sam'l."

"Let's move to the hotel across the street where we can sit down, have a drink, and catch up on all the news Samuel has to tell us."

"You always were the man to take charge, Duncan. What do you say, Jack, do we take up this tight-fisted Scotsman on his offer of a drink?"

"By all means, Sam'l. Offers like this don't come everyday."

Three men with so many questions to be asked. Not knowing which ought to be examined first, they didn't always listen to what was answered. From this confusion, however, Duncan learned that Samuel had left Montreal for two basic reasons.

The merger begun in 1820 of the two largest companies in the fur trade in Canada, Hudson's Bay and North West, all but consigned Montreal to a minor role in the fur trading world. The new company was to be based on Hudson's Bay, not Montreal. Samuel had taken some steps in the management of his financial empire that softened the impacts of the merger, but steps not fast enough or large enough to avoid some serious damage to his holdings.

The decrease in disposable income was reflected in Samuel's personal life. His wife, Jeanette Turmel Rawlinson, did not take kindly to anything that set a brake on her lavish lifestyle.

"Duncan, you knew my wife and her devotion to the grand life of Montreal society. And I think you knew of my indiscretions from time to time. So you will not be surprised when I tell you she left me. Of course, you may have known of her own affairs, but in the end she was the one to leave. She not only left, but she managed with the help of some high-priced legal friends to leave me in an extremely weak position."

Relieved that the conversation did not dwell on the indiscretions of either Jeanette or Samuel, Duncan recovered his composure and said, "I can imagine your time with Jeanette was difficult and the end unavoidable. You have my sympathies, and you have only to ask and I will do everything I can do to get you set up here in St. Louis."

"A friend of Duncan's a friend of mine, so what he said goes double,

Sam'l. But we gotta move quick. We're close on to leavin town ourselfs."

"Leaving St. Louis? Soon? Why, my friends, why?"

The two locals brought the newcomer up to date on plans to get on the Santa Fe Trail and relocate in the Southwest. A friendly drink became a friendly dinner and the talk never stopped. The conversation switched from a blizzard of news, old and new, to plans already acted on, and then to a list of plans needing action.

Samuel was located in a hotel, his luggage reclaimed at the riverboat, and ways and means for staying in contact with Duncan and Jack spelled out. The next day Duncan stopped in at the hotel. He asked for Samuel only to be told, "Mr. Rawlinson is making business calls and said that if a Mr. Ross inquired after him he was to be informed that Mr. Rawlinson would receive him after six o'clock this evening."

"I might as well be back in Montreal," Duncan thought to himself, as he left the hotel. Such formality, such a rush to do business, was so much like the days when Duncan and Samuel were partners in a private bank in Montreal. But it was such a contrast to the easy informality he had with most people in St. Louis. "I can't imagine Jack Gallagher ever telling me he would receive me after six o'clock in the evening!"

"You always talk to yourself? Ever get any answers?"

"Jack, what are you doing here?"

"Might ask you the same. I'm lookin for that Sam'l what's his name."

"So am I, but he's already making business calls and won't be available until six tonight. What do you think of that?"

"Man after my own heart. He ain't been in town twenty-four hours an already he's doin business. I like a feller that's got get up an go."

"He's got that. He's one of the most ambitious men I've ever known."

They walked back to Jack's riverside livery while Duncan filled Jack in on some of the details of Samuel's career in Montreal once he left the North West Company. Since Jack had several years of clerking for James Shaw in the Flin Flon section of the North Country when he was a part of the NWC, Duncan could skim over details knowing that Jack understood how that powerful company operated.

What Jack didn't know was the work Samuel did for several of the wintering partners as agent for them in Montreal during the years they spent in the remote trading posts of the Company. Aside from personal vanities like fine wines and choice foods, clothing, books, and perhaps native maidens to warm their beds, there was nothing on which to spend the annual dividends from the shares they held in the NWC. Having a Montreal agent to manage the wealth and the growth of the partner's accumulations was a very profitable enterprise. Samuel was a knowing agent who commanded a goodly percentage for the services he provided.

"In other words, he's a good one to look after a feller's affairs?"

"Yes. But what would you have him manage? You told me you would sell your livery stables and freight cartage business, maybe even the farms."

"Might do that, but I give some thought to maybe keepin a foot in the door here in St. Louis. Ain't nobody tellin us we're gonna have big success in Santa Fe."

"I feel we'll do well where we are going, don't you think?"

"Well, my friend, I ain't one to find fault, but I always believed in several baskets for my eggs. You sunk everything you got into that school, now you got a pile of charcoal and ashes. No money in that, is there?"

"No money, you're right. But I did make some investments, or rather Samuel made investments with the money I inherited from Jonathan Graham. I'm not ready for the poor house, not yet."

"Figured you had a stash somewhere. I never could get up nerve enough to put my money and faith in pieces a paper. I like to see and hold stuff in my hands like stables 'n wagons 'n horse 'n mules 'n farms. You can have your damn paper. Give me real things."

Jack returned to his stables, Duncan to his house in town. Neither Naomi nor Peggy was home, and Duncan suspected that the growing amount of time the two were together had a lot to do with Naomi's reading lessons. He hoped that was the reason and found his displeasure over not being informed of this event rapidly fading. He was genuinely pleased by this but still at a loss to find a way to tell Naomi of his change of heart. Here they were comfortable, secure, and had friends nearby, yet talk with his wife was difficult. He was mulling over this seemingly perpetual problem when a knock at the door broke his chain of thought.

"Mr. Ross, how nice to see you. Is either Peggy or Naomi at home?"

"Please come in, Miss Wilson. Both women have deserted me for the moment, but I'm certain they will shortly return. I was about to make a pot of tea. Will you join me?"

"That is very kind of you, Mr. Ross, but I ..."

Her excuse was interrupted by another knock on his door. Duncan, somewhat irritated by this, opened the door with a cold eye and a response of rejection, not welcome, on his lips.

"Samuel, you have taken me by surprise. Come in, come in. I'm making tea. Will you join us?

"Miss Wilson, may I present my longtime friend from Montreal, Samuel Rawlinson? Samuel, this is Myrna Wilson, who is also a friend of my family. Now, if you two will excuse me, I will see to the tea."

From the beginning of his career in business, Duncan Ross had been a quick student of situations and opportunities in the world of trading. He was not so quick in picking up on the signals that passed between a woman and a man meeting for their first time.

He found a tray to carry three cups of tea, cream, sugar and a plate of cookies he knew had been hidden somewhere in the kitchen.

"Here we are. I apologize for the time it took and I claim no skill when it comes to fixing tea, but please, help yourselves."

He might as well have addressed his remarks to a picture on the wall. Myrna and Samuel were deeply involved in a spirited conversation. They did take his tea but ignored his cookies. Duncan found no opening for a contribution to their lively talk.

He sat and took a good look at both people. Myrna was an attractive woman, a few years younger than Samuel, and as always she was well turned out. It wasn't anything like the high style of Samuel's former wife, but with taste and colors that complemented Myrna's fresh looks and outgoing manner. As for Samuel, he was an inch or two shorter than Myrna, and had slimmed down from the rather chunky man Duncan had known in Montreal. He wore a fresh stock at his throat and had managed to have his coat brushed and touched up. Even his boots were presentable. But what was this attraction?

The answer to his question was put aside as the two began their words of thanks and promises to return soon to meet with Naomi and Peggy. They left the house together. Myrna had accepted Samuel's suggestion that he escort her to her home.

"Balls of fire," Duncan thought. "In town one day and look what Samuel has accomplished." Business, and Duncan was dying to know what that might have been, locating Duncan's house in a city strange to him, and escorting an eligible woman to her home. He had suggested in his letter to Samuel that "he might find St. Louis a pasture worth grazing." Samuel didn't graze, he made hay.

When Naomi and Peggy stepped into their house they were bursting at the seams to tell Duncan of something they just witnessed. Lines of Negroes in chains were being herded from a steamboat landing on the riverfront to a large barn. Peggy, from her many days of sketching along the riverfront, knew it to be an auction shed. People had lined the streets from boat landing to the sale site. Some began to condemn what they saw, others to shout their support of seeing Negroes in chains.

Both women expressed their shock and anger at this treatment of human beings. Peggy was especially upset over what she sensed was a near riot between ordinary folks over the free-slavery question. Duncan listened attentively, agreed with their outrage, shared their expressions of fear, and suggested they listen to his afternoon story.

"You two had a caller, and I had a caller. Which one do you want to know about first?"

"Why ours, of course, Papa Dunc."

"Myrna Wilson stopped to pay a visit."

"Did she say why she came here? Are we to return her a call?"

"She was too busy to bother with little details. If she did say anything important I missed it."

"Enough, Dunc! Why did she come to this house?"

"I honestly don't know. But if you will give me a minute I might have a solution to our problem with Myrna."

"What problem with Myrna?"

"You must know who my caller was, then we can put two problems together and maybe come up with one solution."

"Who was your caller?"

"Samuel Rawlinson. Hold! I don't why he came, but I know of a way we can get him back here."

"Why do you always make things difficult, Dunc? Tell us."

One sign Duncan had learned to read was Naomi's boiling point. He proceeded to tell them of the two visits, their simultaneous nature, and their leaving without giving any indication of why they appeared on his doorstep. As he continued with his account, he added the idea of asking them both to have dinner with the Ross family.

"If we do that, we will learn all we need to know, won't we?"

"That's a good idea. Isn't it, Mother?"

"I don't know. I remember Samuel the first and only time I met him during a *Rendezvous* at Grand Portage. I didn't like him then, I'm not sure I will like him now."

"Come now. You're talking about a meeting thirteen years ago. Don't you think he might have changed? I think he has, and he has gone through some difficult times that would change anybody. You might enjoy having him and Myrna at your dinner table."

The lively back and forth over giving a dinner and inviting both Myrna and Samuel slipped into a discussion of a possible menu. In the end some sense of agreement was achieved. Duncan was to invite Samuel, Peggy and Naomi to invite Myrna, and various shopping chores were divided among the three.

The evening set for the dinner arrived along with a steady rain. Duncan said he would go to Jack's nearest stable and hire a covered carriage and driver to collect the guests. He was just going out the door when a carriage pulled up in front of their house. It was driven by Samuel with

Myrna seated at his side. Duncan pulled on a Macintosh and rushed to help Myrna alight and took her into the house under an umbrella. He returned to direct and aid Samuel in driving the team to the little barn at the rear of the property.

Formal introductions were not needed, small talk untouched, for all five people found more than enough to engage them in spirited conversation. Naomi despaired of getting all to the table before her expertly done roast went cold on the platter.

It was a delightful evening, one that met every test: a beautifully prepared meal supported with choice wines and topped off with a heavenly dessert and coffee. Duncan was probably the only one who was conscious of everything he ate and drank. The other four were so involved and so fragmented in their conversations back and forth across the table that intake of food and drink ran a poor second to intake of all that was being said and who said it.

By the time Duncan and Samuel retreated to the barn to reunite horse to carriage and bring them around to the front of the house, the rain had stopped. A full moon was hanging out to dry over the group of friends who said their words of appreciation and farewell.

"Naomi, that was as close to a perfect dinner as I have ever had. And Peggy, I know you had a part in this. I tip my hat to you both."

"We Ross women are good at whatever we do in the kitchen or in the studio. Myrna told me Mr. Browning wants more of my sketches."

"Tell me more about that. Just what does he want?"

"The pen and inks I have been doing of local scenes, especially those along the river and the islands in the river, the big river."

"Could you make sense of what Mr. Rawlinson was telling us about Uncle Jack's businesses? I thought he was going to sell out before we leave for Santa Fe."

"I thought so too, but Samuel has convinced him that he can manage his affairs so Jack makes a little money while he is living in Santa Fe."

"Do you two ever think of anything but business?

"Perhaps we do, Naomi, but what would you have us dwell on?"

"Don't you think Myrna and Samuel have become friends rather quickly? Is it possible they have known each other before either one came to St. Louis?"

"I don't know, but I suspect not. I think it a natural thing for them to find each other's company pleasant and something they wish to continue. What do you think, Peggy?"

"I think Myrna is lonely since the death of Thomas, and she has found in Samuel someone she can talk with."

"Does that satisfy your questions about their attraction to each other?"

"I still have my doubts about Samuel. Perhaps I should have a private talk with Myrna and caution her about fast-talking men."

"Please! Give them time to see if there are reasons for them to continue seeing one another, or if there are reasons to break off. I find myself liking the idea of Myrna and Samuel together."

Not only was Duncan pleased with the easy way Samuel had linked up with Myrna Wilson, he was equally pleased with the preparations of the two families for the arduous trek over the trail to Santa Fe. From time to time he, like Jack Gallagher, picked up snatches of conversation concerning the Santa Fe Trail. He was excited and full of anticipation of the new country they would see and the adjustments they would be making in their new life in the West.

Jack had made his deal with Samuel Rawlinson to manage the stables and the cartage business and oversee the two farms Jack had on shares as well as the "home" farm. Like a good poker player, Jack Gallagher was "in for a dime, in for a dollar" – but with a small wad tucked in his britches out of sight.

Duncan's understanding with Samuel was of a similar nature, the managing of property. Only this would be of a portfolio of "paper," not of "hard" assets like those owned by Jack. Eleanor, Naomi, nor Peggy showed any interest in this part of the leave taking from St. Louis.

Duncan had to shift his attention from stocks, as those issued by companies, to stock on four feet. It was Jack's decision to have mules pull their two wagons, and he thought an eight-mule span would do the trick for each wagon. He also wanted ten or maybe twelve mules in reserve so that pairs could be spelled for rest on a regular schedule.

There was another thing Jack liked about using mules. He had been told that crossing streams and rivers could be a "hell on wheels." Being able to unhook a span from one wagon and double up on the other might be necessary to safely cross the water hazards they were sure to encounter. And the more crossings the better, for Jack had learned of the long, dry stretches where water was as scarce as "tits on a boar hog." Duncan learned years ago that Jack's mountain Carolina way of saying things could be more to the point than the formal English he had learned in his Highlands school.

What was the last remaining hurdle to be crossed to make their exit from St. Louis smooth and painless? One night over coffee and bannock, Duncan and Jack pooled their knowledge. From the bits and pieces of talk from men who had been over the Santa Fe Trail, Jack reasoned they should make their first target Franklin, a town in Missouri to the west and a bit north from St. Louis. "We'll make Franklin the place to check over our gear and food supplies."

"Sounds like a smart thing to do, but I thought you said Independence would be the last chance to fill in any shortages."

"Did say just that, my friend. Independence is our back-up to Franklin. If'n we wait til Indy and can't get what we should have there, then we're in a bad way."

"You men have everything worked out but the most important thing!"

"And what might that be?"

"The day we are to leave!"

"Are you ready, Naomi? No last minute items to be made or bought?"

"The answers are yes, I am ready, and no, I have everything I need."

"Fine, now how about you, Peggy? What are your answers?"

"The same as Mother's. I'm ready."

Duncan asked himself the same two questions. For one thing, St. Louis was the place where he had reunited with Naomi. His chance meeting with Jack Gallagher had taken place on the waterfront of this town. On that same waterfront he had met Thomas Archer and persuaded that young man to join his school. Yes, this fast-growing village had been good to him.

Any reasonable man knew there had to be some negatives. Grim pictures like the shooting of Thomas and John and the torching of their school loomed so large and bleak that he wanted to forget the growing divisions that were slowly but surely tearing this community apart.

Again, memories flooded his mind of his years in the fur trade as he worked for the North West Company. Within the company was the jaundiced view of any man who left the NWC to work for Hudson's Bay or Alexander Mackenzie's XY Company – he was a traitor. He was like a soldier who ran away in the face of the enemy – a deserter.

"Is that what I am? A traitor? Am I allowing a current set of failures to obstruct my long-range view of what I might accomplish if I stay with my post, if I do not run in the face of adversity. Would my father be proud of what I am doing, my mother and my sister?"

He poured all these thoughts, jumbled and disorganized, into a letter:

Dear Louise, Rory, and Jennifer

Where to begin? Stay with me as I tell you of what we are about to do. In just a few days we and our good friends, the Gallaghers, will be leaving St. Louis. Let me give you this name and address for letters knowing they could be a long time in reaching us, and our letters to you the same.

We have purchased two large freight wagons and a string of mules plus a couple of riding horses. At the town of Independence, also in Missouri, we will join a caravan of about forty other wagons. Our destination is a village called Santa Fe which is in a Province of the country of

Mexico. I cannot tell you what we will do when we get there after seventy or so days on the Santa Fe Trail.

All we know is that the country of Mexico has made itself independent from Spain, and we have learned there should be many opportunities in Santa Fe. Just as I had to learn French as soon as I arrived in Montreal many years ago, now we will have to learn to speak Spanish, for I suspect we will not hear very much English spoken where we are going.

All of us are in good health, we have good equipment, horses, and mules. And we think we are supplied with enough food for the long trip. We hear that once we are at about the half way point in our journey we should be able to kill a buffalo every day or so to keep us in fresh meat. We also hear that we will have long stretches on the Trail where water could become very scarce and even become a serious problem.

If I sound like I am leaving St. Louis without another thought I am not being truthful. I have doubts, not about our preparations or our companions on the Trail, but about what we will do when we get there. We have made our plans on little firm knowledge and a huge amount of gossip and hearsay.

But please, do not worry about us. We have survived years in the North Country of Canada; we will survive the Trail and the village of Santa Fe. In short we are excited to attempt this adventure. Wish us well. Our love to you all,

Duncan

send your letters to – Samuel Rawlinson
in care of Jack Gallagher's Livery Stable
St. Louis, Missouri, United States of America

The little town of Franklin was just that – little. But it was complete in terms of the needs of the Ross and Gallagher families. They departed St. Louis with a fair portion of their supplies packed into the newer of the two Conestogas. What they bought in Franklin was more of the same – flour, bacon, salt, coffee, tea, and sugar. During the one hundred fifty miles they had logged from "home" to this "jumping off" place they had consumed all of the fancy foods and parting gifts – cakes and cookies, breads and spreads, and even meats – from those who stayed behind.

"Wasn't that a nice party Myrna and Samuel gave us?"

"Yes, indeed, it was very thoughtful of them."

The farewell party was organized by Samuel and aided by Myrna. It was no secret that those two people had found in each other attractions that gave a sense of stability and a promise of the future to their relationship. Even Naomi, who had strong feelings not favorably tilted to Samuel, agreed that this couple had a chance. What they would make of it was something Naomi could never know – until the first letters from St. Louis caught up to them. That might mean as long as a year or even longer.

"Dunc, isn't there a better way to keep in touch? When we lived in the *pays d'en haut* [North Country] we seemed to have closer connections."

"Those connections you remember were of business; the letters I had from my sister in Scotland usually took a year for me to get them and for her to get my letters. No, my dear, I know no way to speed up the system."

"Hold on there, Duncan. We might have luck 'n meet a returnin outfit headin back to St. Louis. Them people would be pleased to carry a letter."

"Wouldn't that be great? I could send some of the sketches I hope to be making along the way back to Myrna."

"You see, Naomi, you thought we'd be going to the end of the earth. We won't, but we'll be close!"

Throughout this run of family talk, Duncan was thinking of the gift Samuel had given him a day or so before their departure.

"Duncan, this is for you, and I expect it to be returned to me on your first visit back to St. Louis."

"Why, thank you. This is a surprise, but what am I to put in this pouch of deerskin so cleverly made with an enclosing thong?"

"Both you and Jack talk quite often of gold mining as one of the ventures you will look into in Santa Fe. I want you to fill this pouch with nuggets of hard gold from the gold mine you will own and operate."

"You always had your eyes open for the main chance, Samuel, but this is going a little far, isn't it?"

"Well, if you're going to be so pessimistic, put any damn thing you want in the pouch. But I still expect it will be delivered to me in person."

"I do thank you, Samuel. I promise it will come back to you full of something representing the best of Santa Fe."

📖 📖 📖

Jack worried that they had not met up with more wagon outfits in this small village. Being Jack, he nosed around the town of Franklin. Several general stores and a blacksmith's shop gave him what he searched for – news of goings and comings on the Santa Fe Trail.

Independence was much closer to the Missouri River than Franklin. It had easier access to steamboats that brought supplies in and took out local goods to markets in St. Louis and beyond. And as far as Jack could learn, it had not suffered the floods that devastated Franklin in 1826.

"Well, that is what I learned. We'll gear up and head west another hunert miles to Independence."

"But remember when we talked with Captain Becknell? He said under no circumstances should we even think about starting out alone. What are we to do? Didn't he give us the name of one of his companions on several trips to Santa Fe who would be heading up a caravan?"

"He did that. We'll form up in Indy under James Peters."

"Let's not lose any time then. I say we get back on the path."

Though they had been on the trail only about nine days, matching teams of mules to wagons was becoming a routine that moved swiftly and efficiently, thanks to the work of the additions to their company.

Back in St. Louis Duncan and Jack had had quite a spirited debate about adding two more people to the group. After seeing the string of mules Jack had put together – buying, swapping, trading – Duncan had had less and less a desire to ride all the way to Santa Fe as the "near wheeler" on the back of a mule.

"What's the matter? You can ride a horse, why not a mule?"

"Can't you see me on a mule with my feet dragging on the ground and the mule caved in from my weight? Come on, we're talking days and days, not a trip across town."

"Well, when you put it that way, guess I ought to pity the mule. I got two young fellers workin at one of my stables burnin with a fever to go West and try their luck. What say we sign em on for a free ride if'n they'll each take a span of mules under their whip and care."

"That's quite a burden to put on the back of untried young men."

"Hell! I never woulda raised the idea if'n I didn't think they was up to it."

"Are they from around here? What are their names? Is it possible I might know these boys?"

"God, school teachers are all the same! Question after question. No, they're from across the river in Illinois, both run off from bad homes. Don't reckon you know either boy. One calls himself Preston Bupp, other one is Leonard Dunkleberger. If'n you was to call for 'Pres' or 'Dutch' you'd get an answer."

"I will have to trust your judgment on this, my friend. See if you agree with this idea: If they go all the way to Santa Fe and do what you tell them, I'll give them a bonus in addition to their keep on the Trail."

"Good as done!"

📖　📖　📖

When the Ross and Gallagher families pulled into Independence they found activity everywhere. News was abundant, and it was no secret that a caravan was being formed. With directions to the gathering place, Jack and Duncan led their two wagons there. Mentioning the name James Peters was like giving the password into a secret society.

Peters appeared before them within the hour. Introductions were made with dispatch and with an air of sincerity. Sets of eyes were at work sizing up and measuring. This caravan would be together as many as eighty days and nights. A sense of responsibility had to be projected as well as received. And it would surely help if all in the wagon train could be decent to one another.

For two days all who signed on to make this trip over the Trail to Santa Fe with James Peters laid up in Independence. He spent hour after hour going over each outfit carefully: Horses, mules, oxen were inspected with a practiced eye. Wagons and people were looked at just as carefully and with detailed questions asked. Peters wanted to know of amounts of food and just which items were in the wagons. He took special note of barrels and kegs that would be ready to fill with water when they reached what he simply referred to as "the dry country." He was not one to scare his people. He just wanted them to be prepared.

"Mr. Peters, we appreciate the care you're giving to this outfit so it's ready, and if there's anyway my partner and I can help, why you just say the word."

"Good to know that, Mr. Ross, but tomorrow morning's first order of business is to get this outfit divided into sections with a leader for each. Who's your partner?"

"Jack Gallagher, the man standing over at that wagon talking to the two young men he's hired to be his black snakers." Black snakers, also called mule skinners, drove mule teams; bull whackers drove ox teams.

"I got him figured as a knowing man around stock. By the way, I am Jim. Plain old Jim, I don't go for this Mister business. But Jim, not Jimmy! Call me that and you might hear my trail bag of ugly words."

It didn't take long for Jim Peters to get his outfit organized with newly elected section leaders getting to know on first-name basis the other members of their groups. He impressed Duncan Ross at once with this mark of leadership and the way the section leaders fell in with his directions. A good omen, he thought. He was not surprised to see Jack elected as one of the section leaders.

Organization was one thing. Having the outfit move out in timely fashion with a sense of order was another. The first command to "circle up" resulted in wild confusion and the exchange of oaths not meant for tender ears. Some people wanted to know why this was necessary when they were days removed from Indian country?

"When we get beyond Council Grove we will be in territory better known to Indians than to us. We damned well better know how to circle the wagons before that. Then ain't the time to learn lessons you'd best learn now. I want to see all section leaders at my wagon. Now!"

The leaders got the plan again drawn with a stick as he traced on the ground the way each section was to move, in what order, and how to break the circle in the morning when he gave the "catch up" order.

"Men, I got some patience with you, for I know most of you have never done anything like this with so many wagons and stock involved. But my supply of patience is limited. So let's make more of an effort to do it right. Agreed?"

The next attempt was an improvement, but not enough to satisfy the wagon master. He set up two more drills, one to break the circle and begin the day, the other to form the protecting circle of wagons for the night's camp.

Practice drills were one thing. Actually starting out on the Trail was another. The Ross family had teamed up with the Gallagher family to head out on the Santa Fe Trail always pointed to the West, but without any real idea of what lay behind that setting sun.

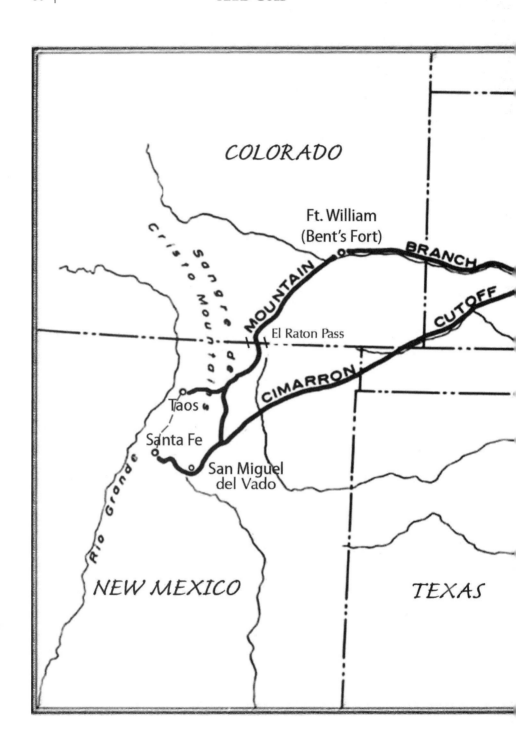

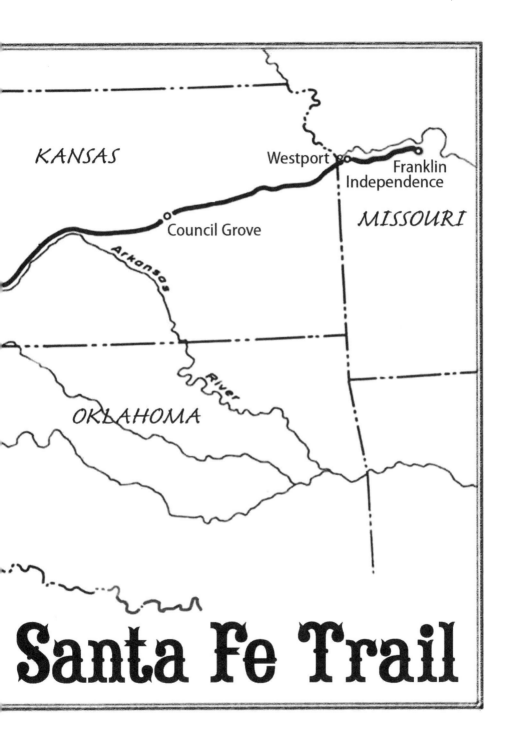

Hard Gold

Even before sun-up there were signs of activity in the loose and some-what disordered circle of wagons drawn up at the edge of Independence, Missouri. Duncan, Naomi, and Peggy Ross stood around one of the many small cooking fires. Jack Gallagher and his two mule skinners, Pres and Dutch, were in the herd of mules rounding up sixteen head to be matched and harnessed. Billy had beat everyone to the pasture and already had his horse watered, fed, and saddled. Also at the fire was Eleanor Gallagher with Grace and little Charley.

This was the big day, the day the Ross and Gallagher families were to actually begin their trek over the Santa Fe Trail. Bacon sizzled in the pan, biscuits baked in the Dutch oven, and coffee was the way Jack had ordered it. Last night before turning in he had cautioned Grace and Peggy, "We take kindly your offer to get up the mornin meal, but let me warn you two, it's the most important of the whole durn day. It's gotta be right! The cof-fee's gotta scald your tongue and curl your hair, the biscuits gotta be hard enough to crack your teeth, and the bacon's gotta be burnt black."

"Well, Pa, did we do it right?" Remembering Jack's description from the night before, Grace and Peggy tried to hold back their laughter.

"Gimme another of them things you're calling biscuits with a second go on that coffee. Man can't hurry an opinion til he's had chance to judge, then I'll tell you after I seen what you did to this here bacon."

"Don't pay your pa no mind, he'll eat anything put before him."

"Now, Eleanor, you know that ain't so."

"I'd be careful about doing too good a job, girls, you might be assigned this duty every morning."

"Papa Dunc, you wouldn't do that to us, would you?"

"Last night I heard Jim Peters say he expected it's going to take about seventy-five days to reach Santa Fe. That means a lake of coffee to boil, a mountain of biscuits to make, and a wagon load of bacon to fry. You girls want to do all that?"

Billy spoke up, "There has to be another way, Uncle Duncan. We'll never make it to Santa Fe on breakfasts made by these two."

"Every one told us how difficult the trail will be. Maybe this is one of those things we were warned about."

The easy give and take around the fire was ended abruptly by the call of Jim Peters, "Sections gear up and be ready to move in ten minutes!"

A red ball of sun showed its face in the east, morning birds began a review of yesterday's news, and teamsters exercised their vocabularies of a persuasive nature as they harnessed, tied, linked, hooked, and chained over three hundred and fifty animals, mules or oxen, to the forty-four wagons all pointed to the West.

"Catch up! Catch up!!"

There were no fanfares, no marching bands, no streets lined with cheering citizens, no pretty girls waving and blowing kisses. None of that. What took place was one massive jumble of wagons, each one striving to be first in line. Jim Peters sensed the confusion milling behind him. He wheeled his horse around and let loose a blast of sulfurous words that blistered the paint off the first ten wagons.

"Get with your damn section and in the order I gave you last night. Any one of you jackasses can't abide that, pull off to the side. We go as a caravan under my direction or we don't go anywhere. Got it?"

It took some time, some snarling, shouting of oaths and threats, but all "got it" and a sense of order settled over the caravan. The trail that began in Independence turned toward the southwest and passed a few miles below the village of West Port, soon to be called Kansas City. It was a well-worn path that demanded several small streams be forded, again with confusion and shortened tempers, as it traced a line up and down over low hills and woods.

As the morning wore on, the sunshine wore out. Clouds began to build in the south and a sprinkle dampened the trekkers and their enthusiasm. The wagon train formed a line snaking nearly a mile in single file. Every now and then it ground to a halt as some wagoneer made an adjustment to the wagon gear or to the animals pulling his wagon. When this happened, everyone behind that wagon had to stop. A few incidents like this and the air became blue with colorful directions to the offender as to where he could go and what he should do when he got there.

Eleanor had gathered up Grace and Peggy, and finally Naomi with Charley in tow, joined them in the "family" wagon. Jack and Duncan continued to slog alongside their wagons to be near to the driver of the eight-mule teams that pulled them. Pres and Dutch were working into the routines as "off-wheel riders" and demonstrated Jack's confidence in hiring them. Billy directed his horse to the back of the line to help herd the loose stock. Rain replaced the sprinkles, and mud replaced the smooth path they followed since daylight. Mud on the Santa Fe Trail usually had two options: to dry up or to get deeper. This day it got deeper and slimier and presented more challenges to dispositions and vocabularies.

Twelve hours on the trail, less than twelve miles in forward progress, and a wagon boss ready to hang by the thumbs any one of his teamsters brought Day One to a close. This was the first of several nights where nothing seemed to go right. No cooking fires could be kindled. There was no sleeping under the stars, no gathering of family and friends about a cheery fire to hash over the day's happenings. Instead, sheets of rain accompanied by bolts of lightning and thunder cascaded down on the miserable bunch of people who at sunrise only hours ago were full of cheerful spirits and bright smiles.

The big Conestoga wagon was designed as a cargo carrier. As a shelter for wet and cold human cargo, it was dry. But that was its only advantage. It was cramped, crowded, and cheerless. The arching canvas top repelled rain and protected passengers from the wind, but it had the warmth and restful colors of a prison cell. In a wooden box twelve feet long, four feet in width and four feet deep packed to the last square inch with family needs – clothing, blankets, food – were two adult women, two teenage girls, and a pleasant little boy of four. They were close and uncomfortable, but what other choice did they have? Duncan had included, at Naomi's insistence, two small tents in their gear. But who was about to pitch tents on ground already saturated with water? The Conestoga had to do for shelter.

"Charley, want to go out and play?"

"I'll go if you play with me."

"Now don't go getting Charley all fussed up. You know you aren't going outside this wagon, Grace. Think of something else to amuse him."

Teasing conversation came to a close, but nothing replaced it. All in the wagon settled down to discomfort and boredom, not realizing a day like this would be repeated several times before they reached the magic village of Santa Fe.

A council of section chiefs was called by Jim Peters the first thing in the morning. All agreed it would be an exercise in futility to gear up and move out in mud that was too much, much too much. Even with sixteen head of oxen or mules hitched to one wagon, forward progress would result in a mile of gain at the cost of an exhausted double span.

Later that day the sun came out, and spirits revived along with three dozen or so cooking fires. Life once again seemed worth living as the aroma of hot coffee and frying bacon spread through the circle of wagons.

Eleven days after departing from Independence, the Peters caravan reached Council Grove. The activity from daylight to dusk was the selecting, cutting, and shaping of logs and partially finished pieces of wagon gear as emergency stock. The grove was a band of oak, ash, hickory, maple, and walnut nearly a half mile in width and stretching for several miles along the Neosho River. It was their last chance to get hardwood, material essential to keep the lumbering wagons in running shape.

Stories explaining the naming of this spot flourished around the fires each evening of the three spent there. Most had the theme of a meeting and agreeing among Indian tribes of the area some years ago, but they seemed of minor importance.

Duncan and Jack finished securing under their wagons the wood they had fashioned at the grove.

"Jack, I have an idea that once we are back on the Trail, we are going to see some changes."

"Changes like what?"

"Flatter ground, fewer streams, and wind that never seems to stop."

"What's got you to thinkin that way? You some sort of a wizard?"

"No magic, just been listening to some of the talk among the men who have been over this trail before."

"Them's the ones you want to pay heed to. Look in your tea leaves. What else you see waitin for us?"

"I see monotony. Day after day of unchanging scenery and weather that only gets hotter and drier."

"Not too much drier. I'm keepin an eye on them iron tires that rim the wheels on our wagons. Once they get loose they'll be hell to reset."

"Does that mean big trouble for us?"

"Don't rightly know, but a little rain now and then would be nice."

A routine soon developed among the wagoneers. Most everyone walked at or near the side of his wagon. Grace and Peggy paired off, but it was Charley, Jack and Eleanor's youngest, who required special attention. His short four-year-old legs couldn't hold to the pace, and he seemed to tire very easily. Sometimes Jack would ease his horse over, pick up the boy, and set him on the saddle in front where he could keep an arm around the little fellow as he rode patrol. Billy and Duncan did the same frequently, but there were times when Charley had to be put in one of the wagons.

Naomi spelled Eleanor in the wagon when Charley had to be taken on board. It was on these occasions that Charley and Naomi became close. He liked the times when Naomi sang to him and the times she held him and told him stories. Eleanor, of course, did the same when she was with her son, but she also had Billy and Grace to look after. And Jack needed her managing skills.

Jack and Duncan did their share of walking, for it was not good, for either man or horse, to be constantly riding. Two weeks before the beginning of the trip each man had selected a horse. Jack let Billy pick a horse he could call his own, too. Duncan and Jack chose big, stout mounts, not because of their speed, but for their endurance and manageability. Billy's selection was a little smaller, a lot faster, and a bit on the frisky side. That was exactly the sort of horse a competent and confident young rider like Billy would choose. The markings on his horse's long muzzle gave it a name immediately – Spook. One half was white, the other half roan.

During one of those times of spelling the horses Duncan walked with Naomi.

"Dunc, I am worried about little Charley."

"And what's your concern?"

"I know he is only four years old, but I think he tires too quickly."

"Does he get sick? Does he throw up when he gets tired?"

"No, I wouldn't say he gets sick. But sometimes when I hold him to tell him stories I can feel his little heart beating."

"Nothing strange about that, is there?"

"It's just that it beats so fast, and it's a long time before I can feel a normal beat."

"Did you say anything to Eleanor? Is she aware he gets so tired?"

"Yes. We talk about it from time to time. She thinks he will outgrow this when he gets a little older."

"I'm sure that's the answer. He's a real trooper. He never complains or fusses."

"Charley's a dear little boy. He makes all of us feel good."

More than changes in the weather were on their minds as they put up for the night. It was the second one after leaving Council Grove. After the wagons were circled, Jim Peters called all the men to a meeting.

"Men, listen up. I ain't trying to scare nobody, but we're edging into Indian country. We must have eyes and ears working twenty-four hours a day. I want more patrols organized amongst you in all four directions around the clock."

"Jim, how many of us do you need?"

"Every one of you that can ride has to take his turn, but no man rides alone. Always ride in pairs."

"There's likely to be a mile or more from front to back when we're moving. How we gonna keep in touch?"

"You'll always ride with a sidearm or a long gun. But nobody plays at being a smart-ass firing off a gun just for the hell of it. A gun is a signal that we've got some Indians near by, not a signal to start a god-damned war."

Peters rode with the lead patrol most days, for that group did more than just look and listen. It selected a site for the night's camp. That meant a place with good grass, water close by, and possibly firewood at hand.

Another duty fell on the advance patrol. If a stream lay ahead that must be forded, a judgment had to be made – where was the safest place to cross? Was there "bottom" to the ford or soft mud or quicksand? Could mules as well as oxen cross with hooves on the ground all the way? Would they have to swim the stock and float the wagons? Would it be necessary to double the teams? Did the banks on either side of the ford need to be shaped with shovels and mattocks for easy entrance and exit of the wagons? Riding in the advance patrol seemed like a badge of honor, but it was also a ticket to damned hard work with little thanks for the effort.

When he was not riding perimeter patrol or herding the loose stock, Billy walked with Peggy and Grace. He insisted the girls take turns riding on Spook. He figured they needed to keep their riding abilities honed, and it kept the horse familiar with the girls' voices, hands, and boots. When it was Grace's turn, Billy was more than happy to make a hand and boost her into the saddle in order to gain time alone with Peggy. Either one would be the last to admit it, but Peggy and Billy enjoyed those precious hours by themselves.

"Billy, do you remember telling me about the big mountains we would see?"

"Sure. But we've got many a mile to tramp before we'll see them."

"You never told me how much grassland we would have to cross."

"Didn't know 'bout that. I think they're called prairies. Some of the old hands tell me they just go on and on, like the oceans. Think you could sketch oceans of grass?"

"I don't think so. I'm not getting time to do any sketching. Until we get up, have breakfast, and set out for the day there's never a chance. At night we're always busy helping with supper, gathering firewood or chips, fetching water. I don't have the time or the energy to do any sketching."

Several days after this exchange with Billy, she found herself walking beside her mother. Naomi was searching for edible greens. She wanted Peggy to learn which greens were not noxious or poisonous weeds.

Naomi had misgivings about their daily meals of beans, bacon, and biscuits. Not all of her greens and the way they were cooked brought smiles of pleasure. Some of her dishes were downright awful.

"I don't want to get you riled, Naomi, but do we have to eat this stuff?"

"No, you don't have to eat it, but do you want to lose your teeth? Would you like to walk with creaking joints all the way to Santa Fe?"

"Is there another way to fix these than stewed in bacon grease?"

"I could boil them, or you could eat them raw. Would you like them fixed that way?"

Finding and feeding fresh greens to both families was only one thing Naomi did for their health. Naomi's reputation as a healer passed through the caravan as swiftly as a sand-devil boiling across the track of the wagons. Nearly every day a man would come looking for the medicine lady. Pinched hands, sprains, cuts and bruises, unsettled stomachs, sunburn, and rashes from something best left untouched were common. And in most cases Naomi was able to give a salve, a potion, or motherly advice that left the recipient in awe of her wisdom and gentle nature.

A bullwacker, Rufus Ferguson, came to the Ross wagon at the end of a long day. "Where's that there lady what does the magic with roots and stuff?"

He was not the ailing one. His partner in the wagon was hurting and needed help. "Could you help him? Soon?"

Naomi went with him. They found his partner sitting on a wagon tongue doubled over in pain with a flushed face and a desperate look in his bloodshot eyes.

"How long have you been in pain, my friend?"

"I guess it's goin on two days, yeah, two days."

"Have you eaten anything today?"

"Not much. Soaked a chunk of hardtack in some coffee. Tried some beans last night, but they come right back up."

"What have you had to drink?"

"Coffee, but not much of that. You ever drink my partner's coffee? I had a sip of water 'bout an hour ago."

"Anything else? Are you sure that's all?"

"Well, ma'am, I had a snort of corn squeezins last night."

"I see. I'm going back to my wagon to fix something that might get you through the night with a little less pain. Can you walk? Does it hurt to walk or straighten up?"

"Yes, it do. Special when I try to stand up."

Naomi turned to Rufus. "Fix a more comfortable place for him than sitting on a wagon tongue." She added, "A spot on the shady side of the wagon with a poncho on the ground and a back rest might give some him relief from the pain."

She went back to what they called the "Santa Fe wagon," the one carrying the merchandise to be sold in Santa Fe plus her medications and Peggy's art supplies. Among the pouches and little bags of dried herbs she found what she wanted.

"Poke up the fire, Duncan, I need to make some special tea for Rufus' partner. Do you know him? He's in pain, lots of pain."

"Anything I can do to help you? The men call him Jerry."

"No. I can manage."

When Naomi returned to the wagon she saw Rufus had made Jerry more comfortable as she directed, but the pains had increased.

"Try this tea, Jerry. Just sip it, don't try to down it like a slug of whiskey. A little at a time, you hear?"

How the man managed to get himself in the wagon the next morning was a mystery, but at the end of the day there was no mystery; he was in bad shape. As soon as the caravan circled for the night Naomi rushed to his wagon. She had to talk to Jerry at the back of the wagon. He could not get himself out, and when friends tried to help him screams of pain were heard all through the camp.

Naomi climbed in. One look told her Jerry's days were numbered. He held himself in a tight, fetal position. He screamed the minute anyone touched him to help him find a more comfortable position. The signs were not good: His eyes could not focus, his forehead was like a hot iron to her touch, his breath was foul, and talking was a major effort. His responses were neither coherent nor helpful.

Jim Peters came to the wagon and took in the sounds and smells. When Naomi climbed out of the wagon he took her aside. "Well, Mrs. Ross, what's your opinion? Does Jerry have a chance? What can we do for him?"

"I think he's close to death, but that's only my opinion."

"That's what I want. But is there something we can do to make his passing a bit more painless?"

"Can you see a way to get him outside? Fresh air will do him some good. Do all of us some good. It might ease his mind if you can move him to a more pleasant place."

Under Jim's direction, a canvas sling was rigged. After much pain and horrible moaning, they got Jerry out and helping hands placed him on a pad in the shade of the wagon. In the process of the moving Naomi placed her hand on his forehead. It was still very hot, yet he shook with chills and drew himself even tighter into a ball. Naomi directed, "Fetch some blankets, and help me turn him into another position."

Willing hands did everything Naomi asked be done for Jerry. An hour before sunrise, Naomi's check on her patient told her it was over. Morning activities, usually loud and frequently playful, were muted and restrained as word of death in the group spread.

Nobody really owned up to knowing much about him. He had a name, Jerome Huddleston. Some thought he came from Indiana, but not much else was ventured. Even Rufus, his partner, didn't recall much. "We got to trading drinks in a waterfront tavern in St. Louis and trading what we knew of the Santa Fe Trail."

Jim Peters had a few questions. "How'd you get your hands on a wagon and a team? How'd you put together a grub-stake?"

"We pooled our money, borrowed some, and here we is."

Jerome Huddleston was buried alongside the Trail, but nobody took the time nor made the effort to erect some sort of a marker on his grave. The wagon train moved on, following the setting sun.

Duncan was assigned to patrol on the right side of the caravan and Jack was riding with Jim Peters on advance patrol when they stopped to view a gently sloping valley directly ahead. "Don't see any problem in crossing this little swale, do you?" Jim ventured.

"Can't see anythin that'll hinder our forward progress, but what's that blob on the far rim of this here dip?"

"Damn! You spotted buffalo. We'll have fresh meat tonight! You keep a lookout here while I go back and organize a hunting party. Can't have every man galloping off and shooting his gun. Those critters are sometimes touchy and scare easily. They can run as fast as you can on a good horse."

"Right, boss man, but I want to be in on the huntin when you give the word."

"You'll get your chance."

For over a week the caravan had seen signs of buffalo. They had encountered places that showed heavy grazing of prairie grasses and tracks by the hundreds, and everyone had learned the value of chips. Buffalo dung, when thoroughly dried, made a fairly good cooking fire, nearly smokeless and, much to the surprise of many, essentially odorless. The further west they traveled the more prevalent were the chips dotting the landscape; they could be found just about everywhere anyone looked.

Watching Jim gallop off, Jack slipped from his horse, led it back a few hundred feet, and hobbled it. Then he retraced his steps to the rise of ground where he and Peters had spotted the buffalo. Figuring he might be too easily seen by the on-coming herd, he lay on the ground and began his first up-close lesson in buffalo behavior.

They never stopped coming. What Jack had spotted was more than a cluster of buffalo; it was an immense herd, an unending stream of beasts flowing like water over the land. Heads down, following closely after the ones in front, they moved on north. Jack lay as though stunned by a blow to his head. He looked to the left as far as he could see, the same to the right, and saw nothing but buffalo. He thought maybe he had had too much sun or had drunk too much "gypy" water, water heavy with gypsum, an alkali that made it risky to drink.

In time he could hear them. Not the bellowing sounds he expected from such a large herd, but sounds of their constant breathing and the occasional grunts of cows and calves trying to reunite. And all left the same aroma as they passed in front of Jack, petrified in his prone position. He knew buffalo fed on nothing but grass, and being around cattle all his life he knew the smell of dung. But he was surprised that here on the open prairie this odor was not offensive. It was the breath of buffalo that offended one's sense of smell.

Jim Peters rejoined Jack and sprawled on the ground beside him. "Haven't they stopped, Jack? Hasn't there been a break, a chance we could drive our wagons through?"

"Not a chance. Nothin's changed since you first seen 'em."

"I've heard of these big herd movements, but never saw one. They tell buffalo in huge bunches move north this time of year and south in the fall. This is something everyone should see."

"Why don't you spell me? I'll mosey on back and send people up two or three at a time."

"Best leave that to me. I have to make sure patrols are out at all times."

The wagons were circled at Jim's direction before he released teamsters in small groups to go forward to watch the passing of the buffalo; all who desired had an opportunity to witness the scene. Jim called all the men together and repeated his instructions about keeping ears and ears peeled for Indian signs.

"Men, we ain't the only ones drawn to this parade of fresh meat and hides. This could be the time some Indian meat hunters put us to the test, so be sharp and stay alert."

Jim's instructions were not ignored. Certainly no one in the group was foolish enough to take a casual view of patrol assignments. But it was only natural that what all had seen with their own eyes was the dominant topic in the group.

"Billy, did you ever think there could be as many of the same wild animals in one group all moving as one?"

"It stretches my mind. I never expected to see anything like this."

Peggy broke in, "I wouldn't know how to begin sketching such a thing as we saw this afternoon. If I did, nobody would believe it came from a real live scene."

"It was real, take my word for it because I smelled them critters. They were real!"

"Why do you always reduce things to their very basics?"

"Well, if you're going to play the grand lady, what impressed you most?"

"The numbers of them, the thousands of buffalo we saw."

Peggy looked over at her mother, who sadly shook her head. "I can't push out from my mind what my people did to the beaver in the North

Country. I think you people will do the same to the buffalo. In a few years there won't be any left anywhere."

"How could anybody get rid of as many as we just saw?" replied Duncan. "A man just returned from his stakeout up on the hill said they're still moving, haven't stopped for a minute."

But Jim wasn't waiting. He picked whom he thought were the best horsemen and the best shots. He told them to pace their mounts to the pace of the herd. They were to ride on its flanks and drop two or three of the critters at the outer edge. He had other men ready with ropes to drag the buffalo killed to the side.

The hunters went to the rise of ground, surveyed the mass of animals still flowing by, eased down on horseback to the level of the buffalo, and began to follow Jim's instructions. Shots could not be heard above the noise of the herd, but four of the beasts were dropped. The mass moved a slight distance away from the fallen, for the four of them were still kicking and bellowing. Ropes found their targets, horses leaned into the task, and the four were dragged away from the main stream of buffalo. Men went to work with knives and axes. The first cuts of buffalo were ready for the cooking fires of the caravan. Hides were stretched out to dry even as they were being scraped.

The rest of the day was given over to a feast while the passing of the herd continued. Just as quickly as it had begun, the vast parade ended. All that remained was the lingering odor, the swath of ground pulverized by thousands of hooves, and a bunch of wagoneers still in awe of what they had seen. What stuck with the Ross and Gallagher group was the taste of freshly killed meat with the flavor and tenderness of the monarch of the prairies.

Another reminder of the passing of the great mass of buffalo was a small pack of coyotes nosing along the path made by the herd. Some traveled with heads up, others with heads down, but all were alert and ready for an easy meal like a stray calf, a sick cow or an aged bull.

Billy was dancing with the excitement of the first encounter with buffalo. "The next time we hunt for buffalo I'm going along."

"It ain't huntin buffalo that your hankerin after. It's the chase. That's got your blood a racin and a boilin."

"How can you say you're hunting when you can see ahead as far as tomorrow and as far back as yesterday on these prairies?"

"Well, Uncle Duncan, whatever you call it, I want in on the next one."

"You thought I was wrong to say the buffalo will be gone in a few years. What will happen to the herds when thousands of men find they can sell hides and meat? Your North West Company sold beaver pelts as fast as it could get its hands on them. Why not buffalo?"

"Why do you think this way, Naomi? What do you see that we can't?"

"It isn't anything I see. It's just a strong feeling I have deep within me that this will happen."

Three days after the passing of the buffalo parade, the caravan experienced another unique episode of travel over this sea of grass. It was thinning grass to be sure, yet sufficient for the grazing of mules, oxen, and horses. Here, however, it was burned grass, mile after mile of it, as far as the eye could see.

"Sometimes this grass is set on fire by lightning bolts that blast onto the ground. And sometimes it's deliberately set by the Indians."

"But, Jim, why would they do that?" Jack asked.

"To make travel through their lands difficult, to discourage us, to put the fear of starvation into us."

Jack wasn't going to be put off by that answer. "But we got enough food in our wagon for at least twenty days."

"But do you have water for twenty days? Do you have feed for your teams?"

"What are we to do? Turn around and head back to Missouri?"

"No. We keep going west. The advance patrol will find a way that gets us to green grass."

"That's not guaranteed. Is it?"

"You know I can't guarantee anything. Prairie fires burn out, they skip and jump from place to place. We'll get through this."

And they did. The three days of tramping over burned and partially burned grass and pockets of green grass affected more than breathing and watery eyes, it penetrated to the soul. Duncan found this mosaic on the Trail disturbing. It was destruction on a massive scale, and to him, it lacked purpose.

Naomi, however, found that the passage over the patches of burned grass affected her quite differently. She saw this burned area as a place for regrowth, for new life. Rather than becoming depressed, she became invigorated. The signs she read were of hope and a bright future. To herself she said, "How can I tell Dunc my people know to fire the prairie to make better grazing which makes better hunting? No, he won't understand."

It was another of those bright, sunny mornings with a breeze to make trudging along the wagons less monotonous and more enjoyable. Naomi and Duncan walked away from the wagons to enjoy the scene.

"There is something we must talk about."

"And what do you have in mind?"

"Do you remember when I took Peggy and went back to the Mandan villages, to the home of my mother?"

"Yes. But you never told me your reason, you just up and left."

"I didn't want Peggy to grow up the child of a trader in the life of a trading post."

"Yes, I learned about that. Not from you, but from others."

"What I want you to understand is why I remained with Armand for nearly three years. After I let Peggy go back with you and Jack, I stayed with him to pay my debt to him."

"Debt? How could you be in debt to a Mandan man?"

"He provided a home for Peggy and me. We had no other place to go. None of the people in the Mandan villages would take us into their lodges."

"Didn't you do the work of a Mandan woman? Cook his food, mend his garments, raise his two boys, and care for his mother?"

"Yes, I did all those things. But he demanded that I be his woman."

"So this is how you got the feeling you were in debt to him? Was he not satisfied with all that you did to make his lodge a home?"

"Among my people when you owe a person for something he has done for you, that person decides when the debt has been paid."

"I see. But you could have left him when you let Peggy go from his lodge to return with Jack and me."

"No. He was happy to see Peggy leave his lodge, but he made it clear I had to remain."

"How did you get away then?"

"Over the time I was with Armand I never let the chance go by to make his pleasure in me anything but pleasure."

"I don't understand."

"When he would come to me and expect me to submit to him, I did everything I could think of to make it scene of misery, not one of passion."

"You came back to us with Jack as he was returning to St. Louis after a visit to his trading post in the villages."

"I told Armand if he didn't release me from my debt to him I would kill myself. I would disgrace him in the eyes of his people. He let me go."

They walked in silence for several miles, each trying to read the other's mind, trying to bring this long, sad portion of Naomi's life to some sort of closure.

"Naomi, you know the great change you brought into Peggy's life and into mine when you climbed down from Jack's freight wagon into my arms. It was real. I think you sensed our joy, our feeling of completeness."

"Yes. I sensed those things, but I felt I could not become a part of you and Peggy. I had disgraced myself by living with a man for whom I had no feelings."

"But that is all behind you. You are with friends, with family. Your debt is paid. Put those years out of your mind."

"I think differently from you and your ways, and you will never understand me and my ways."

Their time together was interrupted when the two men riding patrol on the north flank of the caravan came dashing to the outermost section of wagons and called for Jim Peters. "Indians, Jim. We seen signs of 'em, lots of 'em."

"What direction? How far away? How many? How old are the signs?"

"Off to the north 'bout five, maybe six miles. Looks like last night's cookin fires. Whole passel of foot prints, can't rightly say how many, but there's a big bunch."

"Let me catch up a horse. Then take me where you found signs."

An hour later Jim and the two scouts were at the place of the first sighting. Jim had one of the men hold the horses as he and the other scout walked the area. Jim walked off to the south about a half a mile, stopped and examined the ground, and called the scout to him.

"See these drag marks, like grooves? They're *travois* marks. See how deep they cut into the ground? You men found several families on the move. They've got something heavy on them drag poles. My guess is it's a hunting party going home with meat. Let's get back to our horses."

When each patrol rode in at the end of its watch, Jim alerted the replacement patrol as to the likely direction of the Indians. "Keep your eyes open. Get a count if you spot them, but don't start nothing. They'll have their scouts out, too, but I don't think they want to get into a fuss with us if they're packing fresh meat."

Jack said he would relieve Dutch and ride as "near wheeler" for the afternoon. That was how Billy and Dutch happened to be on patrol together and assigned to the southern flank of the caravan.

"Damn, Billy, you got it good riding way out here to the side. Some days all I breathe is dust and can hardly see the wagon ahead."

"And some days when I'm riding rear patrol with the loose herd all I see is dust and smell ox shit."

"Maybe so, but one of these days we're gonna see the mountains. I made friends with a couple of men who been out this way and they say it won't be but a week or two and we'll see the big ones. The ones you're always talking about."

"Can't wait. I got excited over seeing mountains when we was still in St. Louis."

They walked their horses along for half an hour.

"Damn, Billy did you see that?"

"See what?"

"I swear that was an eagle that swooped down and grabbed that snake. God! They're fast and they don't miss very often. How'd you like one of them soaring overhead and lookin you over for a meal?"

When they were ready to remount, Billy said quietly, "Take a slow look over your left shoulder. Mount up, but don't do nothing."

Billy did the same as the two young men looked at their first contact with the fabled Indians of the Santa Fe Trail.

"Christ, Billy, where'd they come from?"

"Don't know. I see two, how many you see?"

"Two. Think we ought to fire a warning shot, a signal to the caravan?"

"We'd have an arrow in the back afore either of us could get to his gun. Best ride along easy and watch what move they'll make."

Dutch and Billy rode side by side for another mile with an Indian scout off on their left about a hundred yards, the other on the right. Neither the caravan's scouts nor the native scouts made any sort of signal. They just rode on for another hour never taking their eyes from one another.

"Damn, we gotta do something. Nother five minutes and I'll be pissing my pants."

"Hang in there, Dutch. I can still see their traveling outfit moving in the same direction they was when we spotted them. Let them make the first move."

"I say we make a break for our outfit, now"

"They're dropping back. Wait, they ain't notched arrows to their bows, they're just easing down the slope."

"Think you're right. They're heading for their group."

"Good, we'll just mosey back. If they see us racing off to alarm our people they'd be on our ass in a minute."

"I can't wait, take these reins. I gotta piss."

Billy held Dutch's horse while he slipped off his horse to ease his tanking bladder.

"Nothing like a scare to start things to flowing. Did you never see 'em? How in the hell could they sneak up on us in this wide open country."

"Can't say. But they done it."

"What're we gonna tell Jim Peters? How we gonna explain being blind-sided like we was?"

"Why, we'll just tell him we spotted the Indian group at a distance. They paid us no mind, just kept movin on to the south."

"Think Jim will buy that? He'll have a flock of questions, won't he?"

"The less we tell him, the fewer questions. I'm not going to lie to him, but I'm not saying more than he needs to know."

"Hope you're right. There's one man I don't want breathing down my neck when he's mad."

Billy and Dutch eased their horses into the line of wagons, found Peters, made their report, and resumed their places in line. Both young men were bursting to tell somebody of their close call. They agreed that for now they would keep the real story to themselves. Maybe later, Billy thought, he'd share some of this with his father, maybe even with Peggy.

Other than the patrol of Billy and Dutch, it was an uneventful day. That night after supper the men of the caravan gathered around the fire at Jim Peters' wagon. One of them bought his guitar and nearly all brought three or four buffalo chips and a larger than normal fire flared up.

The guitar player was anything but accomplished on his battered instrument and the occasional singing that joined his playing was in the same class. The sense of companionship and the realization that another day was nearly over in peace and harmony was the unspoken theme of the evening.

Duncan strolled over to the man coaxing tunes from the battered instrument and began to clap his hands in a different rhythm. When the player got Duncan's drift, he began to strum out a familiar tune to a different beat and Duncan started to dance. Duncan danced a pattern from his past, a dance performed by men of the Highlands of Scotland, and he did it with precision and style.

As he circled the fire with intricate footwork and arm gestures that told a story, an aura of mystery and remoteness governed his movements. Duncan was no longer on the prairie. He was in a glen tucked into a range of the wind-swept, rugged hills of his homeland. His eyes were fastened far away on his mother and his sister as they clapped their hands to the beat of his dance and encouraged him with their eyes and their smiles. He sensed the pride flowing from the women who had taught him to dance the proud steps of a Highlander.

He finished with the blood-curdling shout of a man who had done well in honoring his ancestors and remembering his homeland. The cluster of men about the fire returned their appreciation of Duncan's effort with nods and smiles.

A deep silence fell over the group as the darkening night and the show of stars overhead took over. About the time the fire was all but burned out, the addition of three or four chips brought it back to life, and the guitar player launched into another round of country tunes. This time his tunes and his playing took on a softer tone. A dreamlike quality set the mood as another dancer circled the fire.

Naomi stood by herself with her shawl drawn about her shoulders. While Duncan had danced, she never took her eyes off his performance. Now she unfastened her long, dark hair and shook it free of her neck. She removed the shawl from over her shoulders and as she danced she used it to add to the grace of her movements. She, too, had her vision fastened on unseen people in unseen places. Where Duncan's steps had been forceful and masculine, hers were light and flowing, as were the movements of her arms and the streaming of her hair, tracing a pattern of soft, imaginary clouds. As she circled the fire in an ever-slowing pace she matched her arm movements and steps until she stood unmoving by the dying fire with her face lifted to the night sky in silent prayer.

The evening came to a close, the fire was but a few embers. No one called for more effort by the guitar player. Men drifted off one by one to their wagons with hearts and minds filled with the gifts of two people who spoke to them, not with words, but with the sharing of souls through their dancing.

Duncan and Naomi drew close together, not by request or invitation, but by a sense of wanting to be alone together.

"Why did you start dancing tonight?"

"No special reason, Naomi. It was just a good feeling that took over, and I wanted to share it with everyone, but especially with you. Why did you dance?"

"You were sending a message to me with your dance. I wanted to return that message with my dance."

Nights on the prairies became the time to escape their monotonous diet of beans, bacon, biscuits, and coffee, the monotonous trudging alongside wagons sharing the clouds of dust they raised, the monotonous view of flat, unbroken seas of grass blowing in a never-ending wind. At night the stars seemed so close they could be gathered by the handful and loud talk was a sacrilege. The night was a time of blessed relief.

Billy and Peggy found themselves drawn into this mystery of the night and the shared need to be with someone, someone special.

"Too bad you can't sketch night scenes on your drawing paper. Think of all the beauty around us and you can't capture it, you can't draw it so anybody else can see it."

"Why, Billy Gallagher, I think you are some sort of a poet. If I can't draw the magic of the night, maybe you should say something about it to put on paper."

"What I'd rather put is my arm around you."

"Why don't you?"

Billy acted on Peggy's invitation and followed that with a kiss and then another. The invitation was not withdrawn.

Duncan and Naomi were also drawn to the display of stars, the total silence, and the faintly discernable line between the ending of the sky and the beginning of the earth. They strolled a few hundred yards from the circle of wagons and felt they were miles from anything and everyone.

"Look, did you see that? It's a shooting star. See it?"

"Yes, I saw it, Dunc. It's not a shooting star. My mother would tell you the children of the night are out to play. They chase around the sky just the way we did when we were little. Did you play chase?"

"Every chance I got. I could never catch my older sister. She was always faster and quicker. Did I ever tell you she liked to dance and was very good because my mother also taught her to dance?"

"My mother taught me to dance. She also sang to me at night. She taught me never to be afraid of the dark, but learn to listen to the night and the stories it can tell."

"Tell me one of your stories now."

"I can't. I'm not afraid of the dark, Dunc, I am afraid of myself."

One fine morning Pres, one of the young men hired as a mule skinner, was walking with Duncan. Jack said he would give him a break from driving his mules.

"Mr. Ross, me and Dutch are thinkin when we get to Santa Fe we're gonna keep headin on west to California."

"Not going to give the *señoritas* of Santa Fe a chance? Why the rush?"

"Well, maybe we'll have a couple of weeks to try our luck at some of them dance things."

"I heard them called *fandangos*. But, seriously, you and Dutch have made up your minds?"

Pres grabbed Duncan and pushed him violently to the side.

"What the hell got into you, Pres?"

"Snake! Didn't you see it? It was one of them damn rattlin bastards that scare the shit out of the mules."

"I thank you, Pres. My God that was a close one. What were we talking about?

"About me and Dutch movin on to California."

"Oh yes. Have you given this some deep thought? This isn't just an overnight fancy idea?"

"No sir. This is solid with us. We got to talking to men in the caravan who's been over the Trail. Ain't a one of them had anything bad to say about California."

"Keep talking and listening. We can take this up when we get to Santa Fe."

Pres went to find Jack and tell him the off-side leader of his span of mules seemed to be more balky than usual. It was acting like something was not right with the harness. Duncan wanted to walk with Naomi and ask her what she meant by, "I'm afraid of myself." This was very much on his mind. He knew Naomi was not one to say something without attaching meaning to it.

After a supper of beans and bacon that everyone wished was buffalo and beans, he took Naomi by the arm and gently steered her beyond the circle of wagons.

"Let's look for some of your night children chasing about the sky."

"There's hardly a night that we don't see them. You have something else on your mind, don't you?"

"You know me too well. Yes I do. You never said why you are afraid of yourself, Naomi. Ever since we left Council Grove I have seen changes in you that are not in any way signs of fear."

"What signs do you see?"

"For one thing, you smile a lot more, and I even hear you sing as you work about the cooking fire or help to get everyone settled for the night."

"Do you see anything else?"

"Yes, but I don't quite know how to say it."

"Try."

"Well, you are a different person than the one I married in the North Country, the one who helped get our school into operation. You've changed, my dear. I like the changes I see, and yet I yearn for the other Naomi."

Naomi walked off a few paces and stood by herself. She wrapped herself in the comforting blanket of the night and seemed unaware of the presence of Duncan. He waited for what he thought was a sufficient time for Naomi to gather her thoughts and return to share them with him. No movement, just the gentle wind of the prairie blowing her dark hair. He slowly walked to her side and took her in his arms. For the first time in many months Naomi did not shrink from his embrace. She put her arms around his neck, pulled his face close to hers, and gently rubbed her cheek against his.

"It has been such a long time since we did this. You asked me why I am afraid of myself. Sit down beside me and let me tell you."

They sat for quite some time in silence as Duncan gently massaged her back and ran his fingers through her long, silky hair.

"I am afraid because I don't know who I am. All these many moons we have been together, and I still don't know who I am."

"You are 'Naomi,' the name I gave you. It was the name of my mother. You are 'She Who Sings with the Birds at the Dawn,' the name your mother gave you. You are the 'Tall One,' the name the people in the compound at our trading post gave you. You are the mother of our child. You are the loved and respected healer, the calm and steady voice of our family. Who would you want to be?"

"I don't know, I don't know. I have been all these things, but which one is the real me?"

"Why can't the real you be all of them? Why do you have to be just one? Your mother gave you a name which I feel fits you as closely as your own skin. Would you want us to call you by your Mandan name? You are as fresh and beautiful as any bird which has the spirit and the soul to sing a greeting to the new day."

"But I like name you gave me. I knew your mother meant so much to you, and when you asked me to carry her name I liked that. I wanted to be Naomi."

"My mother would be so pleased to know you, to love you. My mother was a quiet person who spoke only after she carefully thought out what she would say. Her name also fits you as closely as your skin."

"Neither of us will ever see our mothers again. Both have gone on to another world."

"Yes, my dear, they are no longer with us. But can't we feel their spirits? Not their physical presence, but a sense that they are near?"

"Do you really feel that? Do you truly believe in spirits?"

"Yes, I believe, Naomi."

Time lost all meaning in the magic of the night under a canopy of stars. They sat close, not speaking aloud, but speaking to each other through their senses, through the sharing of the moment. One moment became many as the chill of the night drew them closer.

"The children of the night sky are having a game of chase. Don't try to look now, but let me tell you they are having a wild time tonight. Hold me, Dunc, hold me."

※　※　※

Billy was in a teasing mood as he walked with Peggy and Grace. "I'll bet I seen something when I was riding patrol that you never saw up close."

"Well, I hope you saw something. Why would they send you out on patrol if it wasn't to see everything that was important?"

"Give me a minute, Grace. I saw a bunch of chubby rodents kissing."

"That's important? What have you been nipping? One of the bullwhackers give you a little whiskey?"

"Damn, listen to me. I don't make up stuff. I saw rats kissing right in the middle of their town."

"Peggy, let's find your mother and have her brew some sort of tea to bring this brother of mine back to his senses."

They continued to walk besides the wagons for another hour without another word from Billy. He stopped, looked off to his left, and took the girls by their arms and told them to walk quickly but silently. When one of the girls ventured a question, a sharp glance from Billy ended all thought of conversation.

Billy stopped and pointed. The girls saw nothing. He indicated they should do what he did, take a few steps as lightly as possible, stop, take another step or two, stop. By now the girls realized Billy had brought them to a prairie dog town. Grace and Peggy were at the point of explosion with questions but were afraid to break Billy's imposed silence.

Without any signal the trio of young people were aware of, all the nearby "dogs" disappeared into holes that dotted the plot of ground for as far as the eye could see. Billy continued with his stern glances and gesture of silence. As if by magic the little critters reappeared and town life resumed. Again a signal, and all of the "dogs" within several hundred yards fled to the safety of their burrows. They moved so quickly; one minute there were dozens of the black-tailed critters in sight atop their little mounds, in a second there were none.

Later that night at their cooking fire, the girls tore into Billy with questions and explanations.

"Girls, I told you all I know. Ask my daddy or Uncle Duncan about them little animals."

From those two men the girls gained a bit more information about the rodents that lived in groups, had large families, seemed to do little work to sustain village life, and yet there they were by the hundreds, even thousands. Jack said, "Girls, you pumped my well dry, I never seen these little devils until we struck out over the plains. I'll ask Rufus Ferguson to join our fire tomorrow night. He knowd a lot about them, he lived down Texas way a few years ago, said they was everywhere."

Rufus did add to what the Ross and Gallagher families were learning about these odd little devils that were called "dogs" but were really, to be more specific, ground-dwelling squirrels with a complex social structure.

"An old Indian told me down in the west part of Texas that them prairie dogs ain't kissing when they meet. That's the way they greet and identify each other. I don't know if that old man was telling me straight, but that's what he told me. Nother thing he told me, where you got these little dogs there's a good chance buffalo ain't too far away. The big critters love to hang around them towns."

"Are they good to eat?" Billy seemed to be the most curious one in the group. "They are the same size of the squirrels we hunted back in Missouri. My mother makes good squirrel pot-pie. Why not prairie dog pot-pie?"

"You kill one of those cute, little rascals, Billy Gallagher, and I'll never speak to you again!"

"What are you gonna tell the eagles, badgers, ferrets, and coyotes? They think them little things makes for pretty good eatin."

Peggy thought she had ended the discussion of prairie dogs that night, but Rufus couldn't resist a last comment.

"Miss Ross, I hope to God we never run out of buffalo for fresh meat. But might come a day when a roasted prairie dog will taste pretty durn good. A good night, you all."

⚒   ⚒   ⚒

It started out like any other morning, clear and bright with promise of a hot sun by noon. For the past twenty days the caravan had moved not in one long drawn out line, but in four lines – two lines of mule-powered wagons, two of ox-powered wagons – driven about a half mile apart. But the sighting of a small herd of buffalo changed everything almost immediately. Jim Peters spurred across all four lines shouting as he rode, "Two riders from each section, get your horses and ride to the rear."

Checking each man to see he had a long gun, Jim directed the men to form a single file spaced about twenty yards apart and begin to pace themselves with the herd and shoot as soon as they had a clear line of fire to a buffalo on the outer edge of the herd. Eight riders shot, six buffalo were downed. "Good work, men. Get to work while I bring the caravan into a circle."

That done, nobody need further instructions. The carcasses were skinned and quartered, the meat apportioned. Cooking fires were lit, and a feast began. The next day another small herd was encountered. It met a similar fate; this time five buffalo were reduced to piles of fresh meat.

"Get the meat sliced into thin strips."

"Why not stop and eat it now?"

"Didn't you get a gut full yesterday? We best look ahead to when the bison ain't going to be so obliging and cross our tracks. Hang those slices on a line and stretch it along the sun-side of your wagon."

"Then what'll we do? Feed it to the wolves? Seems like every time we sight buffalo there's always some of them damn plains wolves trailing along behind them. If it ain't wolves, it's them sneaking coyotes."

"Dried meat will keep. Tastes mighty good and gives those sides of bacon a rest. Ain't none of those blowflies to spoil it, but give them wolves a wide path. Never heard of any going after a man, but they are big and travel in packs and can sure scare the hell out of your horses. Keep your eyes open and your ass in the saddle."

Neither Eleanor nor Naomi needed to hear more of Jim's instructions. With flashing knives and deft hands, they had buffalo meat sliced thin. They put Grace and Peggy in charge of drying the meat. "As soon as I tell you the meat is dried, strip the line and hang another go of it. Naomi and I will be packing it away so it keeps."

That night as soon as the evening meal was finished, Eleanor showed the girls how to hang pieces of "hump" meat over the fire to preserve it with a smoke cure.

"Holy Hannah! You two picked up on this meat business like you was born to it."

"Of course," Grace said. "We're good at whatever we do."

"I'll bet you girls never gave thought to the idea the meat you're curin is done over a fire made with the shit of the critter that made the meat."

"Well, Pa. You don't have to eat it."

"I'll eat my share. Don't you fuss your head about that. I just thought you should know what you're doin."

Eleanor walked over to Jack, took him by the arm, and steered him to the back of their wagon. "Now you let those girls alone. They're working hard to put up the meat and they don't need your teasing. Charley's the one who needs your attention."

"Something happen today when I was riding patrol?"

"No. I was busy working with the meat. I don't think anything happened, but he just isn't himself the last couple of days."

"I'll take him for a walk around the circle. Most of the men like to see the little fellow, and he likes to banter with them."

Charley was sprawled in the wagon with Billy, who was trying to teach him how to make cat's paws with some twine.

"Hey, Charley, want to take a walk with me?"

"Can I ride on your shoulders? You walk and I'll ride."

"I guess we can do that. Hop on."

They made it round the whole circle of wagons. After these many days on the Trail there were still some teamsters who seldom spoke to anyone, and if they did it was often a slam or a threat. But with Charley it was different. He knew nearly all the men by their first name, and they certainly knew him. His smile, his open friendliness and the way he responded to the little things the men did to produce that special smile. He liked to watch them at "mumblety-peg" and never failed to be taken in by card tricks. By the time he and his daddy made the full circle, Jack had one sleepy boy in his arms and one relieved mother ready to tuck him into his bedroll.

The travel over this ocean of grass, even of travel over areas of sparse grass, was enjoyable on most days because of the absence of flies and mosquitoes. Everyone noticed each step to the west was a step away from the bothersome flying devils that made life so miserable for both man and beast in the country now lying far to the east. Late one morning as they neared the crossing of the Arkansas River, dark clouds gathered in the south, making angry sounds that warned that changing weather was headed their way. Never had they seen clouds tower so high and move over the land with such speed.

"Circle up, circle up!"

Jim Peter's command was obeyed immediately.

"Get all the stock inside the circle. Pronto! This blow is gonna be a buster. And nobody start a fire."

After unhitching the mule teams and turning them loose within the corral formed by the circled wagons, Duncan, Jack, Billy, Pres, and Dutch checked to see to the security of the canvas tops of the wagons. Not satisfied, Jack had them stretch additional ropes over the tops and tie these tightly to the wheels.

"Don't like the feel of this, Eleanor. I never seen clouds so big and black."

"You get in this wagon right now. You've done all you can."

Duncan gathered his family in the other wagon and ordered Pres and Dutch to join them. "We don't need any heroes. You boys get your tails in here. This looks like a bad one."

In less than an hour the caravan was tested by the worst storm any of them had ever experienced. Blinding torrents of rain driven by vicious winds rocked the wagons and threatened to overturn them. Rain changed to hail, hard and heavy ice rocks which pounded on the canvas tops in an ever-growing crescendo that defied description and put fear in the hearts of all. Talk inside the shelter of the Conestoga was impossible. With the hail came a sudden drop in temperature. Clothing that had been comfortable at the beginning of the day was woefully inadequate in the penetrating cold.

The Gallagher family took shelter in their wagon under the arching canvas of the Conestoga as they watched and listened to the storm. Would the top hold to its fastenings on the wagon bed? Would those extra ropes the men slung over it be of any help? Would the top be torn to tatters by the hail in this gale-force wind?

Eleanor's calming influence was felt by her children, especially Charley. With him in her arms she made a picture of comfort and safety that was shared by Grace and Billy. Jack's eyes were glued to the Osnaburg sheets – the rough, strong, plain-woven cotton cloth that formed the covering of the wagon.

He had followed the advice a Trail veteran had given him in St. Louis. "Was I you, Jack, I'd buy some woolen blankets and have a tent maker stitch them between pieces of the sheeting that'll cover your wagon."

"I might do that, but why?"

"Well, for one thing, they can keep your wagon warmer."

"We ain't makin our trek to Santa Fe in cold months. We're plannin on summer travel."

"You ever spend any nights in the high plains country? It can get damn cold, my friend. And if you get caught in one of them fast-as-lightning hail storms you'll freeze your ass in a minute."

"By cracky, that sounds like a good thing to do."

Jack had the canvas topping for both wagons doubled with blankets between. Now, he crouched at his place at the end of their wagon and let his eyes run over the cover as the rain and hail continued to pound it endlessly. Not only did he have the Osnaburg sheeting doubled, he had the cover made wider so that on either side it could be drawn down on the outside to the bottom of the wagon bed and secured there. In spite of their dangerous situation, he let a smile flicker over his lips as he saw the top was holding and the interior of the wagon was dry and maybe a tad warmer.

Naomi had taken Peggy with her to the front of their wagon and curled up with her arms around her daughter as she closed her eyes and softly sang a Mandan prayer of comfort. Pres and Dutch huddled at the other end and glanced at each other with questioning eyes. "Why did we ever leave St. Louis?" Dutch looked at his friend as he mouthed that very question and shrugged his shoulders in reply.

Duncan never took his eyes from Naomi as she moved her lips and swayed easily to the rhythm of her song. He sensed what she was singing; he didn't need to hear her. The roaring of the winds and the pelting rain and hail could not dispel the security he felt now in knowing he and Naomi were again in tune with each other.

The Ross family and the Gallagher family did what teamsters in the other forty-two wagons of the caravan did. They did nothing. All anyone could do was wait out the storm.

The storm moved on. Heads emerged from under canvas tops as men carefully climbed down onto a lake of white. Hail an inch or so deep covered the prairie in all directions. The circle of wagons was intact, but two had sustained damage. One had the tongue, coupling pole, and double tree smashed. The other had the feedbox, part of the top rail and back boards splintered. This was the place in the circle of wagons where frightened livestock had made their break from the improvised corral.

All the men clustered about Jim Peters as he organized teams of men to begin the roundup of their stock. Mules, oxen, horses fled in a wild stampede to escape the terror of the storm. They scattered to the north, a natural thing to do. The storm came at them from the south so their reaction was to turn tails into the wind and run with the storm.

"I can see some horses. Ease up to those critters. They'll be wild after the beating they took."

Billy was one of the first to leave the circle of wagons. He spotted what he thought was his horse. He walked toward it, talking all the while. It was Spook. After a few minutes of looking and listening, the horse decided this man on foot was his friend. Spook let Billy scratch his muzzle and run his hands over his back and flanks.

After his first attempt to mount, Billy found himself on the ground. The talking, the touching, the rubbing and scratching of familiar hands again worked their magic. On his second attempt, Spook let Billy mount. Riding bare-back holding on to Spook's mane, Billy guided him back to the corral.

Other men walked out to the area where Billy had found Spook and a few were able to lead their horses back to the wagons. Saddled, calmed, and fed a precious handful of grass gathered from under the wagon, Spook, with Billy aboard, led another team of men carrying halters to the place where they could get closer to clusters of horses and mules. The work went slowly but steadily. Mules, horses, and oxen responded to familiar voices and accepted the halters and the guiding hands of old friends as they allowed themselves to be led back to the circled wagons. With sufficient riders ready and mounted, Peters was able to organize a meaningful search.

"Jim, why only to the north? We best go looking in all directions."

"Keep to the north! Buffalo are the only animals that'll turn into the wind. Get moving."

While a part of the men rounded up the stock, others went to work on the damage to the two wagons. Peters felt much better than he had when he first emerged from his wagon after the storm.

"Men, we were lucky, damn lucky. We'll regroup in the morning and see what needs to be done to get full teams hitched to each wagon."

By nightfall the caravan counted its stock. They had lost eleven head of oxen, eight riding horses, and eight mules. As camp routines were resumed, the ring of cooking fires outside the circle of wagons emitted the aroma of coffee and frying bacon that was like a tonic. In spite of the mud everywhere and a sharp wind, spirits revived.

Drawn to familiar sounds and smells, that night five head of oxen, four mules and six horses were led inside the corral by the night watch.

"We was damn lucky," Pres said. "The off-side leader on my span was one of them that wandered in last night skitterish as hell," he continued, "but I'll touch her up a few times with my black snake and she'll feel right at home."

"How about our wagons, Jack? See any problems?"

"Nothin I can see. Any signs of trouble on your rig?"

"Nothing that I could see. Peters said that mouthy feller in the first section of ox wagons is shy a pair. You can't mix mules and oxen. How's he going to be able to keep up?"

"Don't rightly know. Said he try a hitch of six. He might get by 'til we get to the crossing of the Arkansas."

"He'll surely need help there. Then what?"

"I expect all of us is gonna double up, even triple up. They're telling me that there Arkansas can be a real bitch to cross."

It was. And more. Crossing the Arkansas took Jim Peters to the edge of his wits and the end of his temper as he got his outfit safely on the other side of a river that seemed to have a mind of its own.

When the caravan first sighted the Arkansas, it seemed to be just another crossing. The Trail didn't ford at just one place. For ten or twelve miles along the north bank there were signs of crossings. As many as five of them were clearly marked with shaped river banks on both sides. Nor was it hard to identify camp sites of previous caravans.

"This river will separate the men from the boys," Peters had told the group earlier. "She'll rise up three feet in the blink of an eye, and she can go near bone dry overnight."

"What's the secret, Jim? What do we do?"

"No secret, just work as one big team. Ain't no time for bickering. You do what I tell you when I tell you and we'll get the job done. One more thing, and this goes for every one of you wagon men. Soon as you're across, keep moving for at least a half a mile from the bank. Then unhitch in a circle. Takes a lot of space to move teams about, so get those wagons out of the way but ready for the night!"

Jim and his hand-picked crew of men on horseback rode along the north bank of the river looking for a place that seemed right for attempting the crossing. Jim and one or two of his men rode out into the stream to test depth, footing, and easy access on both sides. It took most of the day, but by late afternoon the caravan was camped for the night at the site selected for the crossing.

One of the section leaders asked, "We gonna make use of these few hours of light to start, Jim?"

"We'll wait for morning. Don't want some of the outfit on one side, the rest on the other and then have this river go cranky on us."

An hour before sun-up, activity started in the camp. Breakfast was basic and fast.

"Don't any of you men hitch to your wagon lest I say so. We'll be double and triple teaming all day, so get your teams geared up but not to the wagons. Section leaders, come to my wagon now!"

Organized and moving, members of the caravan watched as the count of wagons safely across to the south side slowly out-numbered the wagons on the north side. This was done at a cost, for repeated drags of teams and wagons over the same places on the river banks churned them into the slipperiest kind of mud where no animal could gain a footing. Peters called to the men on the south side of the river to get their shovels and mattocks and prepare a new place of exit. "Get to it, men, we are needin a new place right now! Move!"

That helped until four or five wagons with their double teams had made that new exit into a gumbo that had to be replaced by another and another. Mud became the universal curse of the crossing and the uniform of all men working the teams and wagons to the other side. It became hard to recognize one man from the other; mud, sweat, torn clothes, and lost clothing robbed people of their easy identification.

"I ain't seen Billy for an hour, Duncan. You seen him?"

"No, but I was told to help Pres and Dutch get their mules to the other side. I'll look for him there."

"Get each of them boys to hitch their mules to a double so's to make a triple hitch on a wagon. Ain't no sense to cross and not have them critters aidin two wagons."

Old Lady Luck drew a black ace from her deck of troubles about then and dealt it quickly. Halfway across, on what seemed an easy passage for a wagon pulled by twelve head of oxen, the snap of a broken axle brought fear to the minds of all and all activity to a halt.

"Dutch, get your mules off to the side so Ralph can get another eight head of oxen out to the lead span on that busted wagon."

Ralph Johnson, a normally quiet man, revealed a salty vocabulary and skills as a bullwacker that took everyone by surprise. He quickly had his team positioned, but not hooked. At great risk to themselves, several men dove among the thrashing, powerful legs of half-crazed oxen to hook the double tree of the hind pair to the lead chains of the damaged wagon. The linkage was completed and twenty-four head began to drag the Conestoga to the south shore.

The wagon did what Conestogas were designed to do. It floated. What should have been an advantage turned into a near disaster. Instead of all those powerful animals pulling the wagon in a straight line, they began to pull it sideways. Movement like this was not a part of the Conestoga design. On the south side of the river Pres and Dutch saw what was happening and immediately led their double hitch of mules upstream and got a line to the wagon bed. That ended the tendency of the wagon to float downstream and gave the bullwackers a chance to realign their oxen to get more of a straight-ahead pull.

As the damaged wagon was dragged up the bank, Peters directed it be parked off to one side. At the same time he called for Jack Gallagher. "You seem to know the most about these schooners. Look her over and tell me what you think. Can she be mended, or do we leave her here?"

The passage of the remaining wagons went along without any more incidents. Wiping the mud from his face and hands and rescuing his battered hat from the rushing river, Jack went right to work on the damaged wagon. With willing muscle and clever blocking with wood from whatever source he could find, Jack got the wagon up and off her wheels. This gave him access to the front bolster and the broken axle. The time spent at Council Grove paid off, for Jack took an axle he had roughly shaped at the

Grove and fitted it to the axle-tree, which was then pinned to the front bolster. Missing spokes of the front wheels were replaced. Other men helped to unload the damaged wagon and spread its contents out to dry.

By mid-morning of the next day the caravan, including the repaired wagon, was ready for word from Jim.

"What's the hold up? Why ain't we movin?"

"I haven't seen every wagon fill up water barrels. Every one of you gotta have everything that'll hold water filled to the brim."

"This seems to be green country. Why the worry?"

"We're just about to begin seventy or eighty miles of the driest country on the Trail. And the soft, sandy ground won't be easy for the teams. See to your water supplies now!"

Some men of the caravan ignored their personal discomfort to carry out Jim's command to fill everything with water; others took the time to leave Arkansas mud where it found them. "I ain't takin this damned mud to Santa Fe, Jim. Give me a minute to wash it off."

"Fine, but do it quick and then see to your water barrels. We've gotta get back on the Trail pronto."

The first day, after the Arkansas River crossing, drew to its close graced with a spectacular sunset. Everyone in the caravan was at the point of exhaustion. Jim roamed the circle of cooking fires with sharp words for anyone he saw wasting a drop of water. "Won't be another chance to fill your water barrel til we get to the North Fork of the Cimarron."

"How long will that be?"

"Can't say. This here soft ground we're going over slows the teams. We gotta save every drop. Oxen and mules can't do anything lest they have water."

The second day on this stretch of their route from the Arkansas was a repeat of the first – long, slow, and dusty dry under a sun that was merciless. A new worry emerged for the trekkers. There were no landmarks, nothing as far as the eye could see in any direction to give a sense of direction. The sun, which had to set in the west eventually, was their sole guide.

"I never thought things could get worse, Eleanor, but they have. How is the little one taking this heat?"

"Charley gets so tired I don't know what to do. He's gotten so he don't want to ride in the wagon, and he says he hurts when Billy gets him to ride on the horse with him."

"Where does he hurt?"

"Says his head hurts and his eyes."

"Why don't you try keeping a damp cloth on his eyes?"

Even a simple thing like a damp cloth was a test of their water discipline. The men came in from their patrol rides at the change of shifts looking like ghosts, but they knew a gourd of water dashed on the face was not possible. A sip or two was the limit.

Dust covered them everywhere; it was in their eyes, their noses, their ears, down their backs, in their boots – nothing escaped a universal dusting. But it was not just ordinary dust. This stuff had alkaline mixed in. It burned the eyes and noses of everyone, especially the teamsters. For them there was no escape. The teams had to keep moving, and those men were the only ones who could do that. Many took to holding small pebbles in their mouths to keep a little saliva going.

By the third sunrise the caravan set out with teams of oxen and mules laying back in the traces. The whips of the bullwackers and blacksnakers were like pistol shots in the dry, still air, but they had little effect. Even the colorful vocabularies of the drivers lost color and distinctiveness. Shouting was not attempted for all it produced was a mouthful of dust. Stopping was not an option. Nobody knew better than Jim Peters what danger awaited the caravan if it was allowed to stop.

"Keep 'em moving, men. You got no choice. Keep 'em moving!"

He alternated riding from section to section, encouraging and flaying out any driver who was not doing all he could to keep those thirty-two feet of his hitch laying them down one after the other. From the section lines he would ride forward to the advance patrol looking for signs of water. Not only was there a problem with no visible landmarks, there was the problem of imagined landmarks.

Mirages!

Every now and then a man would give a shout, raise his hand and point to the horizon, and ride off to find the spring or brook of precious water he was sure he had seen. It was one thing to be disappointed. It was quite another to be shamed in the eyes of fellow teamsters for grabbing at the honor of being the one to find water.

Water. Water. Water.

It could drive a man wild just thinking about it, but to be fooled with those shimmering ponds of sparkling, imagined water was torture. Pure torture.

This passage from the Arkansas to the Cimarron was by far the most demanding test of the caravan. But they made it. Best of all, clear, cold water flowed between the banks of the North Fork, not a river, but a small stream of flowing water.

"Hold up there, all of you!"

"Ain't no man in this here outfit can hold himself or his stock. We're needin water now."

"I hear you, but we have to do it right. Stock will water at least a half mile below our crossing, people above. You have to control your animals and yourself. You both can founder on too much water drunk too fast."

Not only was precious water in front of them, green grass was everywhere on both sides of the little stream. From the confusion of teams and people, Jim brought some sense of order and began the crossing. A circle was formed on a slight rise, and oxen, mules, and horses were corralled within the circle of wagons. That evening he called everyone together and found complete agreement; the next day would be one of rest and washing.

That evening, wanting to avoid the rush in the morning, Naomi and Eleanor gathered their families and set out for a place about a mile upstream from the camp. Taking turns guarding the bathers and assisting the little one, the Rosses and the Gallaghers cleansed bodies that were badly in need of a thorough scrubbing. They resumed their places in the camp feeling like new people. A drink of water, a bath, a change of cloths, the aroma of dried buffalo meat in the cook pot – for now they felt no one could possibly want more than this.

Basic things still had to be provided. Patrols were organized for the overnight stay, and small groups wandered the prairie always within sight of the camp to harvest buffalo chips for the evening cooking fires.

After all the necessary things had been attended to, the caravan could afford the luxury of thinking about the past eighty or ninety hours. And if a sense of pride, a sense of accomplishment crept into their conversations, well, it was earned.

"Tell us, Jim, do we face another stretch like this one we've just finished?"

"I don't know, and I'm not going to guess. But I think the worst is behind us."

And for the next six days Jim's idea that the "worst is behind us" held true. There was still some grazing for the stock, and water was not critical – but what they found was not always the best water. The alkali that had put the sting in the dust the past week had put a harsh taste in the water.

"I'm telling you men, keep them critters moving west and we're gonna strike water that comes from the high mountains."

"How soon, Jim, how soon?"

"Another day, maybe two, you should see a mountain they call Rabbit Ears."

"What does that mean?"

"Means we're on the right track, and it means the big mountains ain't too far ahead of us."

The experienced trail boss wasn't one to fool his men, but he felt it necessary to give them something to look forward to. Monotony had become a problem in the caravan. He had noticed a laxness in tending the stock and checking on the wagon gear. Some patrols did not extend out from the caravan as far as they should, and some riders cut their time short while on patrol. He thought in a few days he'd call a halt for a day of rest and refit to allow the men to rethink the group's safety and security.

The one person who frequently went far out while riding patrol was Billy Gallagher. He heard Jim's talk of big mountains not another month ahead of the caravan, but maybe only days. He kept pushing so he could be the first to say, "I seen em, they're big, bigger than anything I could imagine."

"Damn it, Billy, we're out far enough from the wagons. We kin see plenty of ground around."

"Come on, Pres, you been laying back ever since we started out on this patrol."

"None of the others're going out as far, ease up."

"Ain't what we're supposed to do. Wouldn't be a bad thing if we found some decent water. Last couple of days the water's been pretty gypy."

"Only place you're gonna find water might be at a spring over to the left, down in that little swale."

"Looks like there might be some sort of water. I see some small trees and maybe brush. Come on."

"Hell with it. I ain't ridin way over there. I'm headin back in."

"We got another two hours. We best keep on riding."

The two young men on patrol split. Pres turned his horse to take him on a wide, looping arc that would have him back with the caravan inside an hour. Billy turned off to the left and began a long, easy downward lope that would take him to what he thought were signs of water.

About the time Pres was back with the caravan, Billy was sitting on his horse looking at a seep of water that fed a stand of small trees, brush, and tall, reedy grass. He let Spook lap at the water, then rode around to the other side of the spring. He dismounted and knelt to get some water for himself. It was good water, sweet water, and not laced with alkali. He emptied his canteen of old, brackish stuff and refilled it with this really fine water. Gathering the reins, he led Spook to a level place on higher ground a few feet above the spring. His wandering survey of the area was stopped by a cluster of feathers tied to sticks and pushed into a swath of bare ground.

He began talking to himself. "What in blue blazes have I stumbled into? Must be some Indian thing. There's twenty or thirty of them sticks with feathers of all kinds and colors. Wait til I tell Peggy. Bet she's never seen anything like this."

Experienced riders know the importance of taking care of business before remounting. So Billy tied Spook to one of the small trees and walked to where he could look at those strange sticks, being careful not to step on any. Unbuttoning his britches, he let loose a stream. It was the last thing on this earth he would ever do. He never heard anything, never saw anything, but possibly he felt the whiz of the arrow that tore into his throat.

⚡ ⚡ ⚡

Duncan was more than happy to have Pres relieve him as "near wheeler" of the eight-head hitch of mules pulling the Ross wagon.

"You knocked off a little early from patrol. Any problems?"

"Naw, me and Billy come in about on time. I think he's drifted to the rear with the loose stock."

"Here's your blacksnake. Mule driving's not my favorite thing."

"You done alright, Mister Ross. They're going in a straight line and they're in step. Ain't much more a feller can do with em."

"You can do a helluva lot with them. Not everybody can get a hitch of mules to move the way you say when you say."

Duncan fell back to the side of the wagon to walk with Peggy. "Well, my dear, what has you looking so worried?"

"I didn't see Billy ride back with Pres when he came in from patrol."

"Pres thought he was with the loose stock."

"But he always lets me know when he's back."

"You two have become quite close on this never-ending trek."

"He's my best friend, and we always have a lot to talk about."

"The smell of something on the fire for supper will fetch him."

It didn't. Both families were used to Billy's hours and his activities, knowing that he frequently worked on his own schedule. But it was not like him to miss a meal.

"Pres, you were on patrol with Billy. Where were you two riding? How did you happen to split up?"

"Hell, Mr. Ross, you know Billy, he's got to stick his nose in every little thing. He thought he saw signs of water and rode off to have a look."

"You were told to always ride as a pair, weren't you?"

"I stayed on the high ground, he went trotting off to see if there was any water in the low ground."

"Did you wait for him?"

"No. I just started back thinking he was coming in behind me."

"I'm going to see Jim and get a search party together. You stay right here. You'll lead us to where you last saw him."

"I want to ride along."

"We got plenty of eyes riding out, Peggy. Best thing you can do is keep a fire going to give him a landmark. He's probably just lost. We'll have him back here soon."

It was after sundown when a dozen men set out with Pres in the lead. They started off in the general direction Pres said they had covered on patrol. The gnawing in his gut and the pressure of everyone in the group expecting him to lead them right to Billy brought on confusion that became panic in the total darkness of a night without a moon.

"I think we come too far. Let's bear off to the left and circle round to the higher ground."

They followed after Pres, but found no signs, heard no answers to shouts, nothing. After another half hour of riding on a different track, they paused, gave a shout, got no response. At this last stop the group was joined by the two men assigned to regular night patrol. Duncan said, "You two to continue on the usual circle of the wagons, but ride as easy as you can, stop often to listen. If you hear or see anything stay where you found it, shoot one round from your pistol and wait for us."

After another hour of fruitless search, they had another council. In a brief give and take among the group all decided the best thing to do was go back to the wagons and resume the search at first light. "Keep your horses saddled, just hobble them inside the circle. We may need to leave in a hurry."

Duncan tried to talk Jack into riding back with him. "I know how you feel, but the best thing is to wait for daylight. Come, I'll ride in with you."

"I still got ears. I can hear better'n I can see on a night like this. I'm stayin right here."

"Consider this, my friend. Pres got himself turned around several times. Suppose you stay here the rest of the night, but find it was the wrong spot? Come on, we riding in."

"Billy's out here somewhere. I ain't leavin."

"I'll saddle a fresh horse and lead him out to you at daybreak."

The next morning what greeted the caravan was the rising sun and a line of thirty Indians mounted in a straight line facing the wagons. They were armed but did not have painted faces or bodies, nor did their horses have any of the decorations of a war party. They held their place in silence, without movement, but ready for a signal from the lone rider who sat his horse twenty yards ahead of the line.

"Hold your fire. Don't anyone shoot! No shooting!" Jim Peters took charge. His commanding air gave a sense of order as half-dressed men struggled into pants and boots while seeing to their long guns or hand guns and checking on cartridges. Some men lay under the wagons to give them a clear field of fire, other gathered at openings of the circled wagons.

"Where's Genet? The man we call 'Frenchy'? I need him to talk to their head man. He knows their lingo."

Peters walked out from between two wagons with Philip Genet three paces behind. Jim raised his hand with palm out, the Indian leader did the same. In a low-pitched but loud voice the older man began to speak. Genet translated. "He say, 'His warrior only kill warriors, he not kill children.'"

"Ask him, 'Who did your warrior kill?'"

"He say, 'He kill boy who looks like man, rides like man, dress like man. Not know he kill boy.'"

"Ask him, 'Why did he kill boy?'"

"He say, 'He make his water over sacred place of our people.'"

"Ask him, 'Where is boy?'"

"He say, 'He with us. I bring him. You no shoot.'"

"Tell him, 'Bring boy, be no shooting.'"

As the line of Indian braves parted, two men led Spook to the old chief. Slung over the saddle like a sack of grain was Billy Gallagher. Angry voices and the cocking of guns were silenced by Duncan, who ran up and down the line of wagons shouting and shaking his fist, "Don't shoot. Any man who fires a gun will deal with me. Is that clear? No shooting."

At a signal from the chief, the men leading Billy's horse slipped from their mounts, took Billy in their arms, and slowly carried him to Jim. Laying him carefully on the ground, they walked back to their horses.

Without a word to anyone, Peggy stepped to the side of Jim, looked at the body of Billy, saw the ragged hole in his throat, saw those brown eyes closed forever. Not saying a word, she advanced another ten yards, then held out her hand to the chief. He gave no sign of recognition; she never changed her stance. Two, three, four minutes passed. The chief nodded ever so slightly and the two men holding Billy's horse let the reins drop to the ground. Peggy spoke, "Spook."

The horse gave a soft whinny, bobbed his head, and advanced two paces. Peggy stepped to meet him, gathered the reins, and with Spook following she stopped to look up at the chief mounted on his horse. He looked down at her, reached out his hand, and touched her on the shoulder. Peggy never took her eyes off the old man as he turned his horse slowly and rode to his line of warriors. They did the same, turned their horses, formed two lines, and followed after their leader.

All those backs presented a tempting target to men thinking only of avenging the death of their young friend. Duncan sensed the mood and again walked in front, not saying a word but letting his red hair, his face flushed with anger, and his clenched fists do his talking. Guns were lowered as hammers were eased down. The crisis had passed.

Peggy walked the few steps to Billy's body and looked down at her friend as Spook lowered his head, sniffed at Billy, then drew back and reared to break Peggy's grip on the reins. She held fast and calmed Spook enough to allow her to lead him to the Gallagher wagon, where she tied him to the hitching ring bolted to the back. She pulled aside the canvas at the rear of the wagon and threw herself inside on a pile of bedding.

To the cluster of men standing around Billy's body, Jim Peters asked, "Where's Jack?"

"He refused to come in last night when the group rode out with Pres to look for Billy." Duncan continued. "He's still out there. I said I would bring a fresh horse for him this morning."

"Don't you go riding out there alone. Ain't we had enough troubles with men riding alone? You stay here. I'll get a search party gathered up to fetch Jack."

The search party found him an hour later, way to the north, miles from the caravan and on the opposite side from where Pres had led them the previous night. Haggard, red-eyed from loss of sleep, and with a face creased with worry, Jack heard the group before he saw them. They rode to where he sat his horse. "Find anything? What's took you men so long?"

"Come along, we're riding back in. We got Billy."

"Good! How is he? I'll bet that boy's hungry enough to eat a whole buffalo by hisself."

If Jack was surprised when his rescue group rode to a bunch of men standing around and not to the make-shift corral of the circled wagons, he did not show it. Before anyone could prepare him for seeing the body on the ground, he sprang from the saddle. With two strides he was at side of his son. He reached out a shaking hand and gently stroked Billy's cheek, tousled his hair, and kissed him on his forehead. He got to his feet and asked, "Where's Eleanor?"

One of the men pointed to the silhouettes of the Gallagher family as they slowly walked on the prairie. They watched Jack join his family, they saw him take Charley in his arms, then put him on his shoulders as the family continued to walk.

Duncan brought a blanket, covered Billy's body, and stood there thinking about the steps that had to be taken, but not until Jack and Eleanor told them what they wanted done. Naomi waited for a little while, then slipped in beside Peggy, not saying a word, and took her daughter in her arms and held her close. Neither woman paid any attention to all the activity in the corral as horses were saddled and men made plans as to who would be on patrol, who would manage the mules and oxen as they were geared up. Mostly they speculated over how Billy got himself killed and what the Gallagher family would do about his burial.

Duncan, sticking his head in the back of the wagon, saw that Peggy was with the one person who understood fully what was most needed at this time of terrible tragedy. Unspoken messages flowed between Naomi and Duncan. He pulled the top covering of the wagon to close the opening and insure privacy for those locked in a comforting embrace.

When the Gallagher family returned to the circled wagons, they found some preparations underway. Pres and Dutch were hacking at the hard scrabble ground trying to dig a grave. Jack joined them and told Pres to give him the pick. "Gotta do this for my boy. You dun good work boys, but this here is my job."

After a few minutes of furious pick swinging, Jack straightened up and said, "This here ground ain't wantin to be busted into. Can't nobody dig deep enough, so I'll tell you what we're gonna do."

Jack told the men to fashion two *travois* with a buffalo hide stretched between the poles and hitch them to a mule. With a party of five or six men to each *travois*, Jack sent them on a rock-gathering detail across the prairie.

Eleanor came to the site and began to prepare Billy's body for burial. She refused all offers of help, even from Naomi, and singing softly to herself made Billy ready for his final trip to that other world she knew awaited him.

Duncan was not idle as he saw the essential steps were taken. He went from wagon to wagon and borrowed pieces of the back-up wagon repair wood slung under some of the Conestogas. This wood had come all the way from Council Grove. It was testimony to the good fortune of the caravan that so much of it remained unused. He gathered what was offered, returned to the site, and stacked the lumber into a crude altar. Eleanor told him that she had done for Billy all that could be done. The two of them lifted Billy's body onto the altar.

Without any visible signal to do so, the men clustered in small groups began to walk by to say their goodbyes to Billy. For most it was just moving lips that said words no one could hear. "He was a fine, young man." "He was a damn good horse man." "He's one to ride the long trail with." "I'll miss his smile, his easy way." And more.

Jack also made the rounds of the wagons until he found what he wanted: one piece of hardwood that he could fashion into a stake and another thinner board on which he could burn this memorial to his son. With a piece of iron heated in as hot a fire as he could manage, Jack wrote:

Billy Gallagher
1811-1829

Again the Gallaghers found solace in walking over the prairie. This time it was just Jack and Eleanor who ventured out. Here in the vastness of this land Eleanor's spirits could find her, to talk to her of the good life her son had lived and shared so generously with others. Her spirits reminded her of the life beyond death that waited for all mortals, reminded her of the meaning of the big mountains in Billy's mind. His vision of something he would never see on earth would be his reward in his new life. She and Jack exchanged a few words and returned to the burial site.

"Duncan, we want a word with you."

"What do you want?"

"I guess it's more something we don't want you to do."

"Whatever you say."

"Eleanor and me, we just want to put Billy in the ground. We don't want no kind of service. It wasn't his way of doin things. Billy just went and did what had to be done. That's what we want for him."

"I understand. I'll tell Jim what you have in mind. He's sort of planning something for the caravan."

"No. I'll leave it to you to explain what we want. Give us a few minutes with Grace and Charley and then we'll all go to Billy."

The two families met at the altar. Eleanor and Naomi sang a native chant as they sewed Billy's body into a shroud of rough canvas sacking. Jack and Duncan lifted his body and ever so gently laid it in the shallow depression in the hard ground. Jack took a shovel and sifted ground over the shrouded body of his son, then passed the shovel to Eleanor, who repeated her farewell. Grace and little Charley, who turned to Naomi for help in managing the shovel, did the same. Then Duncan and Naomi followed Jack's example and added their tribute to Billy as did Pres and Dutch. Last to take the shovel was Peggy. As she passed the shovel back to Jack after adding her token of ground, she knelt and took a rock from the pile brought to the site by the men working with the *travois*. She set it firmly in place, added three more, then fled from the scene. Other family members did as Peggy had done; they placed stones on the body and left to go to their wagons.

Jim Peters saw to the completion of the cairn that marked the burial of his young friend, the boy who became a man in such a short time. Satisfied that all who wished to do so had added their stones and that the grave marker that Jack had fashioned was securely anchored in the rock pile, he turned and called, "Catch up, catch up!"

Wagons resumed their unvarying line to the West.

Three riders separated from the caravan and pointed their horses in a southerly direction. It was Pres in the lead, followed by Peggy and Duncan. This time Pres was not confused; he rode directly to the spring with its little trees and reed grass. "This here's the place."

"Now, be good enough to hold our horses. Peggy and I are going to walk closer. I don't think we should make a lot of tracks here."

Father and daughter slowly walked the area. They did what they knew Billy had done – they took a drink of water from the spring. Then they walked to the slight rise of ground and saw the feathered sticks.

"Anything new and strange would catch Billy's eye. What do you think he said to himself when he saw these?" Duncan asked.

"I think he would say, 'Peggy should see this. She'd know how to capture this scene on paper.' And some day I will, I promise you, Billy, I will."

A cough from Pres standing with the horses made both Duncan and Peggy turn around. Not twenty feet away was an Indian brave dressed only in leather leggings, breech-cloth, and with an eagle feather in his hair. He was a fine looking young man who gestured to the decorated sticks. Not understanding his meaning, Duncan and Peggy stood still. He stepped to them and made signs for Peggy to join him. He waved his hand over the cluster and held up one finger. She stooped, selected one of the feathered sticks and showed it to him. He nodded, turned, and strode off.

The three rode back to rejoin the caravan.

The westerly direction the caravan had followed ever since passing Rabbit Ears Mountain two days ago now turned more southerly. The grass seemed a little greener and streams more frequent with the gypy taste of the water left behind. These positive signs were lost on a group of people still in shock over the death of Billy Gallagher.

Henry Willis, the man whose wagon Jack had repaired after the accident during the crossing of the Arkansas, became friendlier with him.

"Why you didn't call a bunch of us together and stage a raid on the Indians who killed your son?"

"What good would that do?"

"We might'a got the one that did Billy in."

"Maybe so. How many graves do you want to dig in one day?"

"Any man worth his salt would give his life to avenge Billy."

"I don't wanna hear no more talk like that!"

Shock appeared in the group in ways other than tough talk by vengeful men. It surfaced on a perfectly beautiful day as Peggy walked with her mother at the side of their wagon.

"What is wrong with me? I haven't shed a tear since Billy's death. Mother, why can't I cry like other people?"

"Most other people didn't know Billy the way you do. Even I don't know him as well as you do. My grief is not just for him, but for Eleanor and Jack and their children, but especially for you."

"I cried and cried when Thomas and John were killed the night the school was torched. I felt very close to them, and I cried for them."

"Billy is and always will be a very special person to you. His spirit knows of your love for him."

"What can his spirit know? I never told Billy that I loved him."

"You don't always have to say certain words for the other person to know what you feel for him. I think Billy knew what you felt, why you always wanted to be with him, wanted to share with him. He knew that."

"I want to cry. I want to cry for him."

"Someday that spirit will tell you it's time to shed tears, to let all the sorrow and anger you have kept to yourself find escape in your tears."

Though the conditions for travel had improved on the ground, every morning clouds piled up in a most threatening manner and by noon a cooling shower followed. By mid-afternoon there were only clear skies. This cycle of clouds and clearing broke on the morning that the sun rose in a clear sky and birds in all directions saluted the glorious dawn in song. The last mist of morning burned off and there they were. The mountains.

Etched sharply against the blue of the sky were those guardians of the West that had filled Billy's mind and heart mile after mile. Yes, there they were, all he imagined them to be. Tall, majestic, remote, yet so inviting. The snows that mantled the highest of them had melted in the summer's sun, but reappeared in the sweet water that refreshed the caravan as it slowly but steadily paced off the last one hundred miles of its journey.

Duncan watched as Peggy saddled Spook for the ride she usually took each morning after the caravan got underway. She seemed to prefer the north side of the group for this solitary ride. "Wouldn't you like somebody to ride with you? You know Jim's instructions that we never ride alone."

"I know. I don't go beyond the circuit of the patrol riders. I just want to be alone for a little while."

That answer was respected, but on this morning Duncan sensed a change in Peggy's routine. On most mornings when she reached a place far enough from the wagons that gave her the solitude she searched for, she matched her pace to that of the wagon train and rode parallel to it. This morning she stopped and sat unmoving in the saddle while she gentled Spook, who sensed the change from her usual routine. She sat, Spook stood, and together they worshiped the mountains, Billy's mountains. The tears came and they never stopped. Spook began to stomp and whinny as he showed his impatience to this rider who seemed not interested in giving him the accustomed morning workout. Duncan saw this and reasoned that Peggy needed to have someone with her. She had become too good a horseback rider to allow her mount to wander untended.

He eased his horse beside Spook, gathered the reins from Peggy's limp hands, and set a slow pace for both horses. He did not need to ask questions; her tears told the story. They must have ridden side-by-side for more than hour when Peggy looked at her father, managed a weak smile, and nodded at the wagon train, wiping tears from her cheeks.

Back with the caravan Duncan took over. He unsaddled Spook and turned him out with the loose stock that followed the wagons. He untied the flap that covered the back of their wagon and gave Peggy a boost into the Conestoga. He then rode out to the patrols to find Jack and take up station with his friend.

Naomi was another one who had observed Peggy's changed morning routine and wondered why Duncan had ridden with her for such a long time. She waited for a few minutes before going to their wagon. She called softly to Peggy and asked if she might join her.

"Billy's spirit visited you this morning, didn't it?"

"Yes. And I did what you said I would do."

"Do you feel better having cried for him?"

"I think so, but I miss him so much, Mother. I can't tell you how empty I feel without him around to tease and boss and laugh with me."

"Nobody will ever replace Billy. It is foolish to think so, Peggy."

"Well, there is something else I must tell you."

"And that is?"

"I think I am missing that time of the month."

"I know that, my dear."

"How can you know? I've told no one!"

"I too am a woman, remember? I read your signs."

"Signs! Mother, are you some sort of witch?"

"Did you and Grace not have a spat over who would make the biscuits two days ago? Did you not lay out Pres for being too quick with his whip on the mules? We women have a way of speaking without saying anything."

"I thought maybe it was because of all that has happened to us in the past month."

"Yes, my dear, that is probably the reason for your worry."

The whole caravan, not just section chiefs, was called to join Jim around his evening cooking fire.

"In another day, maybe two, we will be at a little village. It ain't much of a place, but we're likely to have some soldiers from Santa Fe meet us there and escort us into town."

"Why, what have we done wrong?" Ralph Johnson, the expert teamster who demonstrated his skill in managing a span of oxen at the crossing of the Arkansas, continued, "I ain't letting no damn soldiers near my outfit. I can manage without an escort."

"Did you forget that we are in a foreign country?"

"Hell, I ain't seen no change in the country. Where did we cross a border?"

"When you crossed the Arkansas River you entered Mexico. This here is their country, and you do what they say."

Johnson muttered to himself, yet loud enough for several men to hear, "What if I don't like a stranger messing in my wagon?"

"You smile and let him do what he wants. You resist, and you put the whole caravan in a bind. Maybe make it impossible for any wagon train that comes after us to get into Santa Fe."

"Hell of a way to greet people who come to trade in peace."

"I'm telling you this now. I don't like surprises any more than you. So do what they tell you. I'll bet there will be chances to give a gift or favor that makes our entry into town a little smoother. Get my meaning?"

Back at their own cooking fire, the two families began all at once to figure out all that Jim's talk to the group implied.

"We knew when we left St. Louis we'd have taxes to pay on our trade goods. But damn it, Duncan, I don't like this idea of havin an escort."

"I hear that some of the Mexican officials who will look us over, put a value on our goods, and say how much tax we pay like a little something to cross their palm."

"Maybe so, but I don't do business that way."

"That could be the only way we can get into their town." Pres was the more excited of the two mule drivers and didn't want anything to slow his chance to meet the *señoritas* he dreamed of.

"Don't look at me like that, Dutch. You talk about them gals as much as I do."

"I'm not sure I follow what you men are talking about."

Duncan was quick with his explanation. "Naomi, it's an old game and it's played everywhere. You help me, I help you."

"That sounds too easy. What's the real problem?"

Jack spoke up. "It's timin, Naomi. You gotta know when to spread a little grease. Just like a squeaking wheel on your wagon, that's the one you dab a gob of grease on."

"I don't think much of this game. How are you going to know which one to approach?"

"Chances are that man will let you know he's ready to do business. He'll have his own way of squeaking. He won't want you to grease the wrong axle."

The conversation among the Ross party was repeated at most of the cooking fires that night. But in the end, all came to the same conclusion.

"We'll have to wait to see what happens at this town."

"I heard it's called San Miguel del Vado."

"San whatever. There better not be no hold up. I want to see this Santa Fe place. I ain't tramped all these miles for nothing."

The caravan did not have long to wait. Two days after Jim's meeting they came upon San Miguel del Vado. There were no signs or sounds of greeting from the small crowd that gathered on the village square. Rather, they met a bunch of people who looked them over with some curiosity, but mostly with speculative eyes looking for the greenhorn. This small village of eight or nine hundred people had seen just about every caravan headed for Santa Fe over the past eight years. They were not impressed by this one.

About an hour before sundown, a small band of nine men rode into the village from the west. Now it was the turn of the caravan people to look them over. They, too, were not impressed. One man, obviously their leader, rode on a fine horse. It was outfitted with a saddle of top quality and its master had all the gestures and attitude of a man in command.

Underneath the coating of dust one could catch glimpses of a uniform, old, well-worn and frayed, but still denoting authority. Something was lacking. Eyeing the other eight riders provided few answers, for the image they presented was the exact opposite of their leader. Common horses carrying worn out, shabby saddles with indifferent, shabby riders. Could this be their escort into Santa Fe?

The leader barked an order to his troop and they formed into single file and rode around the circle of wagons looking, occasionally grinning to each other, but saying nothing. The next command to his troopers was to follow him into the village where they disappeared one by one into a variety of small, mud huts. Word was sent to Jim Peters by a ragged street urchin: "You will form all of your wagons in a single file one hour after sunup prepared to begin the trek to Santa Fe. No wagon may remain in this village." The order was signed by José Archuleta, Commanding Officer.

Commanding what? This handful of miserable looking men would be the caravan's escort into the fabulous city of Santa Fe? Into the city of their dreams? The city where they would make fortunes from the sale of the merchandise carried in nearly every wagon? To the city of storied *fandangos* where beautiful *señoritas* would be waiting to dance with handsome *Americanos*?

Surely the caravan would meet with a real escort. This ragtag troop of clowns would be replaced by mounted men in splendid uniforms on spirited horses and they would be presented to *el Jefe* in style befitting the occasion.

Word quickly spread among the wagoneers that this indeed was their escort and that its task was to prevent the smuggling of goods into Santa Fe that had not first passed through the customs house. More hints of their escort came from Jim Peters. "You men be easy on this bunch sent out to escort us into town. Chances are these men get little pay, and chances are even greater that they have not been paid in a long time. Might be a good thing to ask them to share from your cooking pot tonight.

"Just keep your eyes open and your stuff in the wagons. They think if you leave an axe or lengths of rope lying around you don't need them. Such things become theirs."

The morning following their entrance into San Miguel found the Peters' wagon train lined up ready to precede on the last leg of their long journey, but no sign of the escort. The little, round man who command-ed the bedraggled troop was nowhere to be seen. The sun was more than up; it was well overhead and hot! It was a contest between the men of the caravan and the sun as to which was the hotter.

Jim ordered the men to unhitch, turn the stock out to pasture, and find places with shade, leaving guards to watch over the wagons as well as the stock. They found that watering the stock was easy to do. A fast run-ning stream of clear, cold water coursed through the village.

Peters approached several of the local people to ask where José Archuleta might be found. He received a shrug of the shoulders, a blank stare, a rolling of the eyes, but nothing helpful. Nobody seemed to know anything.

"Jim, what's keeping us from striking out on our own? If we get mov-ing maybe that bunch of misfits will catch up to us. Let's make them play our game."

"I hear you, and I'm just as pissed as you. But I can promise you that you'll never sell a single item in your wagons that doesn't go through their customs station."

"What the hell are we gonna do?"

"We'll wait. That's the only thing we can do."

Several women appeared on the main square of the village with nap-kins filled with rolled pastries of some sort. Gestures of offering and shy smiles were clues that a trade might be made. But for what? Duncan pulled a small coin from his britches pocket and showed it. A shake of the head in refusal. He produced another coin and matched it with the first. A smile, and Duncan had a warm, somewhat fragrant something in his hand.

It looked inviting, if one forgot the not too clean napkin that had been its home, and it did smell tempting. Grace and Peggy were at his side and offered to taste it for him. "Let us have it. If we think it is tasty, then you can buy another for yourself."

About that time Jim Peters saw the transaction Duncan made and the deal the girls were trying to make. "I'll take that off your hands. I know what it is."

"Not so fast, my friend, if it's good enough for you, it's good enough for me or the girls. But what the hell is it?"

"Well, *gringo*, it's called a *tortilla y frijoles.*"

"Jim, you're testing my patience. What is a *gringo* and what is a *tortilla y frijoles*?"

"Get used to being called *gringo*, for that's what you are. A foreigner. And many things can end up in this thing, but usually it's made from a thin, baked flour piece wrapped around beans."

Within the hour nearly everyone in the caravan had a *tortilla y frijoles* in hand and a satisfied smile on his face. They were good, but as comments flew around the circle of men about this introduction to local cooking, a growing ripple of anger began to surface.

"Christ, but I hate to be taken for a ride."

"How's that, Philip?"

"Why, them troopers that we're waiting for dun this on purpose."

"Why so? What do they do? Make these things on the side?"

"No, you dumb bastard! They lay up overnight with the locals and make us wait until the women can make a batch to sell to us. I bet they do this to every caravan that comes through this miserable little village."

It was well into the afternoon when José Archuleta made his appearance at the wagons. "My apologies, *Señor*. My duties consumed the morning, for I am a man who follows orders given to him. Get your wagon train prepared to move out in thirty minutes. Those are my orders to you."

Grumbling, choice descriptions of the commander of the escort, and speculations as to why they were ordered to get on the Trail when the day was nearly over mingled with the hooking and hitching of the teams.

Formed in a single line with outriders in close to the wagons – there was no way to spread the patrol miles from the caravan – they moved out.

The country was broken and wooded with trees. Not the towering pines or the full branches of hardwoods familiar to the *gringos*, but short evergreens. As they resumed their westward trek, word passed up and down the line that these were *piñons* and junipers. The pleasant aroma that hung over San Miguel last night came from the *piñon* that had fueled the fireplaces and *hornos* of the locals.

Duncan many days ago had learned not to be amazed at how quickly news, warnings, rumors, and jokes passed along the line of the wagons. In the space of ten hours he learned some of the local names for things, the local ways of doing business, and a different meaning of time and received a rather satisfying taste of the culture.

Was this a repeat of Duncan's experience in Montreal when, fresh from the Highlands of Scotland, he stepped off the "Virginia Planter" in Montreal? Then it had plunged him into the mysteries of French language and French customs. Now it was his introduction to the same, only in Spanish.

Jim Peters and José Archuleta rode side-by-side talking, with many gestures and much arm waving, for over an hour once the caravan got underway. After a few more plodding miles, all heard the call, "Circle up, circle up!"

"Why? We ain't gone more than ten or twelve miles. We got more daylight, let's keep moving."

"We make a night of it here. That's what our escort said we had to do, so get cracking."

That first night after leaving San Miguel del Vado the camp was in sight of what had been a large church at one time. And close by was another large building of several stories stacked one above the other. People at one time lived in this structure. Jim Peters called it a *pueblo*.

The next day was somewhat of an uphill slog. It wasn't steep, but a steady rise had teams of both mules and oxen blowing hard. It took frequent rests to gain the rise. Once there, it was downhill through a twisting, time-consuming pass [Glorieta Pass] to the plain that stretched across the valley floor. The Trail from San Miguel del Vado was a single path with no chance to spread the caravan into four separate sections on paths of their own choosing. The single line forced the caravan to a much slower pace. It was early evening when Jim Peters' call to "circle up, circle up" could be carried out.

"This here's our last night on the Trail. Tomorrow morning our escort will lead us into town, and I suspect you *bucaneros* will want to 'rub up' to impress the women folk. Keep in mind what I told you about being easy on the officials who will be assessing the value of your goods."

As they rode the few miles from the pass in the mountain to the evening camp site, the escort's commander, José Archuleta, found excuses to ride beside Naomi. She told Duncan that morning that if this was their last day on the Trail, she wished to ride, not walk, into Santa Fe.

"*Señor* Archuleta has a wife waiting for him in Santa Fe? Yes?"

"No, my dear lady, there is no *Señora* Archuleta. Perhaps I have a *señorita* who will welcome me, perhaps not."

Both José and Naomi put all their skills of using English and Spanish words to carry on their conversation

"Now, *Señor* Archuleta, do you think I do not know how the women of Santa Fe will be looking for our handsome escort commander? Would it not be wise to have a little something for the special one who waits for him?"

"Alas, my lady, I am worked so hard and have so little time that I do not possess such a gift."

Naomi turned her horse a few feet away from the gaze of José Archuleta and unbuttoned her blouse. She extracted a neatly folded square of fancy material rich in color and design, redid the buttons, and presented it to the commander. "This is a little something you may want to give to your lady. I apologize that it cannot be a finer gift, but I want you to have this."

"*Gracias, gracias,* dear lady. You are too kind to this servant of *el Gobernador.* I shall remember you in my prayers, *Señora* Ross."

To herself Naomi thought, "I would much rather you remember us at the customs house, and I would much prefer to give you a cake of strong soap." And to herself she added, "Don't be too harsh in judging this little man. You gave him a gift, now get on with your own preparations for the entrance into Santa Fe."

It was only natural that the Ross and Gallagher families gather around their cook fire for the last night on the Trail.

"Jack, you have been faithful to your 'knickin stick.' How many days have we spent on this Trail since leaving St. Louis?"

"I added up just this morning and I say this is our sixty-eighth. Now I might have missed a knick, but I'm sure of my count."

"Would you be ready to turn around and start back to Missouri next week?"

"That's a hell of a question to ask. Give us all a chance to sample what Santa Fe has to offer. What I'm looking down on right now ain't too exciting, if that is Santa Fe."

Their evening's camp was on a small ridge that looked over a wide sweeping plain and to the village of Santa Fe. Aside from the twin towers of a church, what they saw was a cluster of mud huts seeping out haphazardly in all directions from a square that had the church on one side and nothing else of size or importance.

Perhaps Jim was mistaken. Perhaps they had yet another day on the Trail before they would see the real Santa Fe.

HARD GOLD

La Tules de Santa Fe

I

She swoops
As she gambles,
Red ruffled skirt
Flashing high.
Scarlet lips frame
a smile of ferocity.
Dark eyes and fingers
snap orders,
survey the cards,
amuse patrons who
intrigued with her
not-quite-niceness,
search pockets
for more silver,
gulp their whiskey,
deal again.
Young man's descent
into the "hall of ruin"
deliciously easy,
part of the game.

II

She swoops
even in private,
glides in silk gowns,
reboso flowing green and gold
like the mountain's brief spring.
Slim fingers dole
gifts and favors
with a light caress.
Behind dark eyes that charm
she watches, calculates.
Stifles stray twinges, thoughts
of babies on the hearth
a man considerate and strong.
Stretches a smile
over gritted teeth,
totes up the scores
of services rendered,
payments due.

This poem, by Patricia Wellingham-Jones of Tehama, California was created expressly for *Hard Gold*. *Muy gracias,* Pat, *muy gracias.*

HARD GOLD

"Come on. Our mothers are waiting for us."

"I'm tired, Grace. I don't want to walk to that dumb, old plaza. I'll stay and play with Charley; you go ahead without me."

"Charley's with Daddy. You can't stay here alone."

"Well, give me a minute to brush my hair."

The female representatives of the Ross and Gallagher families made their way down the narrow, dusty road from their campsite to the town square. Ever since the arrival of the wagon train a week ago, they still had lacked a permanent place. Their wagons had cleared the customs house, and their merchandise had been deposited with shopkeepers on the south and west sides of the Plaza, but that was the end of their Trail adventure.

Finding houses to rent or to buy was yet another adventure for which the Rosses and Gallaghers had neither preparations nor plans. In fact, they hardly knew where to begin. Language was a problem, of course, but that was anticipated. Their attempts at the local mixture of Spanish and some Indian phrases met with encouragement and friendly smiles. Inquiries about permanent quarters were returned by glazed eyes and gestures that said, "*Perdone*, I cannot help you, I have no knowledge of such houses."

This morning's stroll to the Plaza was mainly to buy food. At the west end of the portal at the Palace of the Governors a cluster of vendors displayed their wares in baskets or on blankets. Naomi always looked for fresh greens. Eleanor sought fresh breads, *tortillas*, beans, and items to stretch the fast dwindling store of food that had sustained them on the Trail. Peggy and Grace were drawn to foods already made, *tortillas y frijoles, tamales,* or *tortilla y frijoles con chili.* Those items relieved them of cooking chores back at the campsite. Charley was both excited by the Plaza activities and a bit terrified. He found security in holding on to his mother's skirt.

Once their wagon train had cleared the customs house, the wagoneers had begun to drift off in many separate directions. The sense of group solidarity and security that defined each of the sixty-eight days on the Trail vanished. Every day on the Trail had meant for each member activity with a purpose. Here in Santa Fe activity was a monopoly exercised by the elders, Duncan and Naomi, Jack and Eleanor, as they cast about to find some sort of housing.

Dutch and Pres continued to make their home with the two families who hired them to help on the trek to Santa Fe. Each morning after helping Jack with the mules and horses they disappeared for the day and sometimes late into the evening. Both Jack and Duncan told these two young men to always stay together as they explored the town.

The grand idea of the two mule skinners to latch on to an expedition heading for California had short life. Everywhere Pres and Dutch looked, everyone they asked, all had a similar answer. "Too risky," they were told, "Indians whether Apaches, Comanches, or Navajos, make travel away from towns along the Rio Grande valley unsafe." Raids and ambushes were too real, the losses of life unacceptable. Only under military escort could major travel be planned. The appeal of California remained with the boys, but the costs and the odds of getting there were too high.

Duncan and Jack was another pair who had their dreams dashed on the hard rocks of reality. The weary, time-consuming checking of their merchandise and transcribing of lists of goods from English to Spanish by translators put another drain on resources. The translators made no secret of their expectation of a *gratificacion.* It seemed everywhere Duncan or Jack turned there was an outstretched hand and a demanding eye that retreated only after a gift or a coin found new ownership.

Then there was the problem of locating a place around the Plaza to display their goods for sale to the local population. This was not as difficult as the clearing of the customs officials. Duncan had selected their stock of merchandise with care and the practiced eye of an experienced trader and it carried the unmistakable mark of quality. Shopkeepers around the square quickly learned that the tall, rugged, redhead was a man who knew how to deal and who had goods that were worthy of the prices he set on his goods. All of this required more paperwork, more translations, and more trust on the part of both parties to close a deal.

Jack took the lead in profitably disposing of their string of mules and horses. He planned on keeping Billy's horse, Spook, and two of the larger riding horses he and Duncan bought in St. Louis. The rest found willing buyers, but not always with money in their pockets. Men of Santa Fe were equally good judges of horses and mules, and a bond of mutual respect based on that was quickly established.

It was the search for housing that became the biggest source of frustration and deep concern. More than two months of pain, suffering, and the monotony of day after day over the Trail to Santa Fe were to end in a mud hut? This was their reward, the fulfillment of their dreams? A one-story, flat-roofed mud hut! Something was wrong here, very wrong.

"Dunc, we have to do something! We can't camp out in these two wagons much longer. We'll be at each other's throat. Maybe we should try to buy back our mules and sign on with the first caravan heading back East."

"Don't be so gloomy, Naomi. Surely some of our asking about a house will get noticed."

"I think we are not asking the right people."

"You may be right about that, Eleanor, but whom haven't we asked?"

"Where have you seen the most money change hands in this town? Just like bees are drawn to honey, let ourselves be drawn to money and see what happens."

"I like your logic. Just where is this money you're talking about?" Naomi joined in the conversation and added, "When I go to the Plaza to buy a little food all I see are poor people trying to make a few *reales*. I don't think they can help us."

"Damn! Eleanor's right and I know where to go."

"And where will that be, Dunc?"

"Remember the third night we were in this town and we heard music drifting up from the Plaza?"

"Yes, and I remember what we did. We strolled down to find a large room with the doors open and music pouring out. What makes you think we will find money in a place full of dancers?"

"And didn't we dance a round or two? And didn't I slip a few coins into a box on the floor beside the man who scraped away on his fiddle?"

"Yes. But where did you see a lot of money? All I saw was some of the men from our caravan dancing with women who had paint on their faces and not enough clothing to cover their bodies."

"Behind the room where we danced there was another room with tables where men played card games with stacks of coins on the table."

"And you're going to walk up to some stranger and ask him to sell you a house just because he has money to gamble?"

"At this point, I'll do anything that will get all of us a place we can call our own."

"Good. Tomorrow morning you just march yourself downtown to that gambling hall and make a deal!"

"Not so fast, my dear. I'll bet that place will be empty until dark."

"But remember, you're going to do business, not to gamble our few remaining coins on the luck of the draw."

The next day it was Naomi and Peggy who decided to go to the Plaza to buy a little food for their evening meal. As they strolled from vendor to vendor they drew attention from nearly everyone doing business in and about this long, low Governor's Palace with its portal extending the full length of the building. The two women made a handsome pair: Naomi tall, slender, and graceful; Peggy not quite as tall but with a certain grace and a winning smile.

Their presence in the Plaza had not escaped the eye of José Archuleta. With a low bow, hat in hand, he said, "*Buenas tardes, Señora et Señorita.* How may José Archuleta be of service?"

"*Señor* Archuleta, how nice to see you. Have you been well?" Naomi asked.

"Exceedingly so, my lady, and you?"

"Thank you for asking. Yes we have been well, but are dismayed that we have not been able to acquire suitable, permanent housing. Perhaps, *Señor* Archuleta, you hold the answer to our problem in your hands. You are such an important man in Santa Fe that I hesitate to ask of your time, but could you help us?"

"But of course, I would be most pleased to assist in resolving your problem. Would it be possible for you and *Señor* Ross to meet with me here at the Governor's Palace tomorrow evening at say an hour before dusk?"

"*Si, Señor.* We shall await you here at the appointed time."

On the way back to their campsite Peggy was close to the bursting point over asking her mother question after question.

"I know that little man was the officer in charge of the soldiers who escorted us into Santa Fe, but why was he so attentive to you? He acted like you two were old friends. Are you?"

"He was a squeaking wheel on the way from San Miguel del Vado to Santa Fe. I applied a little grease. And, my dear, I suspect José Archuleta can speak more English than he would like us to think."

"Oh, Mother, you are as bad as Papa Dunc! Tell me, why was he so nice to you?"

"Peggy! It's because I am such a nice person. That should be easy for you to figure out."

"I was going to tell you something important, but now I won't."

"Perhaps you don't have to tell me. You have missed that time of the month again, haven't you?"

"Yes, I have. How did you know?"

"I am your mother. Does that not tell you why I know?"

"I guess so."

"Now, about José Archuleta. I followed your father's advice and gave him a gift as we rode the last few miles into Santa Fe. It was a beautifully stitched fancy handkerchief done in vivid colors. It was among the items we brought along to trade."

"Why give such an expensive gift to a not very clean, little, fat man?"

"Because I felt he wanted to help our group get by the customs officials as easily as possible. For his help he would expect a little something in return. I just gave him a payment in advance."

"Was he really helpful? It seemed to take us forever to get by those men who went through our things in the wagons."

"But they were not as thorough with us as they were with some other wagons. Yes, I think he helped us."

"But why do you think he will help us again? Finding a house is a lot different than looking through a wagonload of trade goods."

"It isn't what he will do, Peggy. It is who he knows. That's what may help us."

The next day was a busy one for both families. Jack made contacts among local men as he made deals over the horses and mules. Two of the locals came looking for Jack and asked him if he was also interested in selling the two Conestoga wagons.

"*Señor* Gallegos, we have come to examine the wagons that are to be sold. Are we talking to the right man?"

"Yes. The name is Gallagher, but I ain't sure we're gonna sell these here wagons."

"*Perdone usted, Señor.* I have not ease with foreign names. But it was my understanding these wagons were to be sold."

"You understand correctly, but we ain't had no luck findin a place to live in your town. We might have to turn them Conestogas around and go back where we came from. I heard there's an outfit gettin together to make the trek in another month."

"That would be most unfortunate for you and your families. Perhaps we can help solve your problem. You will remember us, *Señor*, and our interest in buying these wagons. Like you *gringos* say, you scratch my fleas, and I'll give you mine."

"Sure, that's what we say, more or less. You men see what you might turn up in the way of a house for us. I ain't sellin nothin 'til I hear from you."

Around the cooking fire that evening the two families began to examine what the day had produced in the way of a solution to their big problem – getting settled in permanent housing.

"I just told two would-be buyers of our Conestogas they ain't for sale 'til we have something real to move into."

Duncan asked, "What's this about a caravan forming up to make the return trip?"

"That's what I'm hearing, and I'm also hearing that Jim Peters is gonna be the wagon train boss. Only a few wagons, mostly a big drive of mules and sheep."

"Well, don't get your hopes up about this, but Dunc and I are to meet the commander of the escort that led us from San Miguel del Vado to Santa Fe."

"Him! What does that shopworn misfit know?"

"I think he knows everybody in this town who might have some money, and they all know him, Jack. That's how he keeps himself alive and well fed. He knows every one's business, and he trades on that knowledge."

"I wish you good luck, but be careful, damn careful!"

Duncan and Naomi took their time in walking down to the Plaza on a lovely evening. They had learned very quickly in their short time in this mountain village that when the sun went down behind the western hills the temperature sank with it. They made no attempt to dress up for the occasion, for they really had no dress clothes to put on. They made themselves as clean and neat as possible and set off with confidence. They had little else to put on but confidence.

As they walked under the portico of the Palace of the Governors there were only one or two vendors still at their stalls. A few other people strolled about the Plaza.

"Perhaps José forgot about his promise to meet us. I see no sign of him. What shall we do?"

"I think we should look calm and unconcerned. I have the feeling he is watching us to see if we show any sign of anxiety. Take my arm and let us cross the street, walk slowly and look straight ahead."

A full turn about the Plaza produced no José. "Now what do we do?"

"Take another turn. We can play his game, we've no choice."

They started to do another turn about the Plaza and nearly bumped into their man. "A thousand pardons, *mi amigos*. My business with *el Gobernador* required more time than expected. Follow me, *por favor*. We have someone to meet who can be of great assistance, if she so desires."

"If she so desires." Duncan turned that phrase over and over in his mind. What did this man have in store for them?

They traveled a few steps down San Francisco Street and into the building Duncan and Naomi recognized as the place where they recently danced. No dancers were in sight, just a *peon* sweeping the dirt floor and sprinkling clean sand over it. José marched straight to the back room where again there was no sign of activity and not much light. He tapped on a door in the far corner of the room. It was opened an inch or two and José said quietly, "It is I, José Archuleta. *La Doña* Tules is expecting me at this hour."

"Bid him enter, Santiago."

They were ushered into a well-lit room sparsely, yet elegantly furnished and were greeted by a woman whose glamorous style stopped Duncan and Naomi in their tracks. José stammered, "*La Doña* Gertrudes Barcelo, may I present *Señor et Señora* Ross. They are newly arrived from the East and wish to have a minute of your time to make you aware of a problem of great importance to them."

"*Gracias*, José. Santiago, will you not take José into the other room and have him taste the new wine we have acquired? We would appreciate his opinion as to the value of this purchase. I know him to be an excellent judge of wines.

"Please to seat yourselves. Our humble *sala* is indeed graced by your presence. May I offer you refreshment?"

"You are most kind. I know you are a woman of many talents and a woman upon whom many demands are made. May I be direct and tell you of our problem?"

"Please, Señor. I appreciate a man who can come to the point without first making a fancy dance about his mission. How may I help?"

Naomi took over the response. "We have come over the Santa Fe Trail after an exhausting trek. We came here to resettle. Unlike many wagoneers who will return to the East, we plan to make Santa Fe our home."

"You are very brave and I am sure you and your husband will add much of interest to our modest village. But what is it you need?"

"A house, a place we can call a home. It seems to us a reasonable thing to seek, but we have had no success in our search." Duncan went on, "I shall continue with my directness. We came to you because you are a woman of wealth and influence who must surely know what might be available for purchase, if not purchase, perhaps to rent or lease."

"Yes, I have met with some success in dealing cards, but you certainly know, Señor, one loses as well as one wins. No?"

"What I see, *Doña* Tules, tells me of the latter not the former. Yes?"

"*Bueno, mi amigo, bueno.* Tell me, what are your needs in a house? You have family, servants, and horses?"

Again Naomi spoke. "We have but one child of seventeen years. We have acquired no servants, and have but three horses."

"Not possible! You two cannot have a child of that many years. You both look as fresh as a pair of colts. How is that possible?"

"You are too kind, *Dona* Gertrudes. It is true, we have such a family."

"You must bring him around so I may meet this young man."

"We should be happy to do that, but we have a daughter, not a son."

Gertrudes got to her feet and paced around the room. Naomi

thought to herself, "This woman is a practiced, calculating vixen, and my husband is her target. Well, when the game reaches a certain point I will know how to play my cards, and *Doña* Gertrudes, I do hold some aces!"

What they watched was a woman of medium height, with an eye-stopping figure encased in a dark green taffeta skirt and a reboso of green and soft yellow stripes. Was it the magenta red hair pulled back and held in a knot with jewel-studded combs or the seductive, dark grey eyes that held Duncan's interest? Perhaps both. Naomi was equally entranced. *La Doña* Tules was not a woman easily dismissed from one's mind and certainly not one to underestimate. Naomi was sure this woman knew where she was going with this parade about the room staged for Duncan's benefit, and she hoped it would lead to a solution of their problem.

"I must speak frankly. In this town we welcome the *gringos* who come to us each year over the Trail. We also harbor suspicions of those who come to say they wish to live among us, for we have been harmed, deeply hurt in fact, by some of them. I myself experienced the cold reception given to 'outsiders.' I am in sympathy with your situation. I wish to help, but I must plead the need of time. I shall make inquiries, assess the potential for a satisfactory deal, and get word to you. More than that, I cannot do. But do not despair, I have contacts in this town. *Buenas noches, mi amigos.*"

The ever-present Santiago was there to escort them through the card room, through the dance hall, and out to the street. Both Duncan and Naomi were relieved to find that José Archuleta was not there to join them.

"What an interesting woman, Dunc, would you not agree?"

"Interesting is not the word, my dear. Dangerous might be a better way to describe her."

"But do you think she will really help?"

"I would like to think so, but at what price?"

"Duncan Ross! Why do you think she will put a price on helping us? Have you put a price on everything you have done to help people?"

"Don't misunderstand me. I think we just met a hard woman who has been treated harshly in the past and has learned to protect herself. Pricing a favor is one way of achieving such protection."

§   §   §

Grace and Peggy were helping Eleanor with a tub of clothing to wash and peg out to dry. "That boy has been watching us for five minutes, Grace. Do you know him?"

"Never saw him before, but he is kind of cute, isn't he?"

"If you think so then why don't you ask him what he wants?"

"No, you ask him."

Eleanor ended their curiosity. She walked over to the boy, probably about fifteen years old, and asked him if he was hungry. He stood and dug his bare feet into the sandy ground and shuffled them about as he shyly took a folded slip of paper from inside his shirt. He handed it Eleanor and turned and ran down the hill, but not until he had sneaked another glimpse of the girls.

"Here, you both read this."

> *Señor Duncan Ross*
> *It would please me to have you and your*
> *wife join me for refreshment this afternoon*
> *about the time the sun is at IV on the dial.*
> *We may have things of interest to discuss.*
>
> *Gertrudes Barcelo*

"Run and see if you can find your Aunt Naomi. Tell her she has a note from that gambling house lady"

"But it was addressed to Uncle Duncan."

"He's off somewhere with your daddy. Find Naomi."

They finally found Naomi trudging up the hill with a sack of onions and those new green things she called "chili." They showed her the note; she read it as quickly as she could and gave each of the girls a big hug.

"Does this mean we have a house, Aunt Naomi?"

"I don't know. Our new friend wouldn't bother to send a messenger all the way up to this ridge if it weren't about a house."

Again brushing of dust from clothes, brushing of hair, washing of face and hands and arms, and then fitting the invisible cloak of confidence about her slender figure. Naomi wondered, "Where is that man of mine? We can't miss a meeting with Tules. If he isn't here by III on the dial, I shall go to her by myself."

He wasn't, and she did. Naomi neither rushed down the trail to the Plaza nor did she let her steps lag. She walked across the Plaza with her head up, a faint smile on her lips, and determination in her eyes. A knock at the door of the dance hall was answered immediately by the wiry, dark haired, dark-eyed man who ushered her into the back room and announced, "*Señora* Ross. She informs me that *Señor* Ross will not attend this afternoon."

"Very well, Santiago. That is all."

The two women stood facing each other with waves of hostility emanating like heat from cook stoves. After a long two or three minutes Naomi broke the spell with a big smile. "Well now, Gertrudes, I think we are women who understand each other. We have no need of testing and we have nothing to prove. Shall we be open and honest as we pursue what it is you have to tell me?"

"Naomi, I know I am going to like you and trust you. I seldom feel this way about other people, man or woman, as I do about you. I hope the absence of *Señor* Ross does not mean some ill has befallen him."

"My husband is tending to important business at the moment. He may join us at any time. Please proceed."

"There is the possibility of a house that might be made available to you. Not to buy, but to lease. A long-term lease. Is that of interest to you, or had you set your mind on buying a house?"

"I am certain that we would be interested in a lease. Can you give me some idea of where this property is located, and its features?"

"A short distance east of the Palace of the Governors the street becomes a dusty path and continues into the foothills of those large mountains back of our town. Wood cutters frequently use it as they bring in their loads of firewood to the market on the backs of burros."

"I have taken notice of these wood cutters and their wares."

"This is a rather large property. Perhaps it is too much of a house for just three people."

"That does not dampen my interest. Please, go on."

"It is located with a fine spring nearby and a few acres of pasture. Did you not tell me you had horses?"

"Yes, we have horses. What else can you add to your description of this property?"

"The house was built some years ago and was considered to be in the country. Now our village grows out to meet it, and someday may surround it. I know the present owner has cared well for his place and will be most particular as to whom he will lease it."

"And have you any indication of the rent the owner will fix on his property and the length of the lease?"

"Now, my dear Naomi, you are taking me into an area where I lack a firm understanding of terms. Perhaps we should leave this negotiation to your husband. No?"

"Gertrudes, you should know from the beginning, my husband and I are accustomed to working out our problems as one."

"How fortunate to have a man so close to you."

"No one knows better than I how fortunate I am."

Naomi would have liked more time with this woman so filled with charm and unknown power, but she felt *La Doña* Tules was not about to share anything more with her. It would be up to Duncan to gain additional information.

All thought of a house becoming available was rekindled when

Duncan and Jack gathered the families about them over the evening fire.

"Tomorrow prepare to take a long walk, or if you will, a short hike to view a house. What do you say to that?"

"Uncle Jack, you found a house for us?"

"Easy, Peggy, I said to look at a place. That's the first step."

"Is it in town? How far out in the country is it? How many rooms does it have? Does it have dirt floors?"

Duncan felt it necessary to take over the conversation. "Slow down and put your questions on hold. There is something that must come first. As we were walking to the west of town to look at some mules Jack was asked to buy for another man, we happened upon Jim Peters. He told us in two, maybe three days he would be heading back to Missouri. He promised to deliver letters we may have to send back to the East."

That evening until it became too dark to write and into the next morning the Rosses and the Gallaghers, all save Naomi and Eleanor, were bent over their writing pads. While Naomi had learned to read, she had not mastered writing; Eleanor had learned neither reading nor writing.

Duncan was the first to produce a completed letter. It was to his sister and her family back in Scotland.

Dear Louise, Rory, and Jennifer

It has been such a long time since I have written a letter I hardly know where to begin. We are in Santa Fe with the Gallaghers, still together as two families, still looking for housing, but forced to camp out in the two Conestoga wagons that we used over the Santa Fe Trail.

Our trek to Santa Fe took sixty-eight days in weather that varied from beautiful, bright sunny days to some of the most violent storms I have ever experienced, through some of the driest, dustiest, miserable miles over desert, and over endless miles of grass, oceans of grass, all under blue skies that defy description.

But we made it. We really had only one misadventure. And that proved to be a tragedy, a tragedy that has left us all with permanent scars. Billy Gallagher, Jack and Eleanor's oldest boy, was killed by an Indian. We were able to recover his body and give him a proper burial, but that is of little solace to the Gallagher family. He was a most enjoyable boy who rapidly became a man, and he is missed, terribly missed, by all.

Throughout our travels Naomi became the caravan's medicine person. Some days she was quite busy. Her insistence that we all eat some sort of greens every few days kept our teeth in place and our joints flexible. Peggy continues to grow and is nearly as tall as her mother. She and Billy Gallagher became very close friends in our days on the Trail.

Jack's family, aside from the loss of Billy, survived the trip and is adjusting to the strangeness of Santa Fe and the customs of this country. One thing that is not strange, this town requires cash, and we are running very short of that. I will be sending a letter to our friend in St. Louis to see what he can do to get funds to us in such difficult circumstances.

Be assured we are well, adjusting, and looking ahead to a full life in this town. One of the brightest things that could happen is to get a letter from you when next summer's caravan rolls into Santa Fe. Send your letters to Samuel Rawlinson as I suggested before we left St. Louis. He will see that they are forwarded to us.

Our love to all,
Duncan, Naomi, and Peggy

His next letter was to Samuel Rawlinson.

Dear Samuel

We are here! Yes, we are in Santa Fe but not yet into permanent housing. We hope to change that into one more problem resolved in a few days. Another major problem is one only you can resolve. Santa Fe is a town that operates on a cash basis, especially for newcomers like us.

Will you review my portfolio and select some paper for conversion to cash? I am thinking $1,000 should put us in a better position. You will have to determine the best way to get it to me, for I see nothing that resembles a bank in this town. Banking, such as it is, is done mano y mano, and not through established institutions. Remember this is a Province of Mexico, so certain practices must be followed.

I am pleased to tell you we are well. The only real black mark to our sixty-eight-day adventure over oceans of grass was the death of Billy Gallagher. You will remember he was Jack and Eleanor's oldest son. He was a fine boy who very quickly became a man as we worked our way West. Billy and Peggy became very close, and his loss has changed her from the bright, sassy girl you knew in St. Louis to a very thoughtful, attractive, but deeply saddened young woman.

Naomi says she has a hundred questions to ask, especially about Myrna Wilson. Answers must come from you. I am asking Jim Peters, the boss of the wagon train soon to depart for St. Louis, to personally deliver these letters to you. He in turn can tell you how to contact the next wagon train to head for Santa Fe, probably not until this coming spring.

And Samuel, you should keep close watch on the caravans returning to Missouri from Santa Fe. There are business opportunities waiting for development for the Trail is a two-way street.

My regards for your health and well-being, and our best to friends in your circle of friends.

Duncan

Peggy wrote her letter to Myrna Wilson.

Dear Myrna

We have waited for such a long time to write to friends back in St. Louis. Now we have the chance to send mail with a wagon train leaving Santa Fe for Missouri in just a few days.

I regret not having some sketches to send to you. Our sixty-eight days on the Trail were crowded from the minute we arose, many times before the sun even showed its face, to evening camps that came to life after sundown.

We are all hoping in a few days to be able to plan on moving into permanent housing. We have had to use those big Conestoga wagons as our homes since coming to Santa Fe.

I would have to say our trek West was easier than we expected but for one thing. And that hurts so much I am not sure I can write about it without soaking the paper with my tears. Billy Gallagher was killed by an Indian when we were about one hundred fifty miles from Santa Fe. Billy and I became the best of friends. By the time you are reading this letter what I am going to tell you won't be a secret, for it would be impossible to hide. I am carrying Billy's child. Mother thinks I will have it in late March or early April. I feel fine, but I know changes are taking place. I am not ashamed to tell you this. In fact, I am glad that a part of Billy has become a part of me. Wish me all the good things that new mothers are supposed to receive from friends.

I know you will want to have a letter ready to send to us with the next caravan to leave for Santa Fe. Samuel Rawlinson will know how to forward mail to us. Is he still your friend?

All of us send our love to you.
Peggy

Jack wrote a letter to Samuel Rawlinson, but chose not to share it with anyone. He did say he asked Samuel to send him some cash from the profits that came from Samuel's management of the livery stables.

The two families trooped down the path into town the next morning, located Jim Peters, and turned over their mail for him to deliver at the other end of the Trail. "I'll be happy to do this. I am not surprised to hear of your difficulty in getting anyone to sell or rent a house to you."

"Why is that? What do you know that we should know?"

"Duncan, it ain't exactly you people. It's just that you are foreigners, you know, *gringos*."

"How do we go about convincing them that we just want to live at peace in their town, nothing more than that?"

"I don't know, but what ever you decide to do, do it slowly and give them a chance to see you mean no harm."

"Thanks. I know we'll be in town to give you a send off when you lead your caravan out of town."

The families regrouped after their exchange with Jim Peters and started out on the path just beyond the Palace of the Governors. A natural pairing began: Jack and Eleanor, Grace and Peggy, Pres and Dutch, Duncan and Naomi, with Charley dancing among the elders testing where the best chance for a ride on somebody's shoulders might be found.

After a half hour of walking, Naomi turned to Duncan and said, "Do you know where we are going?"

"All we have to go on is the description one of the mule buyers gave us."

They turned off the main road and onto a lane that led up a little hill to a large clump of trees that surrounded a large house. They were not surprised to see it was a mud house hiding behind a mud wall. Three horses in the pasture next to the house trotted over to give them the eye, snorted and pawed the ground for a minute, then turned their tails and went back to being horses accustomed to ignoring strangers.

Jack went to the gate and called out, "Hello! *Hola! Oye!* Anybody to home?"

No answer, no sound of movement within the house. Another round of calls. This time they could hear the sounds of a door opening. Duncan tested the massive gate set into the wall that enclosed the compound. Much to his surprise it gave way and he could see a very old man standing not more than thirty feet from him with an ancient blunderbuss in his shaking hands.

"No, *amigo*, no shoot. See, no gun, no shoot."

Even at thirty feet an old musket in the hands of a shaky, old man could do some harm. Duncan eased toward the guardian of the place slowly and deliberately. He then tried his best smile and offered a rough, hand-made cigarillo and waited. The old man slowly lowered the gun as much from its weight as much as it was a sign to "come in peace."

The old man reached for the cigarillo and Duncan reached for the musket. Both got what they wanted. Beyond that point there were no more exchanges for it was obvious the old man knew no English, and it was equally obvious he was in very poor health.

Duncan laid the old gun on the ground, put his arm around the man and half carried, half led him to a bench under the portal surrounding the four interior walls of the house. Naomi began to assess the old man's condition. His clothing hung on his emaciated frame. His breathing was shallow and irregular, and the smell of death hovered over him.

The others eased into the courtyard, and Naomi put them to work at once. "There has to be water here, find it, and bring a cup or gourd. Find a basin and some sort of a clean cloth. This man is burning with fever." Everyone scattered to carry out Naomi's orders.

Jack went into the barn and came out with a bridle and saddle and set them on the ground near the gate to the pasture. He gave a low whistle and got a response from the largest of the three horses. His coaxing voice and patient manner brought results and the horse allowed Jack to touch him, rub his nose, stroke his flanks, and stand while the bridle was slipped over his head.

Jack had Grace hold the reins as he worked the saddle onto his back. A few more minutes of low talk passed before he tightened the cinch. For the next twenty minutes Jack walked the horse up and down the lane that led from the path. Satisfied that he had won the confidence of the critter, Jack mounted. He stayed in the saddle and tested the horse with some simple commands. "Dunc, this here horse has been broke to neck reins, I think you can manage him."

"You must ride into town and find that Barcelo woman and bring some help," Naomi added. "This old man is badly done in."

Duncan eased into the saddle and found he had a well-trained horse under him that was more than ready to gallop into Santa Fe. He slowed his mount to a walk as he guided the horse around the Plaza to San Francisco Street and dismounted in front of the door leading to the dance hall. His banging on the door brought someone from the inside to see to his summons and any number of loafers from the Plaza to see what this was about. "Yes, what is it you want? *Señor* Ross isn't it? Please enter."

"First, tell me which of these men can be trusted to hold my horse?"

"Felix, *retendré el caballo!*"

"*Gracias*, Santiago. *La Doña* Tules, is she here? I must talk to her at once."

Santiago led the way to the back room where she sat at a table going over what appeared to be ledgers. At the moment, not the glamorous lady he met a few evenings past. Gertrudes Barcelo was dressed in a faded, shapeless robe, her hair uncombed, and a cigarillo dangling from her lips.

Duncan was oblivious to her state of dress; he lost no time in pouring out his story. She was equally quick to respond. "Santiago, fetch my carriage at once. *Señor* Ross you will ride back with me. You can fill me in on the details of this tragedy as we ride."

"No, *Doña* Gertrudis. While you prepare yourself to go out in the public I must ride to our campsite. Naomi told me to bring the medications she brought over the Trail. She said if there is a doctor in Santa Fe, you should bring him with you."

The compound was alive with activity. Eleanor and Naomi had bathed and dressed the man in cleaner clothes they found in one of the rooms. Grace and Peggy were boiling water over the fire Jack made outside in the courtyard. Charley skipped back and forth making sure everyone did what they were told to do.

Duncan was the first to return from town with a large sack of the medications Naomi had prepared for their trek over the Trail. She and Eleanor agreed that weak tea would be the first thing they gave the old man. A search of the kitchen yielded some food; much of that was beyond use. The best thing Naomi and Eleanor could do was to kill and dress one of chickens scratching around near the barn. The one they caught didn't seem to be any better fed than the old man. At least some broth could be coaxed from its carcass.

When Tules arrived without a doctor she went immediately to Naomi and asked how and why it was the Ross and Gallagher families were here. "My last words to you were that I would make the contacts concerning this place. *Sí?*"

"It was only by chance my husband and his friend, Jack Gallagher, were told of this place. Even I did not know we were coming here until I walked up the hill and realized it fit your description."

"Most unusual, don't you think? You come asking for my help, and you go behind my back."

"Gertrudes, curb your anger! Help us to deal with a very frail old man. Why is he here alone and neglected? Has he family? Do his friends know of his situation? Help us first. Then we will deal with your anger."

"*Pues.* Perhaps you are right. Forgive me of my hot words to you. I shall have to contact the owner who spends much of his time in Rio Abajo. That will take days, but this old man's needs are immediate. What do you suggest, Naomi?"

"Give us a few minutes to talk this over among ourselves."

Tules returned to her carriage where a torrent of conversation flowed between her and Santiago. The two families stood about looking at one another as each person mulled over the questions, "What are we going to do? Who will do it? What are we getting ourselves into?"

Duncan began to outline a plan. "Suppose we do this? Naomi and I along with Peggy and Pres will stay here with the old man. Jack, you and your family go back to the wagons and keep Dutch with you."

"Sounds reasonable, but how will we keep in touch?"

" Jack, you have two horses plus Spook, and you have proved that one of the horses here is manageable. Let Pres and Dutch be the messengers."

Duncan went to the carriage. "*La Doña* Barcelo, how long do you think it will be until you can get word to the owners of this place about what has happened?"

"It will take about three days to get word to Manuel Lucero, the owner, and three days for a reply. I shall word my message to him in such a way he will see that he must come to Santa Fe."

"Fine! Please do this immediately. Before you go would you walk through the house with us? My wife and I cannot just move into this place. We need only to know of the basics. We have no desire to take over completely. We will do only what is required to keep this man alive. Agreed?"

"Again, *Señor* Ross, I admire a man who can act directly. I shall do as you suggested."

"One other thing. We have become aware in the time we have been in Santa Fe of the resentment of *gringos* and of the imperious ways some of us choose to follow. Will you make an effort to quietly spread the word that we are in this place as strangers, but strangers who have only the welfare of a sick man at heart?"

"I am amazed at your grasp of the problems here. I shall do everything possible to aid you and Naomi. Tell me, is your wife a *curandera?*"

"I'm not certain I understand that word, but Naomi can be very helpful in the use of herbs and natural things. May I suggest that when you have reason to contact us you make your first effort to locate Jack or Eleanor? They will know the quickest way to get word to us."

"As you say, *Señor*. I think you wish to avoid me, *si?*"

Duncan's answer was lost in the clatter of her rapidly departing carriage and her laughter floating back to him on the morning breeze.

Outside, a puff of wind was followed by a shower of light snow; snow, wind, snow, wind. And it was cold. Already water was frozen in the pond at the side of the gate. In the pasture the horses stood as close to the barn as they could. Inside the house it was warm and cozy. The largest room had a fireplace around which gathered the Ross family, the Gallagher family, Pres and Dutch, and Jorge Moreno. Jorge was the reason for this scene of comfort and security. The old man's responses to the medications of Naomi and the care of Eleanor had been slow and steady. The signs of his recovered health cheered everyone, but one thing he could not do was to grow new teeth.

It took several days until Naomi could make sense of what Jorge tried to say. In the process she also learned many words in Spanish and became expert in preparing his food. *Atole* for breakfast, mashed vegetables at the noon meal, the same plus shredded meat for his supper. And never did he fail to reward with a toothless smile and a bob of the head anyone in the two families who made his life in this compound pleasant.

Charley adopted Jorge as his own, and the old man retuned his friendship by becoming Charley's *abuelo*. To say they became inseparable would be too much; Charley's pace was always at full speed, Jorge's at near to no speed. But tonight Charley's place was secure; he sat on Jorge's lap to lean back and listen with contentment the wheezing of the old man as he nodded at the side the fireplace.

"I miss camping out in the Conestoga. Don't you miss it, Grace?"

"Uncle Duncan, you are impossible! How could anybody miss that?"

"But think how close and snuggly warm it would be under the canvas top with not a care in the world."

"Aunt Naomi, what is wrong with him?"

"Not to worry, he gets like this once in awhile. Ignore him."

Grace was massaging Peggy's back as she lay sprawled on a buffalo robe in front of the fireplace. For a month she had complained of her back becoming so tired and at times painful. Gentle massages gave her the relief she sought and the sense of acceptance given her by everyone in the two families. When all in this circle knew Peggy was carrying Billy's child she became the center of care and concern.

"Enjoy all of this attention now, Peggy, for when your baby arrives you will be replaced by a few pounds of wet, wiggly, hungry, screaming joy."

"Did you feel that way when you were having me?"

"Some questions are best left without answers, my dear."

The conversation drifted to other topics. Eleanor expressed herself on the plan of Jack and Duncan about a month ago to assemble a wagon load of trade goods and join a caravan going south into Mexico to the city of Chihuahua.

In the few years since the arrival of the first group over the Santa Fe Trail in 1821 the local market became saturated with goods coming in from the East in ever increasing quantities. Caravans were organized in Santa Fe to go another six hundred miles south to Chihuahua, Mexico and profitable markets there.

"Aren't you two glad you changed your minds? Think of where you might be now. It wouldn't be in a warm comfortable room like this."

"Probably not." Duncan broke into the exchange between Jack and Eleanor. "But we must have something to do, something that will generate some income for us. The chance to get in on the Chihuahua trade seemed worthwhile."

"Is that the only thing you might have done? Aren't there other ways to get the income you say we need?"

Jack said, with a touch of bitterness, "We was told them people in Chihuahua wouldn't be any happier to have us than what we find here in Santa Fe."

"But Jack, you've made some money dealing in mules and horses. Isn't that enough?"

"That well's gone dry, Naomi. Until spring comes, if it ever does, there won't be any action in the horse market. Them local men will be as hesitant to deal with a *gringo* in the spring as they was in the fall."

Another period of silence fell over the group. The crackling of the fire and the wheezing of Jorge were the only sounds mixing with the winds blowing every so often by the windows and causing back-drafts in the fireplace when for a minute the room filled with the aroma of *piñon*.

Naomi said, "I think it is time for the treat Eleanor and I have ready. But I don't suppose anyone here is interested in a mug of this liquid people here call *chocolate*."

Naomi and Eleanor smiled. They expected exactly what happened. All were on their feet asking for a mug of the hot drink they learned to accept as delicious. Jorge, who seemed to be sleeping the evening away, held out his hand at the mention of *chocolate*.

Duncan took his mug and turned to the group, "Let us toast Manuel Lucero, the man whose house we enjoy."

"Yes, we owe so much to that man for insisting that we remain here in recognition of the aid we have given Jorge." Naomi continued, "But there is another part of that story you should know. Tules told me that

Señor Lucero was going to ask us to leave. She reminded him that the *alcalde* expected a report from her about why Jorge Moreno had been so badly neglected. Señor Lucero could not risk having to explain that."

"Do you think she has that much influence in this town?"

"Dunc, you know she does. Why even ask?"

"Well, you and she have become very close, so I shouldn't question your version of why we are in this house. But for how long?"

"I think it depends on the care we give Jorge, how long he lives, and whether or not Tules gives an unfavorable report about us."

Several times Naomi had tried explaining to Duncan the strange life Tules had led and the circumstances under which she came to Santa Fe. As a native of this country, Tules told Naomi that she knew of the love of gambling in the make-up of most Mexican or Spanish men.

"Dunc, you see what Tules does as immoral because you come from a culture that respects saving and frugality."

Duncan did not see the point Naomi was making. "But what of your culture? What of the Crees you lived with?"

"Cree people were not given to gathering in extra things. We moved three or four times each year as we went to the sugar bush country, to the planting fields, to the fishing waters, to the hunting grounds. We did not want more than we could easily carry on our backs or in our canoes."

Jack broke in by saying, "Santa Fe was a big mistake for all of us. We can now see what a beautiful part of the country this here Santa Fe occupies. It's the cost of livin here that riles me."

"Cost, what cost? We don't have to pay a *reale* for this place," Duncan said with some heat.

"It cost Eleanor and me our son. It cost me any chance for a business of my own. It's costin your daughter her chance to do any of her art. I suspect the Devil ain't done with totin up his bill."

"Don't you think it's time for all of us to get to our beds?"

Eleanor found that all too many times of late she had to damp down the tension that cropped up between her husband and Duncan. Much of

Naomi's time seemed to be divided between Peggy and her pregnancy and this Tules person in town. For Naomi, it was more than just time in Tules' company, for she found herself going with Tules to tend to a friend, usually a woman, in need of Naomi's skills as a healer.

Shortly before Christmas a big *caretta* load of firewood was delivered to the compound. The driver said he knew nothing of the person who ordered him to bring the wood here. He refused Duncan's offer of payment, saying that had been taken care of. Again no names were offered, but he left with a generous tip in his pocket.

Duncan, Pres, and Dutch tackled the pile of firewood and soon had it split and stacked between the door to the kitchen and the necessary at the side of the wall surrounding the compound.

Snow came frequently but not in huge amounts at any one time. The air blowing down over the village was cold, cold as only air off high mountains can be. But it was dry air, and when the sun came out it seemed warm, even when it wasn't. Grace said, "Winter in Santa Fe is as much a challenge to the mind as it is a challenge to the body."

"I think we have a philosopher in the family," Duncan said teasingly.

"Uncle Duncan, you and I are going to do something this afternoon that will make you a philosopher, too!"

"What are we going to do?"

"Wait, you'll see what I mean."

The day was filled with chores in and around the compound, the barn, and a trip to market to buy some *posole* and *tamales*. Try as they would, neither Eleanor nor Naomi was able to make these dishes quite the way they were meant to be. When Naomi asked Tules what the secret was to making *posole*, she laughed and said, "I can't tell you. *La Conquistadora,* who looks after the welfare of her children in Santa Fe, forbids us to reveal our secrets."

"Is she also the one who taught you how to deal cards with such great success, Gertrudes?"

"Some things I will never tell you."

Just as the sun touched the tips of the hills to the west of Santa Fe, Grace came to Duncan and said, "Dress warmly, Uncle Duncan. We must go outside for your lesson in philosophy."

"Why can't we learn it here in front of the fireplace?"

"Come on, we can't lose a minute."

Once they were outside the house Grace led Duncan away from the compound and walked him to the path used by the wood cutters. "We have to get away to a place where there is nothing to obstruct our sight of the mountains."

"This is growing in mystery every minute, but can't you rush things? I'm getting cold!"

"Hush! Now turn and face the mountains to the east."

"But how can we see the sunset if we face to the east? Aren't you getting your lesson mixed up?"

"Face to the east, Uncle Duncan. Now!"

They stood and watched one of the miracles of Santa Fe unfold before their eyes. At that magic moment, the sun setting in the west casts its last rays on the snow covered mountains east of the village. Those mountains hold the rays for just a few moments and bathe the snow-covered high peaks the color of blood.

"Jorge showed this to me a few days ago. He said, as best I could make out, that is why they are called the *Sangre de Christo* Mountains."

"This is amazing, Grace. And to have learned of this secret from an old man who watched this miracle every winter of his long life adds to its beauty and mystery."

"Now, do you feel like a philosopher, Uncle Duncan?"

"Yes, and I also feel like a racer. I bet I can beat you back to the house."

"I don't think we should do this."

"Do you know of anyone else in Santa Fe who is in a position to help?"

"No, I don't. But isn't there another way to solve this problem?"

"I have some ideas, Naomi, but they will take time to develop. Even then there is no guarantee they will be profitable."

"Well, shall I make an appointment to talk to Tules?"

"I'm certain she would prefer it. Walking into the middle of a card game may not put her in the right frame of mind."

La Doña Tules received them in her usual gracious manner, but her cold grey eyes belied her outward charm. "My dear friends, how are things with you and with that dear, old man, Jorge?"

"Fine, to both questions. But we can dispense with the usual exchange of pleasantries, can't we?"

"Are you Scotsmen always so abrupt? Tell me, Naomi, is he always like this? Quick and to the point?"

"Oh no, Gertrudes, he can be very indirect when he wants something that he doesn't like to ask for outright."

"Like money, perhaps, or the favor of a lady?"

"You two talk to each other far too much. You know me better than I know myself. You have me at a disadvantage, *La Doña* Tules."

"That's the only way to deal successfully with a man, is it not?"

"We are short of cash. Now, is that being openly honest?"

"Yes, and it needs only for you to say the amount and it will be in your hands."

"Splendid. But at what interest?"

"Always the business man, aren't you, my red-headed friend?"

"That way keeps friendships. To borrow without some demonstration of the value of the gesture robs it of meaning, *si*?"

"Enough! The amount?"

"The interest rate? Deal?"

On the way back to the compound, strolling along with the bag of coins slung over Duncan's shoulder much like a sack of *frijoles*, they exchanged opinions of their visit with Tules. "I think she likes you, Duncan. I don't think she would loan that sum of money to any man who asks."

"I think it because she likes you and the help you give to her ailing friends."

"Is it not better to have her as a friend? I would hate to have her regard me as an enemy. Remember you told me after the first time you met her that Tules was more than a glamorous lady, she was also dangerous."

"Did I say that? Well, I see no reason to change my opinion."

"Tules lives by her wits, mixed with her charm, and tempered by her daring to get and stay where she is in Santa Fe."

"I'll admit I find her exceedingly charming."

She couldn't resist teasing a bit, "You never said anything like that to me, Dunc. Why?"

"It's because you go far beyond being just charming, my dear."

"How far, my red-headed friend? Isn't that what she called you?"

The loan from Tules made it all the more important that the first wagon train into Santa Fe in the spring have letters from their friends back in St. Louis. Duncan was counting on Samuel Rawlinson to forward money. If he failed to do so the Ross family would be in a really tight financial crisis.

Living on borrowed money also made it all the more important that Duncan and Jack plan for their trip to the gold mining area south of Santa Fe. Stories of the wealth in the Ortiz Mountains were put on hold as their caravan worked its way over the Trail.

Their first effort to establish a steady flow of income from trade with the merchants of Chihuahua had faded fast in the harsh light of reality. The distance and the time involved in a round trip between the two cities of Mexico was nearly as much as a round trip over the Trail. Then there were the risks of unfavorable prices for their goods, and the attitude toward *gringos* – all these factors worked against them.

Jack and Duncan had talked of gold mining frequently in St. Louis as they planned for this western adventure. Now it was time to put plans into action. Duncan led off the discussion, "It seems to me we can't sit here in Santa Fe and talk about gold mining. We have to get ourselves to the Ortiz scene."

"Won't argue that point with you, but when do we go? Are you talking just the two of us? I ain't going down to that Ortiz place without some sort of a guide."

"You're right, we don't know very much, only gossip. But where is this guide to come from? Who do we know to get us there? Who can we trust to give an overview of the whole area and not just one or two places that turn up with an ounce or two of gold?"

Their discussion spread to include Eleanor and Naomi. "I'm not going to be any good to you men, for I seldom see more of Santa Fe than the Plaza and the markets around it."

"Maybe so, Eleanor, but I've learned to trust your judgment on a good many things. You ain't never let me down."

"Well, one thing comes to my mind, and that is a question. Are you and Duncan going to do the actual mining? Are you going to hire men to mine for you?"

"Can't give you an answer 'til we get ourselfs down to Ortiz and do some lookin around."

"Naomi, it is not like you to sit and not have something to say."

"I can't say much for I don't know much about gold mining. But I can pass on some of the stories Tules told me of her time in the Ortiz Mountains."

"Tules actually worked in the mines there? Incredible!"

"There's our answer, Duncan. Let's talk with Tules."

"Can you trust her?" Jack was ready with another question. "Why would she want to help us? You may be a friend of hers, but to these local people once a *gringo* always a *gringo*."

After another day of debate, Duncan and Jack smothered their doubts, swallowed their pride, and went to see Tules – Gertrudes Barcelo – who ran the richest card game in Santa Fe.

"I understand why you men want to go to the gold mines. The lure of gold has always drawn men to seek it. I can only caution you to go into this with your eyes wide open, and keep them open."

"Is it that dangerous? You know both of us are veterans of the North Country of Canada and the fur trade posts we called home for many years. I think we know how to take care of ourselves."

"I know practically nothing of fur trading. I do know when men get the idea they can just walk around and pick up gold nuggets they tend to go crazy when they find one or two."

"Fur trading wasn't free of rough characters either."

"I will give you several names of men to talk to about guiding you to the Ortiz area, but I can't speak for them. They will have to do that."

"*Gracias, La Doña* Tules, *gracias.*"

Pedro Carrera and Manuel Hernandez were the guides and packers the two gold seekers hired to get them to and through the mining area in the Ortiz Mountains. The day they departed found the sun warm and the air cold. Patches of snow could be found on the north side of almost any *arroyo* and under stands of *piñon* and juniper. At the end of a long day on horseback Manuel said, "*Amigos,* we are almost there. Where do you wish to begin your explorations?"

"We are open to suggestions. What would you do first?"

"I would go to Dolores Springs. That is where the most activity is centered. And there is a store in that village. The owner will know much about the area."

"We must also find a place to camp tonight. Where will that be?"

After some deep thought, Pedro said, "Now, *mi amigo,* you have touched on a problem. Most of the land here has been claimed by someone. To pitch a camp on a site that looks good to you may be a place protected by a claim owner. That would be *muy mal.*"

"So what do we do?"

"Get to the store in Dolores and see what we might learn."

That night about their campfire the four men drew blankets about their shoulders against the penetrating cold as they sat and pooled what they had leaned from the hour they spent lounging about the store.

"*Señors*, did you not learn that the first decision must be what kind of mining you wish to do?"

Duncan was quick to respond, "I did, Pedro. But I still don't know enough to make a decision."

"Lode mining requires a large claim, many pesos, many men, and lots of patience. But the rewards can be huge."

"Be fair to these men, Pedro, losses can be just as great." Manuel presented the other option to Duncan and Jack, "Placer mining can also be rewarding, but the harvest of gold is slow and comes in small amounts."

"What you're telling us is that lode mining means we need deep pockets to make it profitable. Placer mining also means we need a lot of water and a lot of quicksilver to make it profitable."

"*Si, Señor*. You have the big picture. Do you like what you see?"

"I'm confused," said Duncan. "I think of gold and I think of wealth, but all I've seen so far is poverty. Hasn't anybody in these mountains ever struck a find, you know, a lode?"

Manuel was quick to reply. "If they have, *mi amigo*, they were smart enough to keep it to themselves. Or some *rico* or some agent of *el Gobernador* has taken his claim. What is a poor man to do?"

Another day with the two guides, another day of looking at caves that people called home, another day of watching miserable men lashing even more miserable burros around and around an *arrastra*. Duncan and Jack also saw men climbing up *escaleras* from depths in narrow shafts with sacks of *pepena* slung on their backs. And for what? A few grains of gold that barely bought them a dribble of *frijoles y tortillas* to exist with enough strength to do another day of the same. And for the same reward. They saw women squatted down for hour upon hour with a wooden *batea* washing black sand and gravel in icy water in hopes of finding a few grains of gold.

As they rode back toward Santa Fe both Pedro and Manuel felt they had kept their part of the bargain. They showed these Easterners the Ortiz Mountains and the gold mining operations that were going on there as they had for many years. They were honest in their comments; they made no attempt to hide anything from view.

"Manuel, should we also tell our friends the truth about *gringos* and gold?"

"Why not, Pedro? These men are not fools; they know what they have seen. They now know very, very few men will come out of these mountains with anything that can be called wealth. Yes, we should tell them."

The guides had been conversing between themselves in Spanish as they rode. "*Basta, basta.* Time to rest the horses, *Señors.*"

"Well, *Señor* Duncan, are you ready to make an investment in Ortiz gold mining?"

"Manuel, what I am ready for is a soak in a tub, some good coffee, and a back rub."

"*Caramba!* You will find all this at your home? You are so fortunate, *Señor*, to have such pleasures waiting for you."

Pedro added, "We both feel you should know one more thing about what you have seen. It is for Mexicans only. Government officials are making every effort to see that only Mexicans benefit from our gold mining. Even men from Spain are not welcome here."

"*Sí*, that is the way things are." Pedro continued to explain, "I suspect they will not change. *Los pobres* will continue to do the hard work, *los ricos* will take the profit, and *los gringos* can only sit and watch."

In the compound everyone waited anxiously for the return of the two adventurers. The slow dismounting from their horses, the almost painful way they walked into the house, and the glum responses to the greetings of their wives and children told the story.

"What did you learn that is so depressing it can't be shared?"

"Ah, Eleanor, gimme a minute to collect my thoughts. You should be glad we ain't tryin to scratch out a livin from gold mining. That's all I got to say. Maybe Duncan can give you a rosy picture. I can't."

Naomi could not hold back her curiosity any longer. "Well, Dunc, how do you view the scene down there? How rosy is it?"

"My dear, you would spend days looking for anything in the Ortiz area that even looked or smelled like a rose. Depressing is the only way to describe what we saw. And in the end, what we saw is not for foreigners, for *gringos* like us."

That night when they were in their bed Duncan turned on his side, drew Naomi close to him, and murmured, "We don't know how lucky we are. I have never seen such miserable places for people to live and work. Your friend, Tules, can tell you some details. You said she spent over a year at the mines? That she had washed gravel for gold?"

"Yes. She told me those things and more. She said she had to flee from the Ortiz area, and she had to hide when she got to Santa Fe."

"I, too, would flee the Ortiz Mountains, for I can't believe what I saw. It's grim. No, it's worse. It's pitiable and heart-breaking."

"You and Jack talked with Tules. Didn't she warn you?"

"She said keep your eyes open at all times. We did that, my dear, and we saw reality."

A few days after their return from the discouraging trip to the gold mines, Duncan and Jack had a new problem to confront.

"Me and Pres, we gotta talk to you two."

"It's California, isn't it?" Duncan spoke up. "When do you plan to leave?"

"You're right 'bout us leaving. But it ain't to California. It's back to Illinois for us."

Jack joined in. "Had an idea you two was cookin up somethin. Got a reason you can tell us? That's a mighty big decision to make."

Dutch left that part of the explanation to Pres. "Seems like everyone we talked to was dead set against us going to California. Too risky. Then, we got to figuring out what we was gonna do once we got there. We come up empty."

"We ain't seen no welcome mat laid out for us in this here town." Dutch was ready to let all his troubles tumble out. "If I go back home I might be able to make up with my old man and give him a hand on the farm. He ain't getting any younger. He might like the idea of me helping."

"What about you, Pres?" Duncan was always the one with questions. "Can you go back to, your folks? "

"Don't know, Mr. Ross. But I'm ready to take my chances."

"Remember I promised both of you a bonus if you stuck with us all the way to Santa Fe? I expect the first caravan to hit town this summer will have letters from my business agent in St. Louis. One of them should have the money to pay that bonus and in time for you to have it in your pockets when you head back east."

"That sure would take some of the pain out of the trip."

"Be time enough for thanks when you have the bonus in hand."

Duncan could not help but notice the changing attitude of Jack when he brought up the need for them to continue looking for opportunities in Santa Fe.

"You already have established a good name among men in the horse and mule business. Can't you parlay that into something you could own and manage? Then, we have heard about Taos and the fur trading based there. What do you think? Should we get our arses up there to have a look?"

"You go. I think it will turn out to be just like our trek to the Ortiz. Nothin! A big, fat nothin."

"Shouldn't we ask around this town? There seems to be regular traffic between Santa Fe and Taos. What is that all about?"

"Duncan, I 'member hearing some talk about Taos whilst we was waitin our turn to cross the Arkansas. Some furs and hides are packed out of Taos and brung there to the Arkansas to pick up a caravan headed back to Missouri."

"If furs are coming out, somebody has to be packing trade goods back in, don't you think?"

"Don't know, and to tell the truth I don't give a damn."

"Balls of fire! I thought we were partners. What's got into you?"

"You ain't lost a son, and you ain't got another son who is having a hell of time just getting by in this miserable place."

"We're all concerned that Charley doesn't seem to be growing and running and jumping with other kids his age."

"What other kids? He ain't got no friends. All the boys he's met pick on him and make his life miserable."

"What does Eleanor think?"

"She's a quiet one, you know that. But I know she takes it hard that he's not growing. She said maybe livin this high in the mountains has somethin to do with his having a hard time to breath."

Charley's visible lack of progress and Jack's increasingly negative attitude made for a somber air about the compound. But slowly all in the two families found their view of having to live in a mud house changed. Mud wasn't what the houses were made of, it was *adobe*. *Adobe* was mud, yes, but the right kind of soil mixed with some straw, carefully shaped into bricks, and cured in the sun. When laid up with knowing hands and covered with a leak-proof dirt roof, an *adobe* house was cool in the summer and warm in the winter.

Most of all, they learned the ease and convenience of one floor. A portal protected every side on the interior of the compound, and being able to go from one room to another under that roof with ease was better than having to climb stairs. Yet each room was separate from the others.

Dirt floors were soon overlooked, for they became so much a part of Santa Fe living that nobody gave them any thought. When the floors were covered with colorful woven rugs every room became bright and was enhanced by the white *yeso* plaster applied to the interior walls.

The brightest feature of the compound was Peggy. As she moved through her pregnancy she literally blossomed. Naomi and Eleanor watched over her constantly but were careful not to smother her with too many directions. The natural bond developed over the years with Grace deepened and strengthened. The two girls were inseparable and few secrets were withheld.

"Remember the times we walked with Billy and Spook? The way he made us ride to let Spook know we could manage him as good as he could."

"I remember, Peggy, but one thing you can remember that I can never know is what you two talked about when you strolled hand in hand on the prairie when it got dark."

"Grace, I won't tell you. That was between Billy and me. Besides we didn't talk all of the time. Some nights we just looked at the stars and dreamed."

"Come on now. At one time you two had to do more than that."

"Grace, what are you talking about?"

"You know what I mean."

"I think I do, but it was more than once, believe me."

"Did you like it, Peggy, did it hurt?"

"The first couple of times I wasn't sure."

"But then what happened?"

"I don't know exactly, but I could barely wait for the sun to go down, for the evening chores to be over. I couldn't wait to be with him."

"Will I ever have a man like you did and feel that way about him?"

"Of course you will. And you will know he is the right man to give yourself to."

"How can I get started to learn all the things you know?"

"I think when you meet a man you begin to make judgments about him. When you feel that you can trust him, when you feel good about being with him and not guilty, then you will answer your own questions."

Among the many things the two families learned about living in Santa Fe through the winter months was deception. Most days began with brilliant sunshine, with a warm sun and no breeze. The moment you stepped into a shadow you knew just how cold winter really could be. Some afternoons brought gathering clouds and brisk breezes with a sharp edge.

On one such day, Duncan and Naomi set out for the Plaza in the morning. Peggy was content with Grace and Eleanor as companions for the day, and Charley was into a long explanation with Jorge of what it was like to travel over the Santa Fe Trail. Jack just left the compound without a hint to anyone where he was going.

As soon as Naomi completed her purchases from the food vendors at the west end of the portal of the Government Palace, she and Duncan began a leisurely stroll to the shops on three sides of the Plaza. "What are you needing, Naomi?"

"Nothing, but you never know what might catch my eye."

"Fine, then you won't mind stopping for a minute to talk to Felix."

Felix Chavez was one of the merchants who quickly sized up the contents of Duncan's Conestoga when it finally cleared customs. He was just as quick to begin negotiations with an experienced trader, through an interpreter. In the end, he bought the lion's share of the goods in the wagon; some of Duncan's goods were in his store on consignment.

He and Duncan retained the good feeling that came from the sessions of bargaining, and so when Duncan and Naomi entered his shop the greeting was sincere and warm, warmer than his shop. Felix knew he would not have many customers with *reales* or *pesos* to spend until warmer weather returned. Heating a shop was an expense, and one that did nothing for the profit figures.

"*Buenas dias, mi amigos.* What brings you two out into the chill of the morning?"

"Felix, how are you? I must say you are looking prosperous and content. *Si?*"

"Duncan, you must be jesting. Surely you can see my poor store has not made a sale for three weeks?"

"We sympathize, old friend, but I have a problem on my mind. Have you a few minutes to hear me out?"

"But of course. May I offer you a chair, *Señora* Ross?"

"*Gracias, Señor* Chavez. But I shall stand; otherwise you two men will talk the morning through."

"Felix, I feel I must get to Taos to survey the potential for business activity with which I might become associated. What can you advise me about Taos?"

"I would have to say there is potential in Taos. You will find it quite different up there, for fur and hide trading is the major business of that village. As you know, such trading in Santa Fe is not quite so important."

"That is one of the several reasons I have for going to Taos."

"You should not plan that trip for at least another month, perhaps two. Winter comes earlier and stays longer in Taos. And, of course, you are not planning that trip alone?"

"Is the danger that great? I figure it is a two-day trip, but one free of roadside dangers."

"Yes, *mi amigo,* two days should be sufficient, three would be better. But, *por favor,* arrange to go with others."

That brought the conversation to a close. Duncan promised he would not proceed with plans for a jaunt to Taos without first talking with Felix. As they turned their steps eastward to their compound, Naomi spoke, "You can't be serious about going off to Taos. Have you forgotten you have a daughter who is soon to give birth? What were you thinking?"

"My dear long-legged friend, how could I forget Peggy's time is close? I have a plan that might involve going to Taos with more than empty hands. But miss Peggy's big event? Never!"

"That makes me feel better, but I have another bothersome problem on my mind."

"And that is?"

"You have been rather short when you talk to Jack. He's still dealing with the death of Billy. He needs to know you are with him and not finding fault because he doesn't see things your way."

"Jack is my best friend. How can you say I'm short with him? We've always talked very directly between ourselves."

"Well, just expect to have differences with him. You can't possibly walk in his shoes. You have never experienced the kind of loss he has. Besides all that, he has Charley on his mind."

"Do you still think Charley is in danger?"

"The truth is I just don't know. I think he should be taller and heavier. I think he tires too quickly."

"Eleanor told me she thinks living in the high mountains might be his problem."

"It might. But didn't we see the same signs in Charley as we were plodding over those endless prairies when there wasn't much more than an anthill or a prairie dog mound to call a mountain?"

"You still have a fair amount of the medications you prepared in St. Louis. Could you come up with some mixture that will help?"

"If I knew what would work, I would have suggested it long ago."

Back at the compound everything was calm and secure. But underneath was a sense of impending events unwanted and unexpected. They had to wait only a few hours when the first problem showed its face.

It was Dutch, and his usually cheerful face was one of complete disbelief and anger. "That Pres went and got himself in whole peck of trouble, Mister Jack. He's needin help."

"Out with it, Dutch. What happened?"

"Last night we was at that dance hall with the card room in the back. You know which one I'm talking about. Pres dances with this one girl two or three times and some local man goes up to him and says Pres is trying to take his girl from him."

"Slow down, and catch your breath. I'm right here."

"Pres says something back to this man, and they got into it. Both got tossed out of the dance hall, but then two guys with clubs and badges hauled Pres off to the jail."

"Where is the jail?"

"I think it's back of that place they call the governor's house. They told me to go on home or I might end up the same place."

The three men, Dutch, Jack, and Duncan held a brief confab, grabbed their coats and boots, caps and mittens and headed for the Plaza. About half way between the compound and the Plaza a two-horse rig pulling a stylish sleigh dashed by with a cheery hello from the driver. It was *La Doña* Tules and another woman, both dressed for an outing on a cold winter's day.

Tules got the horses turned around and trotted back to the men.

"You three look like a posse headed for the hanging tree. Why so glum on a gorgeous day like this?"

"*Buenas dias, Señorita* Barcelo. Yes, we may end up hanging somebody."

Pres began the tale of woe, with Jack filling in details. Without a moment's hesitation, Tules gave a command to the horses. As they stepped off toward the Plaza, she called over her shoulder, "Meet me in front of the Palace of the Governors."

The command from Tules was yet another reason for the three men to increase their pace. In a short time they were at the Palace. A few minutes later she strolled out of the government building on the arm of a high official. Judging from his elaborate uniform he had to be important, and judging from the attention he paid to her he must have owed her a considerable sum of money squandered at her card tables.

"Now you understand, my dear Manuel, I must have that young man released immediately! He is the only one who can care for my horses the way I demand."

"Of course, *Doña* Gertrudes. I shall see to his release at once. And will you accept my apologies for any inconvenience his detainment may have caused?"

"Perhaps luck will change when next you come to my *sala, sí?*"

As she got back into her sleigh she told Duncan he was to bring Pres to her place on San Francisco Street. The three men waited for about half an hour before Pres came out of the Governor's Palace from a door at the east side. He looked dazed and appeared to be sick, for he was almost doubled over.

"What did them bastards do to you, Pres, did they beat you?"

"They was a little rough, Mister Jack, but it was the damn food they brought. I tried to eat it, but it was slop you wouldn't feed to a hog."

"Hell! Why did you eat it?"

"They made me. They threatened me. Said it would make a man out of me. Said I was lucky they gave me any food at all. Let me sneak around the corner so I can throw up."

Duncan led them to Tules' place of business. They were met at the door that opened on the street by the man who always seemed to be with or near Tules wherever she went. "Please to follow me, *Señores*."

He led them not to the card room, but to a back door where Tules was having a spirited conversation at her sleigh with her companion of the morning.

"*Señor* Ross, may I present my good friend, *Señorita* Ramona Salazar from Rio Abajo?"

"I am pleased and delighted to meet you, *Señorita*."

Duncan turned to Tules, "This man needs immediate attention. He suffered some rough treatment overnight in that damn jail. *La Doña* Gertrudes, may I borrow your sleigh to take him home? I'll have it back to you within the hour."

"Take it as you wish. But, *Señor*, this young man must work tending my horses. That was the reason I gave my friend at the Palace. I told him I could not maintain my establishment without the services of this man and that he must be released without any charges at once."

"Very well, but I am taking him home for a couple of days until he is fit to work."

"You *gringos* have a way of taking charge, don't you? Return to your home, I will see that this young man is cared for."

"We mean no disrespect, and we do not doubt your word." Duncan was trying to ease the growing tension. "This man has been with us as we came over the Trail. We, too, have need of his abilities to manage horses. Can we not work out some arrangement?"

"No! I will be watched very closely by spies from the Governor. This man you call Pres, he must be seen at my place working with my horses."

"Is this plan acceptable to you? You take him into your place where he can be cared for now. I will return with Naomi so she may give him whatever medications he may need. That will free you of responsibility, and it will assure us that he is well enough to carry out whatever work you need from him."

"Take my sleigh. Do what you must do to get Naomi back here. But no tricks, *Señor* Ross. My patience is near the end. Go!"

All the way to the compound with the reins of a matched pair of fine horses in his hands, Duncan seethed inwardly over his abrupt dismissal at the hands of the notorious *La Doña* Tules.

"Damn her, she gets under my skin! But she did help us." To these thoughts Duncan added, "She got Pres out of a bad situation, she's loaned me money, she found housing for both families, and she made friends with Naomi. When my turn comes, how can I ever even the score?"

Most everyone from the compound was there to greet Duncan as he drove the sleigh through the gate. "Dunc, what have you done? Are you out of your mind? We don't need a team and sleigh like that! How much did it cost? I thought you were going to help Pres. Well?"

"Easy, Naomi. Get yourself dressed for a trip into town, and gather up some of your medications. Pres is a sick young man. He needs you."

Naomi hurried off to get herself and her medications collected while Duncan gave everyone the details of Pres' night on the town. On the way back to Tules' place he filled in the story for Naomi.

"Why is he sick? Was he beaten? Did they torture him?"

"You will be able to judge for yourself when you see him. Talking to him will be the best medicine. He hasn't told us the full story of the fight."

Dutch was waiting to take the rig to the barn back of Tules' place of business. "Jack is inside with Pres. He threw up again, says he's hurting."

"*Buenas diás*, Gertrudes. Where is the young man?"

"This way, *por favor*. I have done all that I can for him, Naomi."

"Will all of you please leave me with Pres? I need to have him tell me what he has experienced so I may know what best to give him."

It didn't take Naomi more than a few minutes, as she coaxed Pres to sip a medication, to get a more complete story of the fight. It was not just fists that were thrown about; the local man pulled a knife on Pres. The reaction of Pres was swift and effective. He had taken off his coat and handed it to Dutch as the two gladiators faced off on the dance floor. The second he saw the knife he snatched the coat from Dutch and flung it about the wrist and forearm of his assailant. Pres stepped in as the man lunged about trying to untangle himself from the coat and planted two hard fists, one to his left eye and the other on his chin.

Older men knew trouble was headed toward the dance hall and faded to the side or out the back door as two *agentes de policia* nabbed Pres and marched him off to the Palace of the Governors. As they left with the help-less boy locked in their grip, they had threatened Dutch, "Stay out of this. Go home or we put you in jail with this *hombre*."

It wasn't food that made Pres a sick young man. It was the repeated punches to his stomach and hard blows to his lower back that made him bend over in deep pain. The men who took him to the *cárcel* were experi-enced in giving pain without leaving marks.

"I made up that story about the awful food I was made to eat. I was afraid if I told Duncan and Jack what they did to me, they would start rais-ing hell and maybe get another fight started."

"You lie down, try to get in a comfortable position, and give this syrup time to soothe your stomach and back. Don't get up unless you have to. I'll get some sort of a jar or bucket to use."

A grim-faced Naomi turned on Tules as soon as she had closed the door. "Gertrudes, that boy was beaten. Not with clubs, but with fists so you can't find any marks. We are taking him home with us."

"No, Naomi. He must remain here."

"I said he is going with us. You cannot care for him properly here."

"I risked my name, my reputation to get him freed from the *cárcel*. I am responsible for him. He must remain here."

"When I think he has recovered we will return him to you."

"No, Naomi. You must try to see my position. He stays with me."

Duncan sensed these two powerful women were at loggerheads, and any more conversation might lead to a brawl. "*Señorita* Barcelo, he will remain as you wish. But every day Naomi and I along with Jack will come here to attend to him. We are as responsible as you for this young man. Does that arrangement meet with your approval?"

"No, it does not!"

"What would you suggest?"

"I have a friend, Luisa, who is a *curandera*. She will see to his needs. There is no need for your presence."

"That is not a plan we can accept."

"You have no choice. You fail to see how things are done in Santa Fe. Spies will watch every move in and out of my place, and even your compound will be watched. That is our way. Do not make more trouble than you can handle by yourselves. Now, leave!"

A dejected group walked slowly back to their compound. Duncan and Naomi said very little, but Jack was boiling with anger. "This is one hell of a country or province or whatever you call it. We come here with a wagon loaded with good stuff, better'n anything they got here. We come in peace; we come to live like neighbors, and what do get? Hands in our pockets every time we turn around, people turn their backs on us, and now this treatment of Pres. I hate this god forsaken hell hole!"

No one had an answer to Jack's outburst, but everyone felt his hurt, for all had some experience with similar problems. That night in bed Duncan and Naomi talked, as they had for so many nights when difficulties had come into their lives that had to be thrashed out.

"Do you see why it is absolutely necessary for both Jack and me to get some sort of a business going in this town? The people in Santa Fe have to see some reason for needing us."

"You may be right, but what will you do? You thought about trade with Chihuahua, and that never even started. You looked at gold mining, and that was impossible for you and Jack. What will you do?"

"I still think Jack and I should get to Taos. There is fur trading going on there. Both of us know something about that."

"But will we have to move there? I hear it is a small village even more remote than this town. And remember any day now our daughter will give birth. Do you want to be there when she wants you to be here?"

Except for occasional bouts of morning sickness, one of the many blessings Peggy was aware of as she went through her pregnancy was time for her art. It had been neglected for every one of the sixty-eight days spent on the Santa Fe Trail. More than just available time, there was a strong desire to get down on paper her impressions and memories of that experience. She brought out the box holding her pens, inks, and paper.

"Mother, some days I feel like I'm just starting! All the instruction that Thomas gave me vanished in thin air."

"Peggy, you are so much like your father. Impatience seeps out of you like the sap from a sugar bush in the spring. Keep doing a little each day; it will all come back to you."

"But Mother, you keep reminding me how busy I will be once I have the baby. I must get all the ideas I have churning inside of me on paper soon. The little rascal inside has his own way of churning. Did I give you so much trouble?"

"How can you call it trouble? He is reminding you that he's a part of your life now and not to forget him."

"We both talk as if it will be a boy. What if it's a girl?"

"Why, we'll love it without another thought! Your baby will always be the most precious thing in your life no matter, boy or girl."

Naomi was right and within a week Peggy produced a few good sketches. Within a month those sketches progressed to very good. Even Peggy was satisfied that she had regained her touch.

$\int$ $\int$ $\int$

He came in the early morning. Duncan said he was like the first rays of the day's sunshine. That was after Eleanor and Naomi assisted Peggy through the birthing ordeal and cleaned and wrapped the baby boy. The mother was a bit groggy, but instinctively reached out her arms to receive her child and hold him close. In a few minutes he had his own ideas of what the next thing should be. Peggy introduced him to her breast and he did what newborn babies sometimes do. He did nothing. It took minutes of gentle stroking and puckering of his lips before he got the idea. But once he did, he immediately went to work.

Everything in the compound seemed normal, for a few hours. Then six pounds of screaming, gurgling, sleeping, squirming, wetting, content-ed baby boy took charge. Every woman in the house – Naomi, Eleanor, Grace – claimed some portion of his needs as her special province. As for the men, they just stood around with beaming faces and did and said fool-ish things to convince each other that in some special way he was respon-sible for the miracle Peggy held in her arms.

When informed that a new boy would live in his house, Charley had his own way of taking charge. He sat himself on the floor propped against the sleeping pads, rolled and stacked against the wall each morning, and demanded that he be given the baby to hold. "It's my turn, and I have some things I must tell him about making so much noise. And I have some secrets he must know about."

"Of course you should hold him," Eleanor said, "but you must let me show how to do it so you don't drop him."

"I won't drop him. I don't want him to break. I'm going to take him to the barn to show him the little chicks that just hatched.

"Quick, Mother, take him. He's all wet. What's wrong with him?

Doesn't he know to go out to the necessary?" Charley decided that the visit to the barn could wait.

That evening all were gathered in the family room around the fireplace. In April at the foot of the Sangre de Christo Mountains evenings could pass quickly through being cool to being cold. A fireplace was the natural gathering place, but the center of attention was the baby. Naomi took him in her arms after Peggy had nursed him and slowly walked to Jorge who was in his usual chair nearest the fire. "Here, Jorge, meet the newest member of our family. Would you like to hold him?"

His toothless smile and nodding of his head were answers. As he held the baby he slowly rocked back and forth and mumbled what must have been an old Mexican song of comfort. With tears streaming down his face he continued to croon and rock as though transported to a place far away and long ago.

It seemed that one problem anticipated by all would never have to be dealt with. One glimpse of the baby's soft blonde hair and brown eyes and his name was on everyone's lips... "Billy."

The most changed person of the two families was Jack. His periods of long silence, of brooding and testiness were replaced with smiles and words of goodwill for all. He adapted his daily routines so that he was always available to walk about the compound with this boy child. It gave the women of the house a rest from a mounting list of chores. Jack was frequently accompanied by Charley, who kept up a stream of advice for the new arrival. The men of three generations presented a picture of solidarity to the world, and a silent message. "We are Gallaghers; don't get in our way."

This world was enlarged the day *La Doña* Tules drove into the compound in her fine carriage with Pres at the reins of the matched team.

"*Saludos, mi amigos*! Is this not the happiest moment for all? Let us celebrate and give thanks for this blessing. Now, where are the mother and child? I must see them."

"Welcome, *La Doña* Gertrudes. And welcome, Pres. May I assist you from the carriage?"

"Why, thank you, *Señor* Ross. Do you think me incapable?"

With carefully raised skirts that revealed shapely legs, Tules descended from her carriage, began her tour of the compound, and quickly appraised everyone present. To herself Naomi thought, "She never misses a chance to impress the men and never misses a count be it cards or people."

"Gertrudes, how good of you to visit. Come in the *casa* to see the newest member of the *gringos* who call Santa Fe home."

"Peggy, my dear, you look so radiant, so much the blessed mother. And your baby, he is beautiful! May I hold him? My heart is so full I think I will cry. But this not the time for tears. It is a time given over to joy, to sing and dance, is it not?"

"It is indeed a time for celebration. When you have a minute, Jack and I would like to speak with you."

"But, of course, *Señor* Ross, in a little while I may find a minute. I came to see happy faces and share a few moments with the women of your compound. Can you not give business matters a rest?"

How women can ever find so much to talk about was beyond the world of the men of the compound, and so they waited, and waited.

"Pres, will you go to my carriage and bring the parcel I left on the seat?"

He did as directed under the watchful eyes of Dutch. He could not believe what he saw, for Pres was always the one who gave directions, who made decisions for the two of them whatever they had in mind to do. Pres was a different young man no longer home to the fire and dash that frequently took that pair of young men to edge of troubles.

The package was handed to Tules who took it, beckoned to Jack and Duncan as she walked to the far side of the compound. "Now, what can I do for you men?"

Duncan started off, "We want you to release Pres from his duties."

"And for a reason? It must be a really good reason, for I find Pres to be very good with my horses and every task I give him. No, I am not in a position to release him."

As firmly as he could Duncan said, "He is a part of our two families, but we are about to lose him. And you, too, will lose him."

"And what will happen to cause us to lose Pres?"

"He and his partner, Dutch, are going back to Missouri with the first caravan to depart Santa Fe this summer."

"He can't do that! I won't permit it."

"My dear *Doña* Gertrudis, he has made up his mind." Duncan went on to explain how he and Jack had tried to persuade the boys to stay in Santa Fe. "You have a frisky colt on your hands. You have no right to deprive him of the chance to make his own way."

"He is a valued man in my service and that is where he shall remain."

Jack began, "I've worked with livestock all my life. I can tell when an animal's spirit been broke. I ain't gonna stand by and watch you do that to Pres. Another thing, we want him with us for the few months 'fore he and Dutch set off for the East. He's family to us, and we want him home."

She turned on her heel and marched off to the house with her package and her head held high. Sparks flashing from her grey eyes sent the message, "Who do this Duncan Ross and Jack what's his name think they are to tell me, Gertrudis Barcelo, what she must do? *Pues*, I will show them who runs Santa Fe."

In the house there were squeals of delight, of awe mixed in with expressions of appreciation. "*Doña* Gertrudis, it is beautiful. Such fine stitchery, and the shade of blue is heavenly. Thank you, thank you. Mother, look at this, isn't it perfect for Little Billy?"

The object of admiration by the women clustered about Peggy was the gift from Tules. It was a silk *reboso*, light and feathery. It was covered with intricate designs in white threads against a background of pale blue, designs so fine that the women could not believe it was not done by the angels. Naomi put an arm around her friend and said, "My dear, it is a treasure, such delicate work, and such generous spirits hover around you."

"I wanted your daughter to have this gift. Some day I may tell you the story behind it. Now, I must be off. Pres, bring my carriage to the gate."

Though *La Doña* Tules left in style, tears filled her eyes.

❧   ❧   ❧

As so frequently happens in the mountain country of the Southwest in a day spring became summer. The change brought a host of different chores and duties needing attention after a dormant winter. Naomi felt drawn to the meadows and streamsides where she might find tender shoots of green lamb's quarters to add to their chili dishes or perhaps some *mariola* leaves she could use to make a tea to relieve stomachache.

Jack, with his renewed vitality since the birth of Little Billy, a name adopted by all in the compound, began to work with the horses in the barn and pasture. Grace and Eleanor co-managed the baby, and all took over the spoiling of Peggy. Charley had Jorge to look after, but those pockets of care and concern omitted Duncan.

Left out of the spring makeover and rejuvenation, Duncan went frequently on foot to the Plaza and engaged in slow, easy going but meaningful exchanges with the merchants there on the merits of trade with Taos. That village was very much on his mind and he built an inventory of views about Taos, prospects for profitable trade, and risks and dangers so much a part of all the advice he received.

"Jack, we just have to get ourselves up to Taos. Can you get an outfit together? You know, riding horses, a wagon or perhaps a *carro* or two, mules, and mule skinners. How about it?"

"I ain't got no great interest in goin there. I'll help you get yourself set up to go to Taos, but that's it."

"Come on, my friend, you like to try new adventures as much as I do. We both remember the excitement of our days as clerks with the old North West Company. Let's give it a try."

"Them days is long gone, Duncan. I don't think you can go back and live in the past. Ain't like you to work over old bones. You was always the one to be lookin ahead to tomorrow."

"Taos is our tomorrow, Jack. I can feel it; it's right for us."

Later that day the appearance of Tules in the compound altered the thinking and planning of the families. "Where is that little boy? I must hold him and sing to him."

"*Hola, La Doña* Tules. How nice of you to visit. Come into the *sala* where Peggy is nursing the little scamp."

"Naomi, how dare you call this little angel a scamp? My, he does grow, doesn't he? You are a wonderful mother, Peggy."

Tears filled Tules' eyes as she sank into the chair usually occupied by Jorge. "I, too, had a little baby boy, Peggy. But he was born dead. I never knew the joy of feeding him. I never could do anything for him. I was a mother, but only for a minute. He was buried with a *reboso* around him much like the one I had made for you. It was the only thing I could do for my little angel."

"Oh, my dear. Such a sad story to have to keep in your heart." Peggy finished with the feeding, and after wiping the baby's lips she indicated to Tules to take him. With tears in her eyes and in her soft voice, Tules walked slowly about the room singing for a child she could love, but could never call her own.

Into the scene of motherhood present and motherhood past walked Duncan and Jack. "A good day to you, *Señorita* Barcelo. I hope this day finds you in good health."

"I would say the same," Jack ventured, "and I'm pleased to see Pres has them horses of yours in tip-top shape."

"How observant you are, *Señor* Jack, for it is Pres who not only drove me here, he is the reason I am at your place."

"Please continue." Duncan was ready to cross swords once again with this woman for whom he was developing a strong dislike. "Would you rather we retired to the portal to continue?"

"*Señores*, what I wish to tell you is of interest to all. My friends at the Palace of the Governors tell me of a caravan with armed escort is soon to depart for Taos. I also learned that you men wish to go to Taos. I am prepared to release Pres to aid you in that journey."

"How generous of you. We have need of Pres and Dutch for the trip we have been planning. *Gracias.*"

"You have not let me complete my message. Pres must return to my service once the journey to Taos is finished. Agreed?"

Duncan and Jack looked at each other, and spoke as one. "Agreed."

The departure of Tules was the beginning of many discussions among the Ross family and the Gallagher family. More than discussions, heated words were passed from Eleanor to Jack and from Naomi to Duncan. The women were angry over not being consulted about this trip to Taos.

Duncan tried to ease the tension by reminding Naomi that he talked with her several times about the need to explore the possibilities Taos might have for business opportunities. "But, my red-headed man, you never said it was so close. That fancy card dealer waltzes in here and you and Jack jump out of your skins to tell her 'yes' before Eleanor and I know what you have in mind."

"What we have in mind is a wagon for Taos with some trade goods to test the waters there. Nothing more."

"Nothing more? Why does that woman know more of what you plan to do than I know? All those trips into town you made in the past weeks, were they only about business?"

"Naomi! What are you trying to say? That woman is the last person with whom I would ever want to get mixed up."

With that outburst Duncan strode out of the room, across the compound to the side of the barn where he began to split and stack firewood at a furious rate.

It took a few days for the storms to pass. But in the end Jack, Dutch, and Duncan were on their way to the Plaza on a beautiful day in mid-July where they met Pres. And it was there they joined with the small caravan headed for Taos.

There was no question that the officer in command of the escort was also the boss of the caravan of traders and a few others desirous of getting to Taos under the protection of an armed escort. His sneering appraisal of the *gringos* he was to guard on the seventy-some mile trek to Taos was an indication of the attitude shared by most other members of the group.

The movement of the caravan began at a leisurely pace and never increased through the day. That first night found them a mile north of a small village named Santa Cruz de la Cañada, only a dozen miles from their starting point. At that rate Jack figured it would take all of three days, maybe even four to get to Taos.

They also met one of the men who was going to Taos enjoying the protection of an armed escort. "I say, men, you are not of this province. What call you home?"

The speaker was a ruddy-faced man of medium build and height, properly dressed for the trail, with touches of the gentry about him. He ate the meal served him by a man, obviously a servant, who also took charge of the horses, his and his master's, the minute they stopped to make camp for the night.

"We're a mixed lot, sir. Scotland was my place of birth, but Canada was where I spent most of my adult life." Duncan ventured this, before the man turned to Jack. "And I am a Carolina man, and these here lads are our mule skinners, both from Illinois."

"Good of you men to tell me of yourselves, I am Bertram Woolridge. I claim Scotland as my birth home, too, thought lately I have lived in New York. And I would prefer that you called me 'Bert.' I find formality is not expected in this strange but beautiful land. Would you not agree?"

"May I be so bold as to ask what takes you to the village of Taos?"

"One Scotsman should respond to his fellow countryman, eh? I am exploring business opportunities in this part of the country. What brings you on this trek to Taos?"

Duncan was quick to reply, "For much the same reason, sir."

"Ah, very interesting. Are you two partners?"

"You might say that, then again, maybe not," Jack said. "We take what chances come our way."

The second day started as the first, slowly and without much of a sense of purpose or pressure. Men of the armed escort seemed to be well-mounted, indifferently clothed in bits and pieces of a uniform style of dress, and armed as suited each man. But they were immediately responsive to their commander, and everyone was capable of managing his horse. Duncan reserved judgment as to their worth as an armed escort, yet he felt secure traveling with them.

The second evening in camp was a copy of the first; the escort made its camp separate from the others, and the 'locals' separated themselves from the *gringos*. Bert Woolridge joined the latter group and was welcomed at the fire. "I say, chaps, we don't seem to be in any sort of a rush to complete our journey. I expected a faster pace. What think you?"

Jack was quick to respond, "I agree with you, Bert. Was we on the Santa Fe Trail our wagon master would be havin a fit was we to poke along like this."

The third day was at an even slower pace, this time for a very good reason. At a place everyone called *el Embudo*, the caravan had entered a deeply cut pass in the rugged hills with a decided up-grade, a rocky one-track road, and a wild mountain stream never more than a handshake away.

The escort showed its training and discipline on that stretch of the trip. The commander divided the troop into thirds, one to lead, one to follow, and a third in the middle of the civilian members of the caravan. Their passage through this narrow cut was anything but a secret. The troopers were calling constantly to one another and snarling at any gaps in the line of wagons, *carros*, and horsemen. By late afternoon the group emerged onto a high plain with a magnificent view of the high mountains, and into a wind that even in July cut right to the bone.

"Close up, close, up. We still have some miles before our evening camp. Close up, *maldito sea*!" A trooper with some sort of decoration on his hat, probably a sergeant or perhaps a corporal, was riding along the line of the caravan, prodding the stragglers, and swearing at his men. The commander rode in silence and appeared to be bored with his assignment. One more night and he could enjoy whatever awaited him in Taos.

By the third night around their cooking fire an easy relationship was evident as Bert and his servant joined the "Easterners" – a name given the four *gringos* by the Scotsman.

"My man signed he would get up our evening's meal. He's been with me for many years, you know. I picked him up in India. He can't speak, had his tongue cut out for some minor offense, but he's been faithful and useful. I wouldn't trade him for ten of the people I've seen here about."

It wasn't important what they ate, what mattered was that it was something they could eat. "Pres, another meal like that, and I'll be lookin to replace you, lad."

"Now, Mister Jack, you wouldn't do that."

"Don't know, but that sure was a fine supper. Bert, can you sign to your man that we all 'preciates what he dun for us tonight?"

"Delighted! Tomorrow we surely will be in the village. Will you keep an eye on my man? I have matters needing my attention most of the day. He's a complete stranger to these parts; even in Santa Fe he was ill at ease much of the time.

"Duncan, you should come with me, for the man I will be meeting, Charles Bent, is an important man of the fur trade in Taos."

The caravan's entrance seemed not to excite any of the locals who went about their business with only a glance at this group. Bert inquired where Charles Bent's store was located and went directly to it. Jack said he would stay with the wagon and keep an eye on Bert's servant. Pres and Dutch were free to explore the town but told to stay together.

Bert led Duncan to the little town square or plaza and went to one of the stores there. "We wish to speak with your owner, Charles Bent. Would you be so good as to summon him?"

The man Bert spoke to reminded Duncan of a French-Canadian *voyageur*. He was no more than five foot five or six inches in height, slightly built, with long dark hair and a skin color close to swarthy.

The man turned on his heel as if to find Charles Bent, whirled around and said, "I am Charles Bent. How may I serve you gentlemen?"

Duncan immediately felt the disadvantaged position Bent placed them in. He recovered first, "Charles Bent, I am Duncan Ross from Santa Fe, and I am pleased to meet you."

"And you, sir, what is your name?"

"Yes, yes, I am Wool..., that is to say I am Bert Woolridge. Excuse me; I am Bertram Woolridge of New York."

"Well, now gentlemen, let us go to my office at the back of the store where we can relax and discover what it is that we should discuss."

The office was much like the store in that it was utilitarian. There was no attempt at style or décor denoting wealth, just two desks, one large sit-down and one stand-up with an oil lamp on each desk, several chairs, and a table piled high with maps and ledgers.

Bert, who for the past three days had been the in-charge person, was slow to get his thoughts gathered, so Duncan took the lead. "We learned in Santa Fe of the expansive business you and you partners have developed in Taos and areas adjoining. I have a Conestoga loaded with merchandise I think will be of use to you, and I also wish to share your opinions of the climate for trade in and around Taos."

"I shall be happy to look over what you have brought, for I suspect you are like me, a trader. Are you not?"

"I was, sir. Some years back I was a wintering partner with the North West Company. Today, I am a newly arrived resident in Santa Fe looking for business opportunities. I am finding it has not been a fruitful search."

"Our two villages, Taos and Santa Fe, are quite different, Mr. Ross."

"Please, I would be more comfortable with Duncan."

"As you wish and I would be comfortable with Charles. What I was about to say is that you will find we are a rather rough, and at times crude, lot up here. Our trade is with native groups and with individuals from all parts of the country. With your background in the fur trade of Canada, Duncan, I venture to guess you had me pegged as a French Canadian."

"I'm afraid you are correct about that. I do apologize."

"None necessary. I would be pleased to have the jaunty airs, spirit, and resourcefulness of a *voyageur*. You, of course, know that business in Taos is seasonal, cyclical, and based on a great amount of trust."

"Much the experience I had with the North West outfit. I'm sure you're aware, Charles, that the North West Company no longer exists."

"Yes, we learned of that happening shortly after the amalgamation was made public. As it worked out, Duncan, it was as though Jonah had swallowed the whale. Do you see it that way?"

"Well put, Charles. The smaller Hudson's Bay did indeed gobble up the much larger North West. But then, we didn't have the Bank of England behind us."

"Nor do we. We have had some very encouraging years and a few we would like to forget."

Bert broke his silence. "Charles, let me come right to the point. Is it reasonable to think that rank newcomers, such as Duncan and I, can get our feet in the door in this fur trade centered in Taos?"

"I shall be equally blunt, Bert, and answer with a qualified yes. But not in terms of one wagon load of trade goods. We deal in wagon train lots with several trains each season between the East and our major trading post about two hundred miles to the east of Taos."

A question from Bert, "I see, but you have a monopoly, do you not?"

"No! We have competition, fierce competition! And not only with other traders. We are constantly straightening out difficulties with the Governor of the Province. Remember you are still in Mexico. Several agencies and departments of the United Sates are also aware of our activities. Many times I finding myself wishing we had only traders to deal with."

"You present quite a different picture than I had imagined, Charles."

"It would be a disservice to do otherwise, Duncan. You said you were a wintering partner, did you not?"

"Yes. I grew up in the vast North Country of Canada. There I learned something of extreme weather conditions and the fickle nature of trade dependent on one of God's creatures, the beaver."

"So you saw both beauty and violence in your passage over our seas of grass and sand and another of God's creatures that rule the prairies, the buffalo. I have to prepare for a trip to our post on the other side of the mountains. Shall we look over what you have in your Conestoga?"

On a signal from Duncan, Jack drove the six-mule span hitched to the wagon to the front of the Bent store. "Charles Bent, meet my long-time friend from our days in the fur trade, Jack Gallagher." The men acknowledged the introduction and went right to work, looking, sorting, judging, and bargaining. It didn't take long for the wagon to be emptied with the merchandise in the hands of its new owner.

"Duncan, it has been a pleasure meeting and doing a little business with you. I shall be in Santa Fe by the end of next month and will settle accounts with you then. Is that agreeable? Fine! And Mr. Gallagher and Mr. Woolridge, it was a pleasure to meet you. Have a safe return to Santa Fe."

"Ah, Charles," Bert stumbled over his words, "I should ... that is I need ... I don't quite know what to say. But what would you advise me about continuing on to California from this village? I see no reason for my return to Santa Fe. I have experienced what Duncan has told you; it has not been a fruitful place for business."

"It seems to me, Mr. Woolridge, you should consider going north from here to link up with a wagon train on the Oregon Trail. Once there you can move down the coast to California. There are quite a few caravans on the road this summer. My partner, Ceran St. Vrain, is much better acquainted with that country. I will ask him to assist you in making suitable arrangements. But, under no circumstance, Mr. Woolridge, should you contemplate making such a journey by yourself."

It took some time for the Easterners to locate the commander of the escort and determine if and when he would be returning to Santa Fe. He made no attempt to hide his displeasure over having them in his caravan going back to Santa Fe. Jack used the three days they would have in Taos to scrounge up some cargo they could carry in their Conestoga.

"Running that wagon empty back to Santa Fe don't make sense, and the few *reales* we'll get might pay for them mule's feed."

"Jack, you're always one jump ahead of me when it comes to business. We should make you our agent."

"You was always the one to be the talker, maybe we should make you the ... – oh, forget it."

"What do you think of this village, Pres? See any *señoritas* you'd like to dance with?"

"About the same as what we seen in Santa Fe. Ask Dutch what he seen."

"How about it, Dutch? You willing to make another trip to Taos?"

Further conversation ended when Bert and his man rode up to them on their horses, each one leading a pack horse fully loaded with gear for a long trek. "I can't leave without saying goodbye to you gentlemen. I met with Ceran St. Vrain and he advised me on what we should have to make the journey to California by way of Oregon country. In this little village I was able to buy what we needed, and here we are. We depart within the hour. *Adieu*, my friends. I wish you well, and may we meet again in another place at another time."

"Bert, we offer our congratulations on your splendid outfits." Duncan was taken with how quickly Bert conducted his affairs. "The best to you and your man along the trail. God speed."

Occasionally in the Southwest, the land of *mañana*, things do happen quickly. The friends of three nights and four days on the trail from Santa Fe to Taos disappeared in the midst of a large caravan of horses, mules, wagons, loose livestock, and men anxious to be under way.

Two nights and three days were all the time it took on the return to Santa Fe. Where the eyes of the escort's captain were dull and lifeless on the outbound trip, now they were alive and full of anticipation on the homebound trip. Jack guessed that the small amount of pay he received would be on the card table in La Tules' place before sunset.

The air at the compound was much warmer when the four men

returned than when they had departed twelve days earlier.

"Papa Dunc, we are so glad you're back with us. Come see how much Little Billy has grown."

"Peggy, my dear, this motherhood thing was made for you. I have never seen you so happy."

"Why wouldn't I be happy? We are once again two happy families. I think even Jorge is glad to have you back."

The joy of the reunion was dampened considerably later that evening when Duncan and Naomi were in bed and catching up on news and things. Naomi told Duncan something that made him angry, very angry. "You missed the big send-off party in the Plaza for the caravan that departed for Missouri four days after you and Jack left for Taos."

"That red-headed bitch! She knew it was going to leave and when it would leave. No wonder she was willing to release Pres to go with us."

"Red-headed bitch? Who are you talking about, Dunc?"

"You know damn well who I'm talking about."

"What are you going to do?"

"Well, I suppose Pres will learn of this. He and Dutch will have to wait for the next caravan that forms up headed east. I feel responsible for this sad turn of events. How can I make it up to those boys?"

"I don't know, Dunc, but what did you learn in Taos?"

"I met a most interesting man. Name is Charles Bent, and I have a feeling we're going to be doing business with him someday."

"But what of the village? How does it compare to Santa Fe?"

"For one thing Taos is higher in the mountains, and I think a prettier place than Santa Fe, but much smaller. But what is really different is the atmosphere. Here everything seems to revolve around the Palace of the Governors and the people who are in and out of that place all day long. Up there, trade in furs and buffalo hides is the center of activity. I got a good feeling just being there, like I belonged there."

"Does that mean we're going to move to Taos?"

"My dear, that's looking too far ahead. Let's get our attention back to how much I missed you.

"I think I would like that. Tell me more."

ₑ   ₑ   ₑ

True to his word, by the end of the month Charles Bent made his appearance in Santa Fe. He inquired immediately for Duncan Ross and how he might contact *el pelirrojo*. Bent was well known among the officials who worked in the Palace of the Governors. Directions were given, and soon he was relaxing with Duncan at the Ross-Gallagher compound and enjoying the hospitality so much a part of that place.

Introductions and related small talk put everyone at ease while Naomi and Eleanor plied their guest with refreshments. Jack was the notable absentee. He greeted Bent, made excuses, and melted into the background. "Duncan, I ain't got nothin to say to this Bent, and I 'spect he's got nothin to say to me. You two need to talk without interruption. So go to it, my friend."

For nearly two hours the two men with so much background and experience in the fur trade did just what Jack suggested. They went at it with thoughtful questions, carefully considered answers, and probes into personal history. By the time Charles Bent was ready to return to the Plaza and the hotel nearby, a vast amount of information had changed hands.

"Duncan, my visits to Santa Fe are not usually this relaxing and informative. An air of corruption and deceit hangs over the Governor's offices. I feel nothing can sponge away the grime that gathers on everything and everybody there. My time at your place has made me feel at home. I am pleased to have you be as open and honest with me as I have tried to be with you."

Duncan was not ready to terminate their discussion. "But aren't more than petty under-the-table deals made in the Governor's offices? Are there not real threats to the Province? You mentioned the hotheads in Texas that want to take over *Nuevo Mexico* at least to banks of the *Rio Grande*. And the problem with Indians, especially the Navajos, never seems to settle down for more than a month or two. How can you conduct business in that atmosphere?"

"Duncan, I see two ways to answer your doubts. For one thing, Bent-St. Vrain does a very large volume of business over a vast area. Troubles in one area do not always impinge on the other. And we find being in Taos a distinct advantage. Up there we can all but ignore these slippery government people down here, so we tend to do business our way. You know, a smile and a handshake. Think about that, my friend. I am sure we will find ways to put our talents to work for mutual profit. My regards to the charming women who make this such a pleasant home. My thanks to you for sharing your thinking and your time. Good day, sir."

The visit of Charles Bent to the compound had long-lasting impacts, and it tapped into a deep well of curiosity. "How can two men ever find anything to talk about for two hours? I thought you said, Dunc, that only women can talk that long."

"But this was business. Everything we talked about was business that was important to us."

"Tell me about it as we walk to the Plaza. I may have need of you to carry some of my purchases."

It took some prodding from Naomi to get Duncan on his feet. Most of his reluctance stemmed from knowing she would have questions. She did not disappoint him. "I must say I was surprised by Charles Bent. I thought I was meeting a *voyageur*. Did you have the same feeling the first time you met him in Taos?"

"Yes. I had that impression. He didn't sing any raunchy songs, and he didn't play any pranks at my expense, but he does look like a *voyageur*."

"What are you going to do? He's in Taos seventy miles away. You're here in Santa Fe. How will you ever get together to do this precious thing you call business?"

"I really don't know, but somehow I think we will be doing business."

"Are you up to carrying a sack of *frijoles* to the compound? Now that we have all learned how good they are, Eleanor and I are amazed at how quickly a sack of them vanishes from the storeroom."

On their return home Naomi gave Duncan a full review of the way she saw things developing with other people who lived there.

"I am more than ever concerned about Charley's lack of growth. His mind is growing, his eyes sparkle with new ideas that bubble up in him all day long, but his energy grows weaker. I don't know what to do."

"Is there a doctor, a man who had some real training and schooling as a physician, in Santa Fe?"

"Tules told me there is such a man. He is French, and he is the doctor the *ricos* turn to when they need medicines or advice. Eleanor said she doesn't want a stranger to have anything to do with Charley."

"Does she still think living in these mountains has some part in his not growing and developing?"

"She does, and she has Jack thinking the same."

"Have they said what they might do? You know, find a place better suited to Charley?"

"You're not going to like this, but they have talked about going back to Missouri with a caravan this summer."

"They wouldn't leave Santa Fe, would they? Perhaps they were just teasing you." Duncan's question was aimed at the heart of his concern for the Gallaghers

"Did you ever know Eleanor to tease? When she says something you'd better listen. We know Jack likes to joke with people even when he's trying to be serious. But not Eleanor."

Duncan tried to absorb all that Naomi told him and added, "Pres and Dutch haven't changed their minds about going back. And they're still angry about your friend Tules and the way she tricked Pres into being away from Santa Fe when she knew he should be here."

"It makes me think a lot less of her, but still she helps people. You have no idea of how many come to her for help, and she can be very generous."

"She can. That's true, but doesn't she extract a price for what she does for people?"

A second caravan departed from the Plaza in late September. Pres and Dutch tried to get hired as mule skinners, but were not successful. There was a muted send-off for the caravan, and a rush of local people who had letters to be delivered along the way. Both Peggy and Duncan wrote letters to St. Louis friends, Myrna Wilson and Samuel Rawlinson, and Duncan added one to his sister in Scotland. On the return to the compound Peggy and Duncan talked about the departure they witnessed.

"I can't understand their leaving this late in the season. Even if they travel at a record pace, the caravan still runs the chance of those fall storms on the high plains."

"I remember some of the storms we weathered, Papa Dunc. I wouldn't want to be caught in one that could change to snow in a second."

"Nor I. And they will find the grass on the prairies is short and dry. No, I think it would be better had they waited for spring."

"I pray they make it through. Our letters might be undelivered."

When they got back to the compound Pres was at the gate to meet them. "Well, Pres this is a surprise. Did that grand lady you work for give you a day off?"

"I quit! I ain't working for her no more. She can go to hell!"

"Easy, Pres, easy. What happened?"

"Well, it ain't exactly her. It's that man that she's takin up with."

"That would be the Governor, wouldn't it?"

"That's the one. He comes to her place and acts like he owns it and tells me what to do and how to do it. I tell you, Mr. Ross, he don't know horses. He beats 'em, lashes 'em, but he don't know how to care for 'em."

"Did you tell Tules that you were leaving her? She will have to get a man to replace you."

"I ain't seen her for a couple of days. But that little, shifty-eyed man who counts her money and watches over the tables when she's dealing cards can tell her. He knows everything going on at her place. Let him be the one."

"Well, don't get yourself worked up, Pres, I think this can be ironed out. Come on in and see what we might find to eat."

Shortly after sunrise the next morning nickering of the horses in the nearby pasture gave warning that someone strange was in the area. Both Duncan and Jack were at the gate to see what caused the commotion. Not a single stranger, but ten strangers, well-mounted, steely-eyed, and arrogant beyond belief. "Them bastards are from the Governor's Guard, Duncan. Best see what's on their mind so early in the morning."

"*Señor* Ross. His Excellency, *el Gobernador* Manuel Armijo, orders that you return the stable-hand, Pres, to his place of duty at once. I bid you a good day, *Señor.*"

The troop clattered off in perfect formation and brought this comment from Jack. "Must cost His Excellency a pretty penny to keep a bunch of thugs up on good horses, in clean uniforms, and trained like a bunch of monkeys."

Duncan laughed, "Maybe it isn't his money that keeps his guard up to scratch. Could be someone else's money. Want to guess whose?"

"Waste of time to answer that. What are we gonna do 'bout Pres?"

"Let's go find some *chocolate* and figure out something."

They sat in the kitchen with Eleanor and Naomi and mulled over the situation Pres created for himself. "Of course he was right to walk away from the abuse of horses. Governor or not, no man should mistreat animals!"

Jack was quick to agree. "Pres was right, Naomi, but how's he gonna defy a man as powerful in this town as the Governor?"

"Why do you think only about the Governor?" Eleanor poured more *chocolate* as she went on with her thinking. "Why not think about the woman who has his ear or whatever part of him she wants? Isn't that the person you should talk with?"

"By crickety! Eleanor, I think you're right," Jack continued with a show of enthusiasm. "Naomi, you're the one closest to that Tules lady. Why don't you see what you can do?"

"Well, yes, I know her. But I can't walk in and tell her what to do. She would turn on me in a second if she thought I was getting into her affair with the Governor."

They were saved from more speculation about the message delivered from the troop of ten in such a forceful way early that morning by the appearance of Tules. She drove her carriage to the gate, "Is there not some one here to hold my horses? I would have a minute with the master of this compound."

"*Doña* Gertrudes, what a pleasant surprise. Won't you come in and join us for *chocolate*? You are looking so ravishing this morning that I envy you. How do you do it?"

"Naomi, my dear, you seem to be the only person here who has not forsaken manners. Of course I will have a *chocolate* with you, but I don't care for the men you associate with in this compound."

As she led Tules into the other room, Naomi gave a knowing glance at Duncan and shake of her head directed at Jack. "Now, what can we do for you? Please tell me as we ignore these men."

"Pres did not respond to the order given by the Governor's Guard. I came to warn you of the consequence of this. I know the Governor to be a man of great temper when he is disobeyed. It is unwise to defy him."

"But, are you not aware that *Señor* Armijo beats horses? Your very own horses are mistreated by him. You cannot expect that a young man who has lived with animals all his life can work under those conditions."

"I expect that any man who works for me will do what he is ordered to do."

"That isn't the point, is it? You told me several times of the terrible conditions you were forced to work under at the *rancho grande* in Manzano. Can you not appreciate that Pres feels as you did? That there are limits? That a man does not deserve to be called a man if he yields to the evil of beating helpless animals. Can you not agree? I know you, Gertrudes, you are a better woman than you realize. I know deep in your heart you know how Pres feels and why he left your employment."

"You speak with such passion, Naomi, and I know you speak truth. But have you not lost sight of my problem? What am I to tell the Governor if I return without Pres at my side?"

"Do we not know how to calm our savage beasts? Are we not women? Women who understand the ways of men, and what they want?"

"You don't know Manuel Armijo. It is easy for you to talk. You do not have to face his anger."

"Consider this and say to him, 'My dear Manuel, I cannot abide having a man work for me who is but a *gringo*. My horses deserve the care of a man of Mexico. I no longer wish to have this Pres person at my place.'"

"He might accept that reasoning, Naomi. And if I wear the daring new gown I have ordered he will find it hard to deny my request. *No?*"

"Gertrudes, you are a delight. You see possibilities quickly and clearly. Now, I think we can find a sweet that escaped the eyes of the men. It will go well with another cup of *chocolate. Sí?*"

The carriage driven by Tules had no sooner cleared the compound when a rider came to the gate calling for a Duncan Ross. "I am Duncan Ross. What can I do for you?"

The rider handed an envelope to Duncan and wheeled his horse around and raised a cloud of dust as he galloped back to the Plaza. "What is this all about?"

"You might find out if you opened the letter."

It was from Charles Bent, an invitation for Duncan to return to Taos as soon as possible and come prepared to spend some time there and at the Bent's trading post on the Arkansas River. "I knew that sooner or later Charles Bent and I would find some area of mutual concern. But what?"

"I found a way to resolve Pres' problem with Tules. Do I have to find a way to Taos for you?"

"My dear, you did a magnificent piece of work on Tules to have her release Pres from an impossible situation. How do you think she made out with the Governor?"

"It's always best to bet with Tules, not against her. I think she is doing just fine in her chosen line of work, don't you agree?"

"Let's talk about Taos. This letter says I am to join a Bent wagon train departing Santa Fe in two days. So, my long-legged friend, I won't have to put my own escort together. Not to worry, I won't be making the trip alone."

"But I do worry, Dunc. I hear about Indian raids on villages all around Taos. And I'll worry until you are back with us."

This trip to Taos was handled with more efficiency and dispatch than Duncan's first one. He no sooner set foot in the Bent store on the Plaza in Taos than Duncan was directed to come back tomorrow at break of day ready to go with another wagon train to the main post, known by most traders as "Fort William."

A few questions here and there in Taos brought answers that filled in more of the background Duncan sought about this family of traders. He learned the new and very large trading post on the Arkansas was named to honor William, the younger brother of Charles Bent, who supervised the building and the operation of the post.

Back on the trail the next day as they worked their way through the mountains surrounding Taos to the east, the Bent caravan came to a stretch of the trail over open country. That was but a short respite before tackling another mountain called by the locals *el Raton*. It was a major undertaking, but the wagon master and his people handled it with relative ease. Perhaps it was easy to them, but to Duncan getting wagons over the pass on a road that barely deserved to be called a road was marvelous piece of work. Once free of that obstacle it was nearly three days over a trail along a half dry stream called *Timpas* to Fort William.

The sparse vegetation of the open country matched the sparse conversation of the trip. It was not unpleasant, this was a business trip. The near silence among the men of the caravan reminded Duncan of the long trips he made in freight canoes shuttling between the North West Company's great central depot at Grand Portage and his home post in the North Country. These, too, were business ventures, and many days passed with thousands of paddle strokes, but without a word of English.

While the remembrance of trips gone by was somewhat reassuring to Duncan, nothing prepared him for his first sighting of the Bent trading post on the Arkansas River. It stood alone amidst the scrub growth of the surrounding prairie. Huge by any standards, being the only structure for miles added to its impression of size and security. The Arkansas flowed a short distance from its south side, and along its banks were stretches of grass nearby suitable for grazing livestock.

Duncan passed through the massive main gate of the post and was greeted by Charles Bent, who immediately introduced him to his younger brother, William. Just as the post gave a sense of power, the Brothers Bent gave a sense of purpose and success.

"Welcome, Duncan Ross. We are pleased to have you here. After refreshing yourself, come join us for a cup in the billiard room."

Duncan followed the servant who shouldered his *musette* bag and *poncho* up a flight of stairs along the inside wall. The room was furnished simply with touches of color provided by Mexican rugs on the wooden floor and the Indian blanket on the bed.

Refreshed and curious, Duncan stepped outside his room and decided to trace the sound of voices he heard on the same level as his room.

"There you are, Duncan, come join us. Do you know the game of billiards? Have a try. We had the table brought out from St. Louis, and it survived the trip in remarkably good condition."

The huge fortress-like trading post, the congenial brothers, and this beautiful billiard table ... do the Bents ever stop in their impressions? A flash of caution raced through Duncan's mind, for he remembered how his uncle, the great Simon McTavish, scored many victories for the North West Company over his opposition simply by the impression he made.

Time passed quickly at Fort William. After a hearty supper that included dishes such as a roast of buffalo hump, smoked buffalo tongue, planked trout, and other items that escaped his memory, Duncan was given a detailed tour of the operation. The post had everything: a blacksmith's shop, carpentry shops, tailor's room, store rooms, kitchens, and living quarters sufficient for a small army. Most importantly, in the middle of the compound was a deep well of excellent, plentiful water

The next day the brothers alternated their time between taking care of their personal business and conversations with Duncan. But after hours of this routine, a question began to form in Duncan's mind. Why he was selected to come here, to be exposed to the grandeur of this truly remarkable place and not asked specific questions of substance? They knew of his background as a trader in Canada, but nothing was ever brought up by either brother that he could relate directly to their business.

On the third day Duncan was a part of a caravan on its way to Taos. Again a trip without incident, or without much conversation. Once back in Taos he was sent on his way the very next day with an escort of three seasoned riders who bade him farewell in Santa Fe without any words of instruction or explanation.

ę   ę   ę

Compared to previous winters spent in Santa Fe, this one turned out to be mild and short. But it was not a winter without bleak days within the compound.

One morning about a month after Christmas, Charley came into the kitchen crying. He sought the security of his mother's lap. "Jorge won't talk to me. I didn't say anything to him to make him mad, Mama. But he won't talk to me."

"Sit up to the table and eat your breakfast while I go to his room and see what has upset him."

Jorge was not upset, he was dead. The old man had died in his sleep. He had not made any sort of complaint nor had he showed any signs of illness. He just passed away. Everyone in the compound was saddened with this happening but accepted it. All but Charley. Jorge had become his grandfather, his constant companion, and always offered an ear when the little fellow engaged the old man with fanciful tales from his active mind.

Eleanor recognized this special relationship between a gabby little boy and a wizened old man. Neither could understand what the other one said, yet they spent hours together in conversation. She understood Charley's isolation from other children of his age and his need to talk, to explain, and to dream. Jorge filled those gaps in much the same way Little Billy helped to fill the gaps caused by his father's untimely death.

Eleanor took charge. "Jack, you must ride into town and tell Tules. She will know what should be done and whom to notify. Best you and Duncan go together. There maybe several things that must be tended to."

Naomi learned of Jorge's death and began immediately to prepare for the care of the old man's body for burial.

"Naomi," Duncan said, "don't get too far ahead here until we learn what are the proper burial procedures. He's no doubt Catholic, and they have their ways at the time of death."

Jack and Duncan went on their mission. The women began their chores. Charley went and sat at Jorge's bedside. "He may wake up and want to talk to me, and I have to be here. There are a lot of things he doesn't understand, and I'm the only one he can ask."

When the men reached Tules they were not surprised at her instant response. "You were right to come to me, for I know Roberto Lucero would want his man to have a proper burial and be laid to rest *in campo santo*. You said you had a request, Duncan?"

"Yes. Jack and I want to fashion a casket for Jorge. We feel it would be one way for our families to share in his final rites. Is that something that can be done by people who are not part of your Church?"

"I would say, do it. If there is any question I will handle it."

On a cold but sunny morning in January, Jorge Moreno left the compound for the last time. He had called this place his home for more years than most people could recall. He left behind friends whose names he never knew, in a casket of wood made by caring hands he seldom saw, and followed with tears he would never understand. But he left without his little friend, Charley, who had developed a severe chest cold. Eleanor kept him bundled in a nest she made for him in the kitchen. She and Naomi took turns caring for him and explaining to him that Jorge need not worry any more about keeping warm.

An early spring followed the mild winter. Now was the time for Jack to exercise his judgment of horse flesh, really of mule flesh, as he assembled a string of top quality mules. These would be hitched to the Conestoga wagons stored behind the barn. Jack resisted all offers to sell them, putting off would-be buyers with a series of excuses. Ever since his arrival in Santa Fe three years ago Jack submerged the thought that someday he would need those wagons for a return to the East. That day was rapidly approaching.

It also arrived for Duncan. He, too, had an unwanted thought – those wagons would again be used to traverse the Santa Fe Trail. But not for his family. He and Naomi watched the lack of progress in the health of Charley and the abandonment by Jack of any sustained effort to find something he might develop into a business in Santa Fe. They could see that Grace was not accepted into any circle of young people of her age in Santa Fe. Grace was one of the most attractive girls in the town, a fact not lost on other girls. And Grace had not made much effort to break into those circles; her life centered on Little Billy and Peggy.

Eleanor was also a part of the puzzle. She never said much nor did anything to give a sense of what governed her thinking. Her daily routines led one to believe that life for her meant her man and her children and now her grandson. But was that all? Naomi as well as Duncan wondered if there were not hidden chests locked full of mysteries and unfulfilled desires to which only Eleanor had the key.

It was not necessary for Jack to make an announcement of his intentions to return to St. Louis. The signs were read easily as his preparations forged ahead openly. Few questions were left unanswered. Jack's actions focused on doing the things that would ensure a safe journey as a part of a reliable wagon train manned with experienced hands. He need not be reminded how much luck and good fortune played in any trek over the Trail be it to the West or to the East.

Talk about the town had it that a large caravan would leave for Missouri in late May. By that time grass would be in new growth sufficient to keep a large group moving and still provide plenty of graze for buffalo.

In mid-April Duncan had another letter from the Bents in Taos asking him to return there to consider business proposals they wished to make. Within a few days he was able to join a small group making the trip with a military escort. Though the group moved with visible speed along the trail to Taos, Duncan felt that time dragged. He was consumed with impatience and spent hours in the saddle speculating about which of the brothers he would meet in Taos and what was on their minds. Getting back into fur trading was an agreeable thought, but on whose terms? The Bents' or those of Duncan Ross?

Once in Taos his curiosity was more than satisfied. He had to pinch himself as he digested what the Bents had in mind for him.

"Duncan, good to see you. Come in and meet Ceran St. Vrain."

Charles Bent's partner was a man who showed clearly the years spent on a variety of trails and paths in pursuit of peltries and buffalo hides. He was rugged, polished-type rugged, well dressed and mannered, with a tendency to use few words. He sat and watched as intently as he listened, but seldom interrupted either of the brothers with questions for Duncan.

Back in his room that night Duncan felt the great weight placed on him by these men. What they offered to him was very much what he wanted – a chance to remain in Santa Fe. It was a town he was learning to enjoy and where his family would always be close by.

Was he willing to accept the costs of serving Bent-St. Vrain while being true to his own interests? All night he tossed and turned in his bed at the home of Charles Bent. In the morning Charles would expect an answer. As he understood their proposition, the Bent group wanted him to take over the office and store they maintained in Santa Fe. Charles and William as well as Ceran St. Vrain openly expressed their desires to be "in the field," honestly admitting their dislike of administrative-type work. It was a forthright statement of the preference of the partners.

But was this what Duncan wanted to do year after year? Office work, working with officials of Mexican government in Santa Fe? He speculated that every day would be spent trying to keep abreast of all the under-the-table deals, the bribery, the punishments meted out by men in Santa Fe who confused personal agendas with the needs of the Province?

In the morning, steaming, strong coffee did little to clear his thinking.

"Charles, I make no attempt to hide the results of a sleepless night. I turned over in my mind the proposition you made to me, but I think it best to give me time to digest it. I have more than myself to consider; I would never make this decision without a thorough review with my wife and daughter."

"Fine! I know my brother and Ceran would agree on the importance of your decision for yourself, your family, and for us. We will arrange immediately for your return to Santa Fe with suitable guard, of course. Get word to us in Taos when you have reached a decision."

ε ε ε

On his return, Duncan found intense activity in the compound as the Gallagher family made preparations for their return to Missouri.

"Jack, you have a man standing in front of you with a pair of willing hands, put him to work."

"Dad gum it, you old beaver skinner, you ought to be packin up and go with us. I can't see you sittin in an office pushin paper around. That ain't the life for you."

"I think there will be more than paper pushing. This Bent-St. Vrain outfit is pretty damn big, and I expect I'll be doing some traveling."

"Maybe so, but I see your daughter's wantin to talk to you. I'll have some chores for you after you see what she wants."

"Yes, Peggy, what can I do for you? Your Uncle Jack doesn't seem to need me to help him this morning."

"Papa Dunc, please walk out the firewood cutters' path with me. There's something we must talk about."

"My goodness, this must be about the end of the earth. All this fuss about where we will walk and talk, what's on your mind?"

Peggy was mum as they walked for about fifteen minutes. She turned to her father and said, "I am taking Little Billy and we are going back with the Gallaghers."

Only once before had Duncan Ross been dealt a blow as severe and as numbing as this. He could not speak, he could not walk, he could not think. He turned to Peggy and held out his arms. She rushed to them and held him as closely as he held her. It was a long time before any words were traded. "I wanted to be the one to tell you, Papa Dunc. It had to be me."

"Peggy, this wasn't something you decided to do without a lot of thought. Will you tell me of your reasons?"

"There are many, but I'm not sure I can get them straight in my mind."

"I just want to hear what you want me to know. It doesn't matter whether your reasons are in order or complete; just tell me."

"This is so hard. It sounds as though I am blaming my mother for what I am doing. Since Little Billy was born Aunt Eleanor has seemed more like a mother to me. She does more for Little Billy and me. She's always there; Mother is off doing her things sometimes when I need her to be with me."

"But, Peggy, both Aunt Eleanor and your mother have many duties and problems to solve. They go about doing those things in different ways."

"I know it hurts both of us for me to say this, but there are times I would rather have my aunt with me than my own mother."

"Are there other reasons?"

"Grace and I are more like sisters than just friends. There's no future in Santa Fe for her. The same goes for me, and I don't want Little Billy to grow up in this town."

"Santa Fe hasn't been an easy place for any of us at some time or other since we came here."

"It isn't going to get any better, at least for me. I can't sell any art. I can't make any friends. I just don't belong here."

Peggy's outpouring ended and the tears began. Duncan noticed a downed tree off to the side of the path. "Come and sit with me. I have some thoughts I want to share. I'm like you; I don't know where to begin."

He put his arm around Peggy and made no attempt to talk her out of her tears. After sobs and sniffles subsided, Duncan began.

"You should know your mother had the same fear about where you should grow up as you have for Little Billy. She did not want you to live the life of a child in a big fur trading company. For many years she was upset over my long absences when I had to go to the annual *Rendezvous* of my company. I tell you these things, Peggy, for I want you to see that you and your mother have reason to think alike."

"I do remember Mother cried many, many tears when she took me and went to her brother's people."

"I cried too, for I realized I was the cause of so much unhappiness in your mother's life. Then there is something else you should know about your mother. In order to protect you, to make sure you were safe and secure, she gave herself to a man, to Armand. Do you remember him?"

"Oh yes, Papa Dunc, I remember him and hate him still."

"She did this because he gave you and your mother a place to live when no other people would take you two into their lodges. It was a terrible price to pay, but she paid it to provide a home for you."

"I thought I knew about her life from the very beginning, but she never explained that part of it."

"Now you know. Does it change your mind?"

"It makes me see my mother in a different light, Papa Dunc, but I am still going back East."

"Perhaps you had best return to the compound. I want to sit here for a few minutes, alone."

Hours passed before Duncan could drag himself back home. He tried to get into the bustle and confusion of all the activities there, but he felt like he was in another world. He wished that what he saw, heard, and felt were happening to another person, not to him.

He was in their bedroom looking for something when Naomi walked in. "She told you, didn't she?"

"Yes. How long have you known?"

"You were still in Taos when she told me everything."

"What did you say?"

"I'm not sure we said very much. There were long pauses when neither of us said a word."

"Are you trying to persuade her to change her mind?"

"No, are you?"

"I don't think so. Should we?"

Naomi didn't answer Duncan's question. Instead she went to the compound gate, stood for a moment, and then walked on the woodcutter's path to the mountains. Alone, yet in sight of the compound, Naomi recalled her last conversation with Rosalia Baca. In her work as a *curandera* Naomi had met this older woman, herself a *curandera* some years in the past. A severely crippled leg made Rosalia's impossible to continue. Her vast knowledge of where the necessary roots, herbs, barks, and grasses were gound was shared with Naomi in return for Naomi's care and concern for her condition.

They were on the upper reaches of the little stream that coursed through the village of Santa Fe searching for *yerba del pescado*, a root that Rosalia said was the best cure for a sore mouth.

"You are very quiet this morning, Naomi. Have I said something that has upset you?"

"No, Rosalia, no. I guess I have been thinking of my own problems instead of the work we have at hand."

"Might it be something I may have an answer to?"

"My people value the judgments of the elders; I should value yours."

"I suspect you have a family problem, Naomi. Will you share it?"

"For some years, Rosalia, my daughter and I find that we have gaps in our lives that we can't seem to fill. I fear something is about to happen. I don't know what it is, but my inner self tells me it will happen."

"Not to fear, my dear Naomi. I know you to be a strong and caring woman. Talk to your daughter, tell her you are afraid. Ask her what she thinks might drive you two apart more than you are right now. Ask her!"

Naomi stood for a long time with her eyes fixed on the high mountains as if the answers she sought could be given her by the spirits she knew lived there. When she returned to the compound she found things just as she left them, but with a firm resolve to follow Rosalia's advice and talk again with her daughter.

From that time until the families gathered for the final meal in the kitchen the morning of departure, everyone went about as though they were walking on eggs. What had to be done was done and redone, checked, and rechecked. Nothing could hold back that dreadful minute, and holding back the tears became a contest of wills that tested everyone's capacity to control emotion.

Somewhere in those extremely tense last hours, Peggy found another time to have Duncan to herself. "Come and see this grandson of yours. I think he has grown a full inch since your last trip to Taos."

"He continues to do well, Peggy. And he continues to favor Billy in his appearance. How about his disposition, is it like Billy's?"

"Papa Dunc, are you deaf? Can't you hear him two or three times a day when he thinks he needs me? Don't you remember Billy and how grumpy he got when he was hungry?"

"I guess you're right about that, but there's something else you want to tell me, isn't there?"

Peggy went to a corner in the room, unrolled a blanket that was wrapped around a small metal box. "You gave me this box shortly after we landed in St. Louis after our long trip down the Missouri River. Remember?"

"Yes, but this box looks like it has been through a fire. My God! This is the box where you put that piece of McTavish tartan your mother gave you when you left Armand's lodge."

"It is. And somehow it survived the fire at the schoolhouse. I want you to have it again. Didn't your mother give this piece of tartan to you when you left Scotland to go to Montreal? Take it. It belongs to you."

"My dear, I can't tell you how much I love you and how much this piece of cloth means to me. But, Peggy, it is equally important to your mother. I wish you would give it to her to keep for you for another day."

Peggy said nothing. Duncan spoke again, "Giving this to your mother will do a great deal to bridge the gap that you feel exists between the two of you. Why don't you see if she will accept it?"

While they were talking, Duncan carefully removed the cloth and just as carefully unfolded it and held it up. "This is remarkable, Peggy. I can't see that the fire damaged it in any way. How very thoughtful of you to salvage this from the ruined schoolhouse. And what is this?"

He handed her a small parcel of clean material that was tied with a bow lying in the bottom of the box. With hands that shook ever so slightly, Peggy undid the bow and with great care extracted the feathered stick she had selected from the place where Billy was killed.

"Papa Dunc, did you ever think that the young brave who let me take this was the one who shot that arrow?"

"He might have been. Maybe it was his way of accepting responsibility for what he had done. What do you think?"

"I think it was him. It has taken time for me to live with that. I can't say what I think of him now, but I know it is not the hatred I felt at first. If he was the one, he showed a lot of character to have me take this reminder of what happened at that little spring of fresh water."

They both stood cloaked in silence, looking at each other this time without tears, but knowing the depth of sorrow and sadness fastened on that stick with a feather. Duncan was the one to break the silence.

"Peggy, will you consider this idea? You keep the piece of plaid and the feathered stick. Some day you can give them to Little Billy. These two keepsakes will help him to understand who he is and where he came from."

Duncan's face suddenly changed from its normal, sober demeanor to one filled with a puckish grin. "Stay here, Peggy, I'll be right back. I have something for you."

Duncan returned in a few minutes with the leather pouch Samuel Rawlinson had given him.

"Did I ever show you this? Samuel gave it to me at our going-away party, and said I was to fill it with nuggets from my gold mine. I want you to give it back to him. Tell him there are no nuggets of gold, only golden memories of Santa Fe. Will you do that? And give this letter to him, please. Go ahead and read it. I want you to know what I am telling Samuel about the way things are working out in Santa Fe."

Dear Samuel

Once again I am writing a letter to you at a critical point in our lives. You will receive it from the hands of my daughter. Peggy and Little Billy are going back to St. Louis with the Gallagher family.

Many things have developed, or in some cases not developed, here in Santa Fe that caused Jack and his wife to make this decision. Some time spent with Peggy will give you the full story, for I know she has her own views of what has happened.

Our parting is not in anger, but with understanding and respect for the need of everyone heading back to Missouri to plan for their own future.

There will be no partnership with Jack. We looked

at three possibilities here but could not develop a single one of them. Grace has to leave Santa Fe, for in another six months she would be facing a life without purpose here in this high mountain village. Eleanor will always be Eleanor, the guide and guardian of her family. Little Charley may have a fighting chance for a more normal life, a healthier life, back in Missouri.

As for Peggy and her child, I will have to admit with great reluctance that her decision, and it was her decision, is the right one. She and Billy will have a more stable and promising life in the East. But then who ever knows with certainty what is right and what is wrong?

As for Naomi and me? We have yet to make defining decisions. I think we will continue to probe and test possibilities in this beautiful but challenging land. We will do it in good health, with the thought of a better tomorrow, but will face our future together. And is not togetherness the most important thing to have in our lives?

Look in on our daughter and grandson from time to time to be sure that they have the essentials, and take care of yourself and be good to your friends.

Our love to you,
Duncan and Naomi

    ʠ   ʠ   ʠ

The next morning all in the compound arrived at the Plaza where places in the line of wagons were found for Jack's two Conestogas. Pres and Dutch walked among their mules with a bit of swagger as they cracked their blacksnake whips and flirted openly with *señoritas* crowding in to wish the travelers a safe journey. Tules joined Peggy and Naomi and took Little Billy into her yearning arms and smothered him with kisses for the last time. Eleanor was more than busy keeping Charley in sight as he went up and down the line of wagons giving each one his nod of approval. And Grace had her hands full trying to keep Spook gentled until the call was given to move out. Eleanor and Naomi found little last minute things to attend to guaranteed to keep them apart. These two Mandan women had shared and endured a gamut of experiences from birth to death, yet were unable to find words or gestures at this time of parting.

During the last hectic days of Trail preparations, Naomi and Peggy said their farewells – not in one emotional, earth-shattering episode, but in many little gestures, touches, and smiles. Duncan's parting from Peggy and Little Billy was of the same nature – a sequence of meaningful, little things that were spoken of, others without words but leaving imprints for a lifetime.

Jack and Duncan stood like two statues, not moving, not speaking, and not even looking at each other. At the call of the wagon master, "Catch up, catch up," they exchanged weak smiles and went about their business, Jack to the wagons, Duncan on the road to the compound.

"Mr. Ross! Can you not wait to walk home with your wife?"

"Naomi, I'm sorry. I was lost in the departure scene at the Plaza. I never was very good at saying good-bye."

"I don't think anybody ever gets good at that if they really mean what they say and feel. In all our years together, Dunc, there has never been a time when we need each other more than we do right now."

Disturbing thoughts can sometimes be diverted by an established routine of daily tasks. Duncan tried, but did not succeed. It seemed like ten times a day he found his mind drifting from the work of Bent-St. Vrain that lay before him on his desk. He relived again and again the departure of Peggy, Little Billy, and the Gallagher family.

What had he done, what had he said, where had he gone wrong to bring about these separations of family and friends? Added to the torment of the inability to answer his own questions was again a sense of tension growing between him and Naomi.

Daily living became difficult in the lonely compound with its many rooms, each one distinct and removed from the others yet together under one roof.

Duncan brought home ledgers and record books from the store in the Plaza. He thought working at the compound might rekindle that sense of purpose and togetherness that existed when the families traded living in two Conestoga wagons for life in Roberto Lucero's compound.

This did not help. In fact, it made the situation more difficult. It forced Naomi and Duncan into many meetings they preferred not to have. Mealtimes were silent and drab, chance meetings in and about the house were tense, and nights were separate and lonely. All of this happened without plan or intent, but it did happen. By the time the caravan with the Gallagher wagons reached San Miguel del Vado these patterns were developing; by the time it reached the pass over *el Raton* they were no longer patterns, they were routines set in stone.

"Dunc, this is not good, being together but so distant from each other."

"I agree. We should get ourselves out of this compound. It was made for family living, not for what we are now trying to do."

"I suspect we won't find it any easier to get a place in the village now than when we first came to Santa Fe."

"You're probably right, but what are we to do?"

"Charles Bent, does he not own property in Santa Fe? I mean places other than the store on the Plaza?"

"I really don't know, Naomi. I work for him, but I am not privy to Bent's personal wealth or holdings. Beside that, I don't think it wise to obligate ourselves to the man who is my *bourgeois*."

"I would like a place in town where we can keep a horse or two. I want a horse trained to pull a cart or light carriage. And you should have a good riding horse for the trips you will have to make for the Company."

"That may add to our problem of finding just a house. A house with pasturage and a barn is a big order."

"Have you not seen José Archuleta around town? You know, the little man who helped us solve big problems?"

"Yes. I seem him frequently about the Plaza, and he's in and out of the Palace of the Governors many times a day. Should I ask him for help?"

"I think you should. But what of Tules? Should we not tell her we want to leave this place? She got us into it. We can't keep her out of the plans we have in mind. Can we?"

"No. I guess not. I'll look for José, you speak to Tules."

Summer became fall with no change for the unhappy Ross duo. One bright spot was the arrival of a caravan from St. Louis on the Plaza in late July. The usual greetings and routines were observed, and on the second day a man recognized as the wagon master made inquires for Duncan Ross. "I have letters for you. Sir, can you identify yourself to me as Duncan Ross?"

"I can do more than that, I will invite you and your wagoneers to drop by my store on the Plaza and negotiate the sale of whatever merchandise you have in the wagons. Now, shall we go to the hotel on the corner of the Plaza and have a meal other than beans and bacon?"

"I see you have not forgotten some of the pleasures on the Trail, Mr. Ross. I shall be more than happy to accept your invitation."

They enjoyed their brief time together and made arrangements for business as quickly as wagons could clear the customs house and its attending sticky-fingered officials. Duncan all but ran to the compound with the letters given him by the wagon master. Part of his haste was his need for news of his family, and friends and part because he had something to share with Naomi. She was not at the compound and left no sign of where she may have gone.

During the time spent with the wagon master, Duncan learned the

Gallagher wagon train had opted for the longer route over *el Raton* rather than the shorter *Cimarron* cut-off route. Duncan knew that Jack was going to suggest to the wagon master that this alternative route be followed.

The meeting of two caravans was by chance, not by plan, along the banks of the Arkansas River. The westbound group with the letters for Santa Fe folks was waiting until water in the Arkansas River dropped to a safe level before attempting the crossing. Members of both caravans hurriedly scratched out letters to be exchanged in their brief time together.

Duncan opened the first letter, a brief note from Peggy.

Dear Mother and Papa Dunc,

What luck. We reached the crossing of the Arkansas at the same time a wagon train bound for Santa Fe was here waiting to cross. Everyone agreed to deliver letters for the other caravan.

We are well, really we are. Little Billy has been a constant worry, but not an undue burden. Charley watches over him like an eagle. Grace and Aunt Eleanor are taking good care of both and, to tell the truth, spoiling me.

Uncle Jack said going over the Raton Pass took longer, but we had good water every day. We stopped for two days to rest, refit, and add more wagons to our caravan at Fort William. What a huge place. The company you represent in Santa Fe, Papa Dunc, is well organized and treated us generously all the time we were at Fort William.

Some of the people in the other caravan said they had seen Indians twice, but had no trouble. They also said buffalo seemed scarce even though grass is plentiful.

I hope the rest of the trip goes as well as this first

part, for there isn't anything I can tell you to indicate we are having a difficult time. It is good to have Pres and Dutch with us.

All our love,
Peggy and Little Billy

There was also a note from Jack.

Hello Mr. and Mrs. Santa Fe,
A chance meeting of an outfit headed for Santa Fe gives us a chance for a letter exchange. Things are going right along, no problems worth writing about.
The little ones, Billy and Charley, are good travelers; Grace and Eleanor are taking good care of all of us. Pres and Dutch are doing a good job with the mules. So I don't have much to do but get in everyone's way.

My best to you both,
Jack

And there were letters written from Santa Fe people. The one from Samuel Rawlinson was more of a detailed review of Duncan's investment portfolio than a personal letter. And there was a letter from Myrna Wilson for Naomi.

🌶   🌶   🌶

It was the winter season before Naomi and Duncan resolved their housing problem. Neither Tules nor José Archuleta played a role in their good fortune in finding a house in town not far from the center of activities important to both Naomi and Duncan.

Rosalia Baca told Naomi of her neighbor who planned to move to Socorro, a small village along the Rio Grande River downstream from Albuquerque. The neighbor was going there to tend to an ailing *tia*, but did not want to give up her house in Santa Fe.

Naomi looked over the house, decided it met their needs, made the final arrangements to rent it, and then told Duncan they were going to move. "You are so wrapped up in your business affairs I didn't think you would want the distraction of having to work out the details of this move."

"I suppose you did the right thing, but it seems very small. Do you see us being comfortable while being forced to live so close?"

Naomi laughed, not for some time had she laughed. "My dear red-headed man, I think you are afraid of me!"

"Maybe I should be. What do you think?"

"I think we should move into this house and we will be happy there. Now, what do you say to that?"

"I think we should do it."

ɛ̆ ɛ̆ ɛ̆

Duncan allowed a foolish thought to creep into his mind. "We have our housing problem behind us, now we can relax and enjoy this unique village." Problems in the affairs of Bent-St. Vrain more than replaced the housing challenge. These Bent problems became major and some of them seemed beyond his solution. Bursts of activity arrived in his office and store with the arrival of each caravan in Santa Fe. Whether one from the East or one from Chihuahua, along with mounds of goods came mounds of troubles.

Hours were spent at the customs house and hours in the Palace of the Governors. Hours of satisfying accomplishment were few; most hours were forerunners of new deals to be cut, more palms to be greased, and more affairs left in the accepted mode of *mañana*. Duncan's training and experiences in the Canadian fur trade did not translate into the methods practiced in Santa Fe.

"Naomi, do you remember our time in the trading post on *Lac de Wapiti*? Did I ever burden you with problems of the business of the post?"

"I would say at least half the time."

"You jest, don't you?"

"All right, maybe I overstated a little. But you are worried now, and have been for most of the winter, aren't you?"

"I should know I can't hide anything from you, long legs. But I have never been confronted with men who spend all their energies on schemes and plots to avoid paying taxes and duties, of beating someone in a deal, and just plain cheating."

"Is there nothing you can do?"

"Very little. The one big thing I can do is go see Charles Bent and tell him I cannot be an effective agent for his company in Santa Fe."

"Would you really want to go that far, Duncan? That doesn't sound like your way of handling problems."

Another two months drifted by. Then a Chinook wind blowing over the town was a welcome hint of spring. It was a sign to Naomi that she and Rosalia Baca should be out in the countryside searching for the first tender roots of *tansy* to make a medication both women knew was helpful to those with kidney problems. After a rewarding day in the field with Rosalia, Naomi was preparing an evening meal when Duncan walked in.

"Was your day as good as mine? I hope so."

"It was, but what made yours so special?"

"I have the solution to our problem. What do you think of this idea?"

Duncan plunged into the proposition he would lay before the Brothers Bent. He and Naomi would move to St. Louis and he would become the resident manager for Bent-St. Vrain. He would distribute the company's incoming cargos off the Santa Fe Trail to profitable advantage; he would organize wagon trains and assemble the company's outgoing cargos destined for Fort William, Taos, and Santa Fe.

Naomi's response was quick and to the point. "This town is really not meant for either one of us. You are serious, aren't you?"

"Never more serious in my life. I will put the details of my idea in a letter to Charles Bent and get it off immediately."

"Before you write that letter, I thought we might talk over the idea that had Pres and Dutch stirred up. You know, California."

"Let me ask you what you just asked me. Are you serious?"

"Of course I'm serious. California could be the answer to a lot of our unanswered questions, don't you think?"

"But what would we do there? Have you given thought to that?"

"Did you really know what we would do once we got to Santa Fe? You and Jack had some shaky ideas, but nothing definite. Yet you never stopped for a minute in your plans to come here."

"I suspect California will prove to be far different from anything we have ever experienced."

"I would be disappointed if it weren't. Isn't that why people are on the move all the time? To find a different place, to do different things, to meet different people?"

"You, my long-legged friend, have given more thought to California than I have. Give me time to catch up to you and your thinking."

"You want something to think about? Read this letter I had from Myrna Wilson. You'll find some things of interest to you, I'm sure."

Dear Naomi

Where to begin? Well, how about this? I am now Mrs. Samuel Rawlinson. Surprised? No more than Samuel; he doesn't realize it yet, but I actually asked him to marry me. He thinks it was his idea, but you know men are sometimes slow to learn what is going on in their lives.

He wanted to live closer to the downtown and riverfront of St. Louis. My little place would have been just great for the two of us, but his idea won out and so I now have a quite large house to manage. Samuel didn't have to coax me to give up my tutoring, but some days I do miss the children. Maybe someday I will have one of our own to worry over.

Though you have been gone for only a few years, you would find many changes in St. Louis were you to return today. The slavery issue is still with us and gets more heated every day. In spite of that, the town grows; we see more boats on the big river and more caravans are returning from places other than Santa Fe.

Samuel and I frequently talk over the brief time we had with you and with the Gallagher family. We agree we miss you people and wish there was some reason for you to come back.

I hope you are in good health and doing things in that far away place that bring you happiness.

Our love to all,
The Rawlinsons

"My, that was full of surprises. So, old Samuel is now among the ranks of the married. I think he picked, or should I say a very nice lady picked him?"

By the end of April Duncan was in Taos talking with Charles and William Bent.

"We find merit in your proposal, Duncan. Having a resident manager in St. Louis fits into our plans very nicely. When do you think our affairs in Santa Fe will be in such a state that we can put your replacement right to work?"

"I have set up company affairs with few loose ends. I can leave with the first caravan to depart for St. Louis this summer and not jeopardize your Company's business in Santa Fe. Are we in agreement?"

Charles spoke up, "It seems to me you are able to settle a personal matter with this move as well as advance our interests, right?"

"Yes. Both Mrs. Ross and I will be much happier there. And that should only result in my getting a better grip on business at the St. Louis end of Bent-St. Vrain affairs."

The escort that returned Duncan safely to Santa Fe left him at the

Company's store on the Plaza. He quickly disposed of some pending business matters, then rushed home to share with Naomi the good news from the Bents.

"Dunc, I'm so glad you are back home. I have such good news to share with you."

"And I with you. But you go ahead with your good news. What is it?"

"There is a large mule train forming up to go to California with a valuable consignment of woolen goods under an armed escort all the way. I have been asked to join it and be its *curandera*. What do you think of that, my red-headed man?"

"Well, my long-stemmed rose, what do think of this? The Bents have approved of my going to St. Louis to be their resident-manager."

Disbelief flashed immediately across both faces. How could two people who so recently felt their tensions had fallen away be confronted with two massive problems simultaneously? Neither problem could be delayed in reaching a decision, yet neither problem held a solution to it.

After long moments of silence, Duncan ventured this, "Well, we really don't have a problem, do we? We will go to St. Louis and be reunited with our daughter, our grandson, and our best friends. Isn't that the only possible answer?"

"No, that is not the only answer. How easily you forget the problems we were so happy to leave in St. Louis. Go back there and I believe those same problems will be waiting to greet you. Don't dismiss going to California so quickly."

"How can you say that? Isn't the chance to be with Peggy and Little Billy the best thing that could possibly happen to us?"

"Part of Peggy's decision to return with the Gallaghers was to get herself and Little Billy away from Santa Fe. And I will add this, Dunc, to get away from me. She needs time to do this. I don't think our going to St. Louis so soon after she gets there will help in her search for an independent life."

A day after this discussion which resolved nothing, Naomi came to

Duncan with an alternative. "We will go to California and explore the possibilities it may have for both of us. If at the end of three years we are not
satisfied and happy there, we will go to St. Louis."

"I promise I will think through your plan. But I must send word to
the Bents in Taos of my decision very soon. How much time has the group
organizing this California journey given you for an answer to their invitation?"

"You must understand this, Dunc. I listened to what they offered, but
I made it clear that it must include you. They welcomed that, for many
people in the caravan know of you and your no-nonsense ways. They must
have our reply by next Monday."

"So we don't have much time. What are we going to do?"

"Dunc, I am convinced that we should go to California."

"I feel this offer from the Bents will never be repeated. It's now or
never with them. I think we should go to St. Louis."

"Let's give this another few days. We have that much time, don't we?"

"We do, Naomi. You must not only think of the advantages of what
you want to do, but the costs of doing it. Not in terms of dollars, but in
terms of what will not be done if we go to California."

"Costs? If there are costs for me, how about you? What will not get
done if we go back East?"

After a restless night Duncan was ready in the morning with a line of
reasoning he was sure Naomi could not resist. "When we get back to
St. Louis we will look for a place along the river. Undoubtedly Jack and
Eleanor will return to their farm with Grace and Charley. Peggy and Little
Billy will have a safe and secure home with them. We can live nearby, but
not close. What do you think of that idea?"

Naomi took her cup of *chocolate* and went outside where she could
see the mountains. After a very long time she turned to face Duncan who
had slowly followed in her footsteps. "Your idea doesn't solve any of our
problems, does it?"

"Why not? I think it solves our major points of difference."

"Look ahead. You are telling me that we will not become an intimate part of Peggy's life no matter what part of St. Louis we choose to live? Dunc, you know better than that! We are the people she wants to live some distance from, at least for the few years she needs to work things out for herself."

"But you seem to forget why we would move back to St. Louis. I will be the local agent for a very busy trading company, and I expect to be just as busy in my work for it."

"Being busy is only a part of living. There must be time for others in your life than that idol you worship, that thing you call business."

"But people must have a purpose, a reason for working, don't they?"

"Yes. But they must also have some balance in their life."

Another restless night, another plan presented over the morning meal.

"Think about this idea, Naomi. Rather than make St. Louis the end destination of Bent-St. Vrain Company we make West Port [Kansas City] the terminus. I'm sure the men back in Taos would agree to that, for we have already discussed that option even before I signed on with them. That way we would not be involved in Peggy's daily life, but still much closer than if we go on to California. Well?"

"I admire your trying to find a solution to our future, and I like to have you share your thinking. But, my red-headed friend, I haven't heard a word about what I will do in your world. Am I not worthy of some consideration?"

"What are your thoughts?"

"I think it is important that each of us continue to do what we do best. You must be involved in some kind of business. I must be into my natural healing medications and working to help people who benefit from them."

"That's a sound bit of reasoning, my dear. But you have overlooked one little thing."

"And what might that be?"

"Geography! There are a few miles between Missouri and California the last time I looked at a map."

"I'm sure there are. But one does not set out on a new route without first setting a direction. Right?

"Right. But in what direction are you going?"

"I want to go forward. What you propose is that we go backward."

"How so? I don't follow your thinking."

"You would have us go back in place, you would have us go back in time, you would have us go back to the old and familiar. At the same time you would have us deny the unknown, the mysterious, and the adventure of things and places that are new and different."

"Well said. But am I not offering stability and security in our lives? What do you offer in your plan?"

"Change, Dunc, change! That is what we need more than anything at this point in our lives. When I am old and gray, stability and security may be attractive goals. But I am not old and I am not gray, and neither are you!"

Naomi's Mandan background plus her years with Cree people showed as she gathered her things to join the caravan forming on the Plaza. She had several parcels of her medications, a trail bag of personal items and clothing, a parcel of dried foods, and a well-organized bed roll and ditty bag all packed on the back of a mule.

"Is that all you are taking, Naomi? Let me rush to our store and put a more complete trail pack together for you and buy another pack animal."

"Dunc, I have all I need."

"Are you sure? There will be damn few trading posts along the way."

"I said I am ready."

This was how you said farewell to the woman of your life, to the one who taught the real meaning of love? His thoughts raced far ahead of his tongue and the words it should speak: "Take her in your arms and tell her you will miss her. Do it, Duncan, do it."

Another line of questions flashed through Duncan's mind. "What kept you from telling Naomi last night all these things which you cannot say now? Was it stubbornness? Was it your troublesome sense of pride? Was it the dread of accepting the fact this might be the last night you held this wonderful woman in you arms?"

At some point in their last days together both Duncan and Naomi realized that nothing would mark this farewell as a memorable event. Several days ago both had accepted the fact the choice they faced – go East or go West – had no solution as they said their goodbyes. Not with words and actions, but with a closing of their minds and hearts.

Naomi stood beside her horse, gentling it with soft words and strokes on its muzzle. But not a word or gesture for Duncan. Was it her ingrained practice of not showing emotion in public? Could it be that she was as stubborn as her man? Had she so hardened her heart after twice before parting from this man that there was nothing to say?

What Duncan did, at Naomi's command, was make a hand and boost her onto the saddle of her riding horse. She gave direction to her mount and guided it to a place in the caravan. At the last minute, Naomi made the horse do a complete turn around. Duncan could see the tears, and through his tears he caught a fleeting smile. She spurred her horse to resume her place on the road to California.

As he was doing his packing, Duncan found time to write a letter to his sister in Scotland. He sat at the table, ink, pens, writing paper at the ready, but no words. He and Louise had always been quite open and at times brutally frank with one another. This time it seemed impossible to put anything on paper. He tried again for the third time. A letter didn't result, but a lot of deep thinking and musing aloud did take over.

"Oh hell! How can I write to my sister about things which I don't fully understand? I'll wait until I am back East and send her a letter from St. Louis when I have a better grip on my situation. Damn it, we survived one separation when Naomi fled with Peggy thinking she could return to her Mandan roots. We survived the separation at Armand's lodge in Mandan country when I returned to Missouri with Peggy and Naomi remained behind with her new man. By God, we will survive this one!

"It seems just like yesterday I wrote to Samuel telling him that the best thing a man and woman could share was togetherness. How little I know!"

THE END

abuelo — grandfather

agentes de policia — policeman

alcalde — mayor

arrastra — a crude mule-powered device and stones for pulverizing ore

atole — corn meal

basta — enough

batea — wooden bowl

buenas dias — Good morning

buenas tardes — Good afternoon

buenas noches — Good evening

cárcel — jail, lock up

carreta — cart for small, short distance loads

carro — two-wheeled wagon for larger loads

casa — house

curandera — healer

escaleras — ladder

gobernador — governor

gringo — foreigner

hola — hello

hombre — man

horno — oven

La Conquistadora — conqueror (female); holy figure associated with the "reconquest" of Santa Fe in 1692

Lac de Wapiti — Elk Lake

maldeto sea — damn (or much stronger)

mano y mano — man to man

muy mal — very bad

pelirrojo — redhead

por favor — please

pobres — poor person(s)

peon — laborer

pepena — gravel, crude ore

perdone usted — I beg your pardon

piñon — short, aromatic pine tree

pues — well, then

retendré el caballo — hold the horse

rico — rich, wealthy

Rio Abajo — South of Santa Fe in the Rio Grande valley

Rio Arriba — North of Santa Fe in the Rio Grande valley

sala — room

Sangre de Christo — "Blood of Christ," north-south range of mountains east of Santa Fe

tia — aunt

tio — uncle

travois — two trailing poles lashed to an animal (dog, horse, mule, oxen) with a canvas or hide sling to carry the burden

yeso — plaster, used mostly on interior walls